British secret agent Geoff Kearney regained consciousness. He was lying on the floor. His gun was beside the brick mantel. He'd had the secret compartment open, was about to reach for the video tape.

He saw a man running past him through the kitchen door, then another. Kearney grabbed for the Smith & Wesson 9mm, firing into legs as they passed him. Something fell on him and Kearney beat at it—a man, his fists hammering at Kearney's gas-masked face. Kearney fired four times, the body thudding upward, rolling onto Kearney's right arm.

A pair of combat boots stood over him, a rifle butt came crashing down. Kearney dodged to the right, the rifle butt hitting the floor. His left hand tore the Cold Steel Bowie from the fabric sheath at his left side. He rammed the nine inches of quarter-inch carbon steel straight up between the man's legs.

There was an inhuman shriek.

Other titles in the Defender series:

DEATH GRIP

Super Defender 9

Jerry Ahern

A Dell Book

Published by
Dell Publishing
a division of
Bantam Doubleday Dell
Publishing Group, Inc.
666 Fifth Avenue
New York, New York 10103

ISBN: 0-440-20528-X

Printed in the United States of America
Published simultaneously in Canada
January 1990

10 9 8 7 6 5 4 3 2 1

*For all the people who have told us
they enjoy THE DEFENDER,
and believe in the spirit
of America as he does, best wishes. . . .*

Prologue:
Night Stirrings

*T*he look in the eyes of the President of the United States as he died in David's arms was unforgettable. There were other dead around him, Marine and Secret Service guards, and of course some of the assassins in Army fatigues who had died in their attempt to murder him. And David had been covered with blood, some of it the President's, some his own.

Thinking of the rooftop death scene again contributed at least as much, if not more, to the spreading gooseflesh on her bare forearms and calves beneath the hem of her skirt. The top she wore was pink cotton knit and had half sleeves to her elbows; the skirt was blue denim and full, and stopped a few inches above her ankles. Her white coat sweater had been lost when they'd navigated the stream a few hundred yards off the road where the van had died, and her white tennis shoes (now a muddy brown) were still wet and squishy from wading across the water.

David had offered her his coat when she'd decided to go out looking for another car, but she'd declined, saying that wearing a man's sport coat would only draw unwanted attention to herself; but she'd really refused because he was running a slight fever and she didn't want him to get worse.

Of the wounds he'd sustained at the sanitorium in the vain attempt to save the life of the President of the United States, the one that had crossed David's right bicep, then punctured his side, was the worst. They'd found medical treatment with sympathizers to the Patriot movement, showered, changed from their dirt-stained black battle dress utilities, then moved quickly on, splitting up to minimize the chance of one roadblock neutralizing them all.

The pink cotton top fit her loosely, and intentionally so, to hide the little white plastic Null shoulder holster for the Model 60 Smith & Wesson .38 Special revolver, the crossover strap secured to her bra. And as she walked along the highway, toward the lights of a truck stop ahead of her about a half mile, her purse with the .45 and the spare ammunition for both guns and a wealth of other vital possessions seemed to grow even heavier. The bag was slung from her right shoulder and her arms were folded over her breasts, fingers splayed over them for warmth.

Rose Shepherd kept walking.

There would be some sort of vehicle at the truck stop. And once she got past the security cops, she'd steal it, then go back for David. She prayed that the car's heater worked, at least a little. . . .

. . .

There was enough of the Irish in Geoffrey Kearney's veins that he knew the wail of the banshee when it beckoned in the night. He sat up in the bed, cold. Enough of the dream lingered at the fringes of his consciousness so that, without thinking, he reached out his fingertips in the fuzzy gray darkness to feel Linda Effingham's throat for a pulse—because the banshee's cry always foretold the death of a loved one. But it was an air raid siren that had pierced his sleep and stirred Kearney's fears. It was a banshee of a different sort, its portent no less deadly.

What was the time? He needed to know the time to glue himself back into reality and put the dream away. Kearney ignored the face of his Rolex, the room not dark enough for the luminosity to be more than a blur anyway, instead looking at the diode readout of the motel clock at their bedside. Two A.M. He'd heard sirens like this in other lands when air raids were imminent, heard them in the United States, but only at specified times, for testing the systems. Church bells began to peal softly. A chill ran along his spine. As he reached for the remote control of the television he heard sporadic, distant gunfire. A voice came before the picture with the crackle of static. ". . . again has confirmed that the President of the United States has joined the ever-growing toll of victims in the violence which still spreads like a plague across the North American continent. A spokesperson for acting President Roman Makowski called the President's death, and I quote, '. . . a tragedy from which the Republic will not soon recover nor will soon forget.' White House sources, which spoke only on condition of anonymity, confirmed that facts so far unearthed in the still-ongoing investigation point strongly to the so-called 'Patriots' as being responsible for the President's brutal murder. The infamous Dr. David Holden, former history professor and Navy-SEAL-trained commando, the Patriots' firebrand leader, may indeed, as one Justice Department source put it, 'be the actual triggerman.' We switch live, now, to Denise McDermott on Capitol Hill." A new voice, sounding jaded and artificially, almost mannishly, resonant, began droning on with suppositions, observations, government-sanctioned trivialities and "updates"—and Kearney was hardly aware anymore of the pretty-enough-looking mid-thirties redhead and her sanitized news.

Linda Effingham, real and beautiful and honorable, still slept, curled up in a fetal position beneath the covers beside him.

Kearney pulled the bedspread over the single white sheet and yellow waffle knit blanket as he slipped from beneath the covers. In darkness, his eyes well accustomed to the dim light from the glow of the television screen, he padded into the bathroom, his pistol in his left hand. Setting the S & W autoloader on the flush-tank lid, he urinated. It wasn't a war, or at least not in the classic sense with bombings and invading armies; at least not yet, it wasn't. But it was a decided escalation on the part of the Front for the Liberation of North America and the FLNA's ultraliberal, far-left minions in the inner circles of American government in Washington.

Still naked, Geoffrey Kearney crossed the room, stubbed a toe against his shoes, and kicked them out of the way, cursing softly. He stood beside the motel room's single window, his body nearly flush against the frame. The faded gold drapery and the white sheer between it and the window were pushed back only inches so he could peer out. The gunshots were more frequent now, no closer; but there was a new sound added to the cacophony of tolling bells and howling sirens—honking automobile horns from the four-lane roadway a hundred yards or so beyond the parking lot. Lights were coming on everywhere throughout the motel complex (several smallish buildings connected by porticos, surrounding a brackish-looking swimming pool), and flaring head-lights were turning up the driveway toward the motel.

There was an uneasy feeling in the pit of Kearney's stomach. He moved quickly to the bed and touched Linda's face with his free hand. "Wake up, darling. We're moving," he whispered just loudly enough to be heard over the television.

Partially masked headlights, mounted omi-nously in the large fenders of two-and-a-half ton military trucks, lighted the weed-studded, blacktop parking apron fronting the abandoned garage/body shop. In spots the light was bright enough to see the unit insignia worn on the shoulders of the men in U.S. Army battle dress utilities who milled about near the trucks. It was the same insignia worn by the men who'd murdered the President of the United States that afternoon on the rooftop of a govern-ment-run sanitorium in rural Virginia.

The deed was done where the President had been

under intensive care, comatose and on the edge of death since his near-fatal wounding during the FLNA missile attack on the international conference called for the very purpose of dealing with the FLNA terror. The Vice President had been killed in the explosion, and Speaker of the House Roman Makowski had assumed the Presidency. But when the President, almost miraculously, began to return to consciousness, the plan to murder him was formulated so Makowski could keep control of the White House.

The plan succeeded, despite the best efforts of the Patriots to foil it. Makowski, a murderer, sat in the Oval Office, the President elected to that office having been assassinated on Roman Makowski's orders.

David Holden held his breath as he tucked back flat against the rough stucco surface of the garage wall. The mumblings of the M-16-armed men, the night stirrings of crickets, and the slipping of gravel beneath the soles of his city shoes were drowned out beneath the rapid beating of his heart.

During the fighting he'd sustained a grazing wound along his left thigh, deep enough to be painful but not so serious as to be incapacitating, only annoying. He took a similar crease over his right bicep, but in this case the bullet had burrowed into the fleshy area beneath his rib cage and out again. When he moved at all, this hurt, but the bleeding had been successfully stopped, the small entry and exit wounds disinfected, packed, and sutured.

He didn't feel any pain now. His instincts for survival forced out all other concerns. When the stolen truck in which he and Rosie Shepherd had escaped broke down, she'd left him here, because of his wounds and against his protests, while she went off to "liberate" fresh transportation. And driving back here now, she might find a death trap waiting unless he could intercept her along the road.

At last David Holden reached the rear of the building, grabbed up his pack, and started limping into the trees. If he could only reach the road leading down to the garage in time—

He was behind enemy lines in his own homeland, the United States of America. And he knew the simple orders under which even legitimate troops, not to mention Roman Makowski's killers, would operate concerning wanted Patriot leader David Holden and his second-in-command and lover, ex–Metro Detective Rose Shepherd: Shoot on sight.

Holden flipped the selector of his M-16 to full auto, more conscious again of the pain as he clambered up the embankment toward the road. . . .

"Roman? Where are you going, honey?"

Roman Makowski belted his robe tightly at his waist, looking down at her in the yellow light of the bedside lamp. With her eyes half-asleep and her makeup ruined, she didn't look quite as good as she had in the heat of passion a few hours earlier. And now he was exceptionally grateful for the back entrance by which she'd arrived and would soon leave. "I'll be gone for quite some time; matters of state and everything—you know. Why don't you get yourself dressed and I'll have one of the Secret Service guys take you home. I'll call you tomorrow," he lied to her, already crossing the bedroom toward the bathroom. He flicked on the light and closed the door.

If Hobie Townes had awakened him, that meant Townes had something that was hot. Maybe the damned evidence that Cerillia'd just been starting to talk about on the phone with that pain-in-the-ass Holden and that goody-goody black FBI Agent Luther Steel—before one of Townes's idiots had cut the line and killed the tap on conversation.

Kearney held the Smith & Wesson Model 5904 9mm in his right hand, just under the goatskin A-2 jacket. With Linda Effingham's suitcase and his own in his left they slipped through the door, all lights inside the room behind them out. "Where will we go?" Linda whispered to him.

The Ford was backed into the parking slot two doors down from their room. "Away from here," Kearney whispered back. "There's wild country not far away. With the current conditions in the United States, being a stranger anywhere might not be quite healthy." He realized he must be sounding horribly depressing. So Kearney tried to brighten his voice when he added, "And, anyway, it'll be like a grand camp-out. I can snare rabbits for us and you can cook them over an open fire. Nature's wonderland will unfold before our eyes." Kearney didn't think she bought it, but he didn't believe it either.

They reached the car. Kearney decided not to call attention to themselves or waste the time opening the trunk. Their two bags could just as easily be flipped into the backseat. "What about paying for our room, Geoff?"

Kearney wasn't exactly worried about that, but reassured her, "They have an impression of my credit card. And the keys are back in the room, darling. They'll be none the worse for us checking out a bit earlier than they expect."

Kearney let her in, starting to cross over to the driver's side as a beer-stained voice called to him from one of the interconnecting porticos. Kearney's pistol was just stuffed into his trouser belt, his hand still quite near to it. "Whatchya doin'?"

Kearney smiled, not knowing if the smile could be seen or not. "My wife's pregnant. Happened just like this the last time, so if I'd had any sense I wouldn't have taken her with me. Three weeks before the damn doctor said it'd happen. Hell—we're in a hurry, unless you're an obstetrician, friend." He was using one of his American accents, a little southern, to go with the Georgia license plate on the Ford's rear bumper, which would be conveniently facing who-ever was speaking to him from the shadows.

Then there was a second voice. "Got them bags full o' towels and shit, boy?"

"You the manager?" Kearney said, his fingertips on the butt of his pistol, his body a quarter turn right from the portico so it would be impossible for the speakers to see him. "And all I'm taking is my wife, to find a doctor. Hell, with all these damn sirens and shit, I couldn't even call out on the telephone." He was playing a long shot that the two voices didn't belong to anyone from the motel, because he hadn't tried the telephone at all and it might be working perfectly well.

"Let's see your wife."

"See this instead," Kearney wanted to say so badly that it almost hurt. But instead of drawing the pistol he responded, "She's not getting out of the car, fellas. What would you do if she were your wife?"

Then he heard one of them laugh and the other say, "What I'm gonna do right now, boy—fuck her."

Kearney edged away from them, to make them feel more bold, draw them out of the shadows and into the meager light. "I don't like anybody talking that way about a woman, any woman. You guys beat it, now," Kearney insisted, intentionally breathing very shallowly so his voice would have the tremulous quality of fear to it.

"We're gonna beat it all right" was followed by vile sounding laughter.

Kearney kept edging back from them; and at last they stepped into the meager light. One of the men wore an out-of-season light-colored staw cowboy hat with high crown and wide brim and a complicated feather hatband. He carried a something in his right hand, behind his thigh, but Kearney couldn't see exactly what. The second man, larger than the first (which was saying a great deal, since the first man was the size of a small bear), was hatless and the way the light caught his face Kearney could see the man's high cheekbones and the corners of a long mouth curled up into a smile. There was a long stick-shaped object in the fellow's right hand, most likely a jack handle from an automobile. He slapped the thing repeatedly into the palm of his left hand.

They weren't exactly weaponless, and it was possible that the first man's weapon could be a knife, or, less likely, a gun of some kind.

Kearney was beside the driver's side door. He heard the click as Linda must have reached across to open the lock for him. He could have tried jumping behind the wheel and getting the door locked after him, but there probably wouldn't be the time. At any event the tire iron could smash out the windshield or side window in a single blow in powerful hands.

Kearney audibly sighed and turned to face them squarely, using his normal voice, but keeping the slight southern coloration. "Boys, push has come to shove. Give it up now."

"You gonna be brave? Hell, I like brave, makes it more fun." The first man, the one with something in his hand behind his right thigh, laughed drunkenly.

"No, I'm not going to be brave; I'm going to be lethal. Get out of here or you're both dead men," Kearney announced. Had they been professionals of even the most minor sort, he wouldn't have wasted his words on them. But they were only drunken bullies.

The first man started to move his hand from behind his thigh. Kearney had no choice but to take appropriate action in the event that whatever the man held was a deadly weapon. But instead of drawing the 5904, Kearney drew the B & D Trading Fazendeiro from the pocket of his bomber jacket. The second man lunged toward Kearney. Kearney had no place to which he could sidestep. He took a step back, instead, just far enough to throw off the second man's balance. Drunks weren't known for keeping a strong sense of equilibrium at any event.

As the second man lurched just slightly off balance, Kearney wheeled right, landing a fast double Tae Kwon Do kick to the second man's right hip and knee. As the man stumbled and fell, the shielding effect of the second man's body between Kearney and the first man was gone. The first man's upraised right arm ended in a ham-sized fist bunched around a jack handle, which crashed downward toward Kearney's face. Kearney stepped over the fallen man and inside the first man's reach, his left arm going up, his left hand catching the man's right wrist as Kearney's right knee smashed up into the man's groin. Kearney's right fist bunched around the Fazendeiro, striking the butt of the still-closed knife to the man's left temple.

As the man caved forward from the first knee smash, Kearney hammered his knee upward again, turning right 180 degrees, slipping the Fazendeiro into his pants pocket as both hands locked onto the man's right wrist. Kearney snapped forward at the waist, flipping the man over his shoulder and onto the ground. The second man was starting to his feet and Kearney wheeled half right, kicking the man in the tip of the jaw, then again, snapping his head back into the door of the Ford. Kearney dropped to one knee beside the first man, the one with the jack handle, ready to deliver a killing downward blow to the Adam's apple if necessary. It wasn't. Kearney merely stood and kicked him as hard as he could in the crotch.

"Are you—"

It was Linda Effingham, half out of the car, her face white as a sheet.

"Hop in, darling, we're moving," Kearney advised, slipping behind the wheel. The front doors slammed almost simultaneously as Kearney turned the ignition. . . .

. . .

The road was all but deserted, as befitted the early hour and the times. An occasional three- or four-vehicle semitrailer truck convoy passed David Holden's position and that was all. No one drove at night except out of necessity, and the truckers had long since taken to convoying for safety. Yet, although such reports rarely made the newspapers or broadcast, the convoys were little safer than individual trucks. Lawless elements—either true FLNA units or gangs that had banded together, since the fighting had begun, for the sole purpose of capitalizing on the nation's misery for a quick, violent profit—would stop the convoys, steal the valuable commodities, destroy the rest, and frequently slaughter the drivers. Because of this pattern, and because of the general torpor of the economy (no factory night shifts, convenience stores closed, skeletal hours for everything from the poorly stocked grocery stores to the overpriced department stores and the resultant loss of sales and revenue), long-distance truck runs were few and far between. There was little to haul and there was real risk of death to those who found work and dared take to the roads in pursuit of a living.

Unemployment figures had not been released by the government since Roman Makowski assumed the Presidency. In the event figures should eventually be released, and *even* if the government sanitized them with creative accounting, such figures promised to deal the economy another serious blow. Orders for durable goods had been continuously dropping, prices for everything were rising, and inflation was at runaway levels while the ranks of the unemployed

and underemployed swelled. As usual a disproportionate percentage of unemployed were from among
the young, women, and ethnic minority groups. The
number of poor grew, the middle-income class being
choked by higher prices, more taxation, cut-back
shifts, and reduced job openings.

Almost daily those few civil liberties that remained
were being encroached upon. Merely to possess a
firearm of any type, for example, constituted a felony, and because of the volume of firearms-related
arrests, fill-in warrants were issued when the provi-
sions of martial law were not considered enough to
suspend the Constitutional guarantees. The jails
were so overcrowded with persons rendered criminals by the passage of ex post facto laws that thou-
sands of genuine felony perpetrators were given
early release, exacerbating the out-of-hand crime
problem and swelling the ranks of unemployed welfare recipients. To finance the bloated welfare rolls,
although the government officially denied it, new
money was being printed at an unprecedented pace,
thereby devaluing existing currency and raising the
prices of consumer goods beyond the levels caused
by shortages.

The nation was ripe for violence on an unprecedented scale.

David Holden sat with his thoughts among the almost carelessly scattered boulders shifted years ago
from the roadbed. Useless, they had remained here,
but now their utility was in providing him necessary
concealment. His right side hurt badly, but he told
himself the wound had not reopened and that the
wetness he felt was merely perspiration from the ex-

ertion of his climb from the rear of the abandoned garage to the roadbed.

It would be easy to spot Rosie, since he doubted she'd steal a semi and she would be alone in the passenger compartment of whatever vehicle she drove. And it was imperative that he did spot her before she turned off the highway into the drive for the garage/body shop. Because none of the vehicles that had brought the Army uniform-clad assassin showed any sign of being on its way, and if he didn't stop her, she'd drive to her death. . . .

Rose Shepherd knelt a few yards back from the barbed-wire-topped, eight-foot-high chain-link fence that surrounded the truck-stop parking lot, her eyes squinted a little against the bright yellow of the lights. Seven semitrailer trucks were parked there along with nearly a dozen automobiles of various descriptions, age, and condition.

Her attention immediately gravitated toward the largest of these passenger cars (although she'd often heard other examples of the same model called trucks), a dark gray Chevrolet Suburban with midnight-blue lower trim panels and light truck-sized tires. Under her breath she almost prayed the Suburban had the big engine. . . .

He'd fallen asleep, but the sounds of crunching gravel awakened him. As he moved, David Holden felt a deep searing stitch of pain in his right side. There was no time to look for blood now. He blinked several times, trying to bring his senses fully awake, his right hand groping at his waistband for the full-sized Beretta. When he found it, the grip plates were sticky and he realized they were sticky with his blood. "Shit," Holden murmured under his breath. To reach the gun the blood had to have oozed across his midsection, which meant a steady flow.

He heard the crunching of gravel again, mingled with the rustling of dry fallen leaves. There were pine trees all about his position in the rocks overlooking the road; the only deciduous trees were in a small stand about twenty-five yards back over the brow of the embankment, a few feet over his head. David Holden, the pain intensifying as he moved, got up into a crouch, the Beretta—blood-covered grips tacky to the touch—in his right fist, the M-16 at his side. He moved gradually, in a diagonal direction, up the embankment, away from the small side road that passed the garage, putting whatever was the origin of the sound between him and the men in military fatigues who'd invaded the sanitorium and assassinated the duly elected President of the United States.

David Holden had no doubt that the origin of the sounds was one or several of these men. As he moved, he put the Beretta away, drawing the Defender knife from its sheath beneath his right shoulder instead. A single shot would bring them all down on him. The knife's handle, too, was wet and slick with his own blood. . . .

If she'd worn nylons, she would have ripped them. As it was, crossing the fence, she skinned her legs almost, but not quite, to the point of bloodying herself. She'd searched the perimeter of the fence, discovered at least a half-dozen sheets of discarded roofing shingles, shaken and brushed away the beetlelike insects living beneath them, then used the shingle strips to protect herself from the barbed wire at the top of the fence.

She dropped almost the full eight feet now, her skirt billowing around her like a parachute but without the same fall-breaking effect. She came down hard in a crouch, falling to her knees, skinning them a little on the gravel.

The security cops—four of them that she could see —were sticking together by the truck stop's entrance gate, this a reinforced section of chain-link fence some eight feet in width and, for some silly reason, at least three feet taller than the perimeter fence. Rose Shepherd got to her feet, looking right and left, the Detonics Servicemaster .45 coming out of her purse, her left hand racking the slide (she'd emptied the chamber in preparation for a hard landing coming over the fence) and stripping the top round from the magazine. Her right thumb brushed the safety upward, then braced under it as she started along the fence line; she carried a gun cocked and locked only when combat was imminent.

She stopped directly opposite the nearest of the semis, brushed her skirt to clean it of the debris of rotted leaves she'd picked up, then glanced right and left again, breaking into a dead run for the rear of the truck. Her hair was down and, as she ran, she could feel it lashing at her face, a wind whipping up across the blacktopped parking lot, and on the edge of the wind came a fine mist of cold rain.

The truck's engine was running.

She shivered all the more, despite the exertion of the run.

The rear of the semi's trailer—Rose Shepherd flattened herself against it, content for the moment that she couldn't be seen from either the gate or the well-lit interior of the truck stop's dining area. The rain was increasing, the wind heightening as well, plastering her skirt flush against her legs. She found a bead-ended rubber band, caught up her hair at the nape of the neck, and twisted it into a ponytail to keep it out of her face, her .45 set on the rear bumper of the semi.

There was an ear-splittingly loud groan, as the air brakes released.

She reached for the Servicemaster, the truck and trailer starting into motion. As her fingers started closing over the black checkered rubber grips, the volume of pouring rain suddenly increased to a torrent, the truck's motion speeding up.

Her fingertips brushed against the surface of the Pachmayr grips and she fell forward, catching herself on her hands and knees as the truck pulled away. "Shit!"

Rose Shepherd looked up.

Patrons taking shelter from the sudden rain were staring at her from inside the truck stop's doorway, and the guards were staring at her from the gate. Aside from the little Chiefs Special under her soaked-through top and her knife, her only real weapon was riding away on the rear bumper of a semi. Leaping to her feet, Rose Shepherd broke into a dead run after the truck. What hair she hadn't caught up with the rubber band sticking to her face, she squinted against the rainwater pouring into her eyes.

"Hey, you!"

One of the guards was shouting at her from beside the gate. She didn't waste energy looking at him but kept running as fast as she could after the truck, the insides of her once white track shoes now awash with a flood of rainwater, so filled that as she bounded through the puddles dotting the black-topped lot, she couldn't really tell the difference.

She was almost up even with the rear of the truck.

It was starting to turn. "Don't do that!"

A gunshot came from beside the fence. "Stand right where you are!" blasted from a battery-oper-ated bullhorn.

She didn't have the energy or breath to tell the man who'd shouted through the bullhorn where he could put it. She veered hard right, trying to inter-cept the truck, slipping, catching herself. Her clothes were completely soaked, her skirt bunched up to her thighs as she ran. The denim material seemed to weigh a ton.

The truck finished the turn and Rose Shepherd was nearly beside it. As the truck veered sharply right again, she saw the Servicemaster. Her right hand reached out for it. Her fingers closed over the .45 as the truck began to accelerate. She fell forward into a huge puddle, but she had the gun.

Rose Shepherd looked up.

Three of the guards from the gate were running toward her through the rain, one of them pulling on his orange slicker, the other two already wearing theirs, those two with revolvers in their hands.

Rose Shepherd pushed up to her feet, spitting puddle water away from her lips. She looked around for the Suburban. There was no chance of stealing it now— But—the truck! She started running again, the three orange-slicker-clad security cops changing direction, running through the rain to cut her off. She heard a pistol shot, then another. Water in the puddle through which she ran splashed upward as the bullet impacted. She raised her right arm, protecting her eyes, the .45 still firmly in her fist.

Rose Shepherd kept running.

The truck was picking up speed.

Her lungs ached from the run and her shins were starting to cramp.

Another pistol shot whizzed past her.

Rose Shepherd stabbed the .45 toward the three security cops and they all dropped to the pavement. She didn't shoot, just kept running. The cab of the semi was fifty feet from her, angling toward the parking-lot gate. The gate was closed, but the truck sounded its air horn again and again, her ears vibrating with it. And the truck was picking up speed.

She kept running.

The gate was still closed, the fourth security guard raising his right hand palm outward in the classic traffic policeman's "stop" gesture. The truck's air horn sounded again, then again, and again.

Twenty feet or less to the cab. She threw her shoulders back, her left hand tearing her skirt upward where it bound across her thighs. The security cop by the gate was stepping back, running out of the path of the oncoming truck, hauling the gate open with him as he ran.

Ten feet.

Five.

Rose Shepherd shifted the Detonics Servicemaster to her left hand, throwing her body toward the passenger side door, jumping as the truck accelerated past, her right hand gripping the grab handle, her purse swinging from the crook of her elbow. Her left hand moved to her waist, ramming the .45 into the waistband of her skirt, then moved to the truck's door handle. She tore the door open, the gate only half open, its leading edge looking only inches away from the nose of the cab.

She threw herself across the bucket passenger seat, hauling her legs in after her, bending them upward from the knees, the door slamming to behind her as the sound of metal tearing metal began and she stabbed the .45 toward the figure behind the wheel. "Keep driving or your dead!"

The driver laughed; and, as Rose looked up, sheets of chain link were skittering over the hood and falling away from the windshield. There was a loud ripping sound and the truck seemed to lurch ahead.

"Honey, I'm not stoppin' for you or anybody; so put the fuckin' gun away and strap in with that seat belt. Wouldn't wanna break us any damn laws!"

Rose Shepherd just stared at the pretty girl with the long blond hair. . . .

Three men, one of them stopping to urinate into some low bushes, one of the other two making some sort of crack about it that Holden was too distant to understand, were some thirty-five yards from him. All three wore the uniform of the men from the roof of the sanitorium. Holden put his hand to his side, holding his breath against the pain as he tried to think.

Ever since the inception of the Patriots under Rufus Burroughs, it had been a taboo to open fire on the police or the military, since they were only Americans doing their job, and the real enemy was the Front for the Liberation of North America. Sometimes the taboo had been incredibly difficult to keep. But keep it they had. But there, in the sanitorium in Virginia where the President had been kept in seclusion to recuperate from the injuries he'd sustained during the terrorist rocket attack on the security conference, it had come down to fighting the men in United States Army uniforms or letting the President die.

The President had died anyway, but so had many of the men in uniform. At the time Holden had rationalized that the uniforms were fake, that the men who wore them were FLNA terrorists. But he'd pondered increasingly over that in the intervening hours while his wounds had been patched, while they'd cleaned up, changed, then separated after learning the bitter truth that Rudolph Cerillia, their one and only true ally in government, was himself about to be killed and they were powerless to stop it.

Luther Steel, special agent in charge of the Metro Task Force, acting directly under the orders of the now-dead President and FBI Director Rudolph Cerillia, now, along with his men, as wanted as any of the Patriots, had wept. Cerillia had been like a father to

Steel, despite the difference in races, Cerillia white, Steel black.

These men in the uniform of the United States were approaching Holden's position. What if . . . David Holden trembled, considering the possibilities. What if they were actual military personnel and part of a unit that de facto President Roman Makowski was fielding to do his dirty work? Had the real President only been their first victim?

Holden was reminded of the *Schutzstaffel* of Adolf Hitler. As an historian Holden had been able to view the SS only as a disgusting abstraction. But was he now seeing its reincarnation, albeit on behalf of a political and social philosophy of the far left rather than the right? Were they a private military force of killers serving only the country's leader, doing only his bidding, no matter how corrupt, how vile?

His right hand, gripping the Defender knife, shook with rage and fear. Despite the pain in his side David Holden started moving again, one eye on the road, looking for Rosie. Light-headedness washed over him as he moved, a sick feeling in the pit of his stomach. He worked his way along the edge of the embankment above the rocks in which he'd hidden earlier, looking at his watch, trying to estimate the time that Rosie would return. If he could avoid engagement with these men until he saw her coming, then he could make it down to the road and intercept her. They might even get away without alerting the force still parked near the garage. And if worse came to worst, and he were discovered, at least with transportation available, he could risk a gun. To try using the knife against at least three men, when he was already faint from loss of blood, was asking for defeat.

As silently as he could, Holden kept moving. . . .

"Who the hell are you?"

"I needed a ride," Rose Shepherd told her.

With a toss of her well-past-shoulder-length blond hair, the girl behind the wheel of the semi laughed in a pleasant-sounding alto. "Fine. My name's Kelly Martin." And she took her hand from the massive steering wheel and outstretched it for a shake. Rose Shepherd took it. "I wasn't about to hang around for those rent-a-cops to shake me down over my load. What's your name?"

"Rose Shepherd." There was no sense hiding her identity. "What's in your load?" Rose clutched the .45 tight in her fist even though it was still inside the waistband of her sodden skirt.

"The Rose Shepherd that's on all the wanted lists?"

Rose Shepherd shrugged her shoulders. "That's me. What's on your manifest?"

"Yeah; I read about you. Ex-cop, right?"

"Ex-cop. What's wrong with your cargo?"

"Ammunition. I work with the Patriots out of Miami. Trouble with a state that sticks out into the ocean like a hitchhiker's thumb like that is they can cut the whole damn thing off too easy. Anyway, that's what they did. The ammunition was supposed to be coming in by boat, but the government's stopping every damn boat and searchin' it. So, I went up for it."

"You're nuts," Rose told her. "I mean, no offense,

Kelly, but you're nuts. What the hell you think they do to trucks?"

"I change plates. The cops are spread thin. Got a group of Patriots from Panama City on the panhandle there—"

"I know where it is." Rose nodded, easing the grip on her .45 long enough to search her purse to see if her cigarettes were still dry. As she lit one with a Bic lighter, she glanced into the big West Coast mirror. No pursuit lights yet, but that would come. The rain was falling in sheets now, the windshield wipers having almost no noticeable effect. Perhaps the rain was part of the reason for their not being followed. "They gonna meet you, and then what?"

Kelly Martin laughed. "Then it's their problem. I change clothes, maybe rinse some dye into my hair, and take a regular passenger car south and join up with my unit again. Got any idea how many creeps the FLNA's sendin' up from Cuba and over from Mexico? God—"

"Who's your boss in the Miami Patriots?" Rose asked her. She'd met the leader of the Miami Patriot cell once. If this self-proclaimed Patriot smuggler knew the right name, it would go a long way toward making Rose believe she could be trusted.

"Why should I tell you? Ohh—I get it! You don't believe me, testin' me, huh? So, prove you're Rose Shepherd, not some damn FLNAer or a cop."

Rose Shepherd shrugged her shoulders. She hadn't yet mentioned anything about the direction in which the truck was traveling, because Kelly Martin was already driving down the right road. Rose glanced at the speedometer, shivering in her wet clothes and at the thought of how fast the woman was driving in this downpour. Every once in a while Rose could feel the rig starting to hydroplane. It would be another ten minutes at least before they'd reach the county-road turnoff to the garage, where David was hiding. "It's not like I carry my old badge, okay? I don't even use the right driver's license anymore. All my ID's are faked. You've probably seen my picture in the post office, though." And Rose Shepherd leaned forward in the bucket seat, pushed her wet hair back from her face, and smiled.

Kelly Martin turned and looked at her, smiled back, and said, "Yeah, but the hair was shorter."

"It was dryer too."

Kelly laughed. "Got a hair dryer in the back there above the bed. There's a plug-in near the cabinet door. Runs off twelve volt, don't worry."

Rose Shepherd looked behind her for the first time. She'd noticed the cab was long but hadn't really thought about why. There was a boxed-off stall on the driver's side, she imagined for a chemical toilet. Next to it there was a double bunk, one high, one low. Above the high one and below the low one were built-in cabinets.

Rose released her seat belt and swiveled the bucket around so she could slip into the rear compartment. She found the hair dryer on the first try, but it took a few seconds to find the outlet. The floor of the cab was built up a little, she thought, and she wondered what might lie beneath it. "Whatchya doin' out this way?" Kelly asked.

Rose stubbed out her cigarette in a clean built-in ashtray near the lower bunk, then sat down. Before starting the hair dryer, she told the woman, "If you're a Patriot, then maybe you know better than to ask a lot of questions. I'll tell you when the time comes, all right?"

"Suit yourself. That mean you're my driving buddy for a while?"

"At least a little while"—and Rose Shepherd started the hair dryer as she worked with her other hand to finish getting the rubber band free of her tangled hair. . . .

Hobie Townes had insisted on watching the entire tape and every single commercial in it: a Three Stooges movie and seemingly endless commercial plugs for an offer of what might well have been every single country music and rock 'n' roll record ever produced. But at the end of the movie, when the Stooges had finally aided Hercules in his triumph, there was the message Rudolph Cerillia sent them from death.

"Shut the damn thing off," Roman Makowski said, standing up, turning his back on the projection television screen and the images of American faces, American air power, the Statue of Liberty, all the while the Star and Stripes in half-dissolve beneath the images, "The Star Spangled Banner" played by the Marine Corps Band. "The son of a bitch."

"That was the only tape in the whole damn house, Mr. President."

Makowski kicked the wooden tray table with the coffee the servants had brought them, sending the coffee spilling across the carpet. "The fucker's laughing at us. Only tape, my ass. If it isn't in the damn house, Cerillia got it out somehow. You realize what he probably knew?"

"Yes, sir," Hobart Townes answered softly, gravely.

"We had him eliminated to shut him up, didn't we, Hobie?" Makowski sneered, turning around, staring Townes down.

"Yes, Mr. President. In the best interests of the nation, of course."

"Yeah, whatever you say." He looked at the blank screen for a few seconds. "You find that damn tape, and find it before some damn reporter finds it or the fuckin' Patriots get their hooks into it. You find it, you're top dog under me. You don't, you're dog meat. You just remember, I can take you down 'cause I put you up there to begin with."

"Yes, Mr. President. Do you have any—"

"Ideas? Where you should look? What the hell are you my security chief for, huh? Ideas! Shit, man! Just find the tape. When they throw the dirt on Cerillia's coffin, I want him buried, all the way, all the way." Makowski kicked at the table again, overturning the creamer that, somehow, hadn't spilled its contents when he'd knocked the tray to the floor. "You plant the stories on the Patriots?"

"Yes, sir. By morning when—"

"It is morning, Hobie. I blew half the damn night watchin' a comedy, remember?"

"Yes, sir. I meant, when you address the special joint session of Congress this morning, well, the papers, the networks, they'll already have the text of your speech. They're already laying the President's death—"

"God Almighty—you have to call him that?"

"What I meant to say, Mr. President, was they're already laying the assassination at the sanitorium at the feet of the Patriots, Holden and all the rest of them. And Cerillia's going to be implicated as selling out to them—and when he double-crossed them, they killed him too. It's all set."

"Yeah—find the damn tape, Hobie, or it's your ass." And Makowski left the Oval Office, wishing he'd had the girl stay in his bed. . . .

The rain started like a fine, cold mist, then suddenly it enveloped him. David Holden could barely keep conscious. He huddled in the rocks, clutching his M-16 against his chest, his body shaking with cold and loss of blood. "Rosie," he repeated, over and over again, under his breath. He had to stay awake long enough—alive long enough, if this was going to be it—to intercept Rosie Shepherd before she drove into a trap and died.

If she died, he wanted death too. Elizabeth, his three children, all he'd ever cared for in his life, were gone from him except for Rosie. What life he had, she had given back to him. With his wife and son and two daughters murdered by the Front for the Liberation of North America, he hadn't cared about living. He'd fallen in with the Patriots and Rufus Burroughs, their leader, when there was nothing else for him and his life could be wasted that way as well as any other, wasted and lost.

But then Rufus Burroughs had died, and he inherited the mantle of leadership for the Metro-Patriots, already the most effective resistance unit against the

FLNA's assault on the United States. And Rose had stood beside him and eventually slept beside him.

More than the cause, which always seemed so hopeless, it was Rose who kept him going, who was his happiness.

David Holden realized he was becoming maudlin and wondered if that were somehow a premonition of death.

He looked up toward the darkness above him. The rain washed his face, renewing him in that instant, and he whispered, "Not yet, God. Too much to do—please."

David Holden lowered his head, held his gun, fought the pain. . . .

Rose Shepherd's hair was dry enough. She glanced at her Timex Ironman, having taken it from her purse and put it on. There was no longer any sense in worrying about appearances. Her clothes were mud stained and soaked, her top still so wet that anyone short of a blind man could have seen the shoulder-holstered revolver beneath it. With the driest portion of her slip she wiped off her .45, sitting down again in the front passenger seat beside blond-haired, blue-eyed truck driver and self-proclaimed Patriot Kelly Martin.

About four minutes remained before the turnoff to the garage where David still waited. "What's in the false compartment under the floor, Kelly?"

Kelly Martin turned her head, the hair moving again. She was very pretty in a wild, young sort of way. Rose Shepherd didn't feel young tonight. "What do you mean?"

"I mean, the false compartment under the floor just in front of the bunks, between these seats and the cabinets under the lower bunk. You know."

Kelly Martin's eyes were back on the road. Under the circumstances that was the best place for them to be, the rain falling more heavily than before, if that were physically possible. "Why do you wanna know, Rosie?"

"Why'd you call me 'Rosie'?"

"What's this, a damn inquisition?"

"That's my nickname. I don't like it, but only a few people I trust use it."

Then Kelly Martin's face lit with a grin. She had high cheekbones, clear skin, a well-scrubbed look that didn't seem to go with her mouth or her attitude, Rose thought. "I had a girlfriend named Rose when I was in high school. She used to hate it when people called her Rosie too. Figured you might feel that way."

"Fine. What's in the false compartment?"

Kelly Martin shrugged her shoulders under the man's flannel shirt she wore. It was open at the front all the way, a pink T-shirt–like top beneath it. "In case of trouble I got some shit stashed there."

"What kind of stuff?"

"Why?"

"If you've heard of me, then you've heard of David Holden, right?"

"Sure, like everybody's heard of David Holden. He as good-lookin' a hunk as he looks like in the magazines and newspapers?"

Rose Shepherd almost felt offended, then said quickly to cover it, "He looks better than the picture they use on his wanted posters. He's with me." She had her hand on the .45 again.

Kelly laughed again. She seemed to do that a lot. "What? You got him in that purse o' yours?"

Now Rose Shepherd laughed, but she didn't feel like it. "No. He's a coupla miles up the road. There's a turnoff. You're taking it." Rose raised the .45 so its muzzle pointed in Kelly Martin's general direction.

Kelly glanced at it, then away. "Yeah, honey, well, you try shootin' me, this truck jackknifes and I'm not the only one who's dead."

"David Holden's out there. You say you're a Patriot. He was wounded trying to save the life of the President of the United States."

"The television news guys say different," Kelly Martin answered, a hard edge to her voice.

"So, when did you start believing them?"

"Who are you to him?—oh, yeah, you're supposed to be Holden's main squeeze, aren't you, Rosie? Huh?"

"That's none of anybody's business but his and mine."

"So I should delay a cargo of ammunition just so I can pick up some guy who's probably dyin' anyway, huh? Well, think again. There's folks down in Miami who're dyin' too. The FLNA's almost taken over the whole friggin' state."

Rose Shepherd had to know, before she shot Kelly Martin and tried to grab the wheel. They couldn't be more than two minutes from the turnoff now. "Who's your leader in Miami?"

"Why should I tell you? If you're who you say you are—"

Rose dropped the safety on the .45. It made an audible click. "I'll blow your damn brains all over the cab, lady, so help me. I know the name of the Patriot cell leader in Miami. If you don't, you're dead. And either way, the truck's turning off onto that side road." Kelly Martin's eyes darted between the muzzle of Rose Shepherd's Servicemaster and Rose Shepherd's own eyes. There was honesty in Kelly's eyes, Rose thought, but she couldn't take the chance. "You've got thirty seconds for that name, or, so help me God, you're history, kid."

"It's not Kelly Martin. It's Kelly Martine. My dad's a Cuban, came here when Castro seized power, knew old fuzz-faced Fidel was a rotten Commie schmuck all along, then worked with that CIA thing and spent a year in a damn rathole jail before he escaped. He's Guillermo Martine. He's the cell leader, all right?"

Rose Shepherd let out her breath. And she raised the safety on the .45 as she shifted the muzzle into a safe direction. "Then you'd better slow down and get ready for that turnoff, or I'll tell your father and he'll whip your butt."

She looked at Kelly Martine.

Kelly looked back. "Shit"—and she started gearing the rig down for the turn.

"It's just ahead," Rose Shepherd told her. . . .

The sound of trucks, not from the road bed, but from behind him, beyond the tree-covered knoll that formed part of the embankment edging the highway.

David Holden was soaked to the skin. His knuckles were white with cold and tension, his hands locked on the M-16 at his chest. He tried to stand up. It wasn't working; a wave of nausea swept over him. He looked into the darkness above him. To the east, a long way away, there was a thread of light weaving between the clouds. He smudged blood and water from the crystal of his Rolex. It was nearly dawn.

Holden shifted the butt of the M-16 from his chest to the ground, then worked his hands upward along its length until he reached the flash deflector. There was a muzzle cap in place.

He closed his eyes, inhaled, then pulled himself up from his knees, the sounds of the Army trucks getting louder now. If they left . . . And then he looked into the roadbed. A solitary semitrailer truck, the yellow light pattern on the grill forming a happy face—it was slowing down, to make the turnoff onto the side road.

"Rosie," Holden whispered.

He dug in the butt of the M-16 and hobbled along the embankment. If he could start a shooting war, now, Rosie would hear, turn off, be saved.

His teeth were clenched so hard against the pain that his jaw, too, began to hurt.

He kept moving. . . .

Kelly Martine had told her to open up the panel in the floor. Using the Phillips head screwdriver blade from a Leatherman tool identical to the one David always carried, Rose Shepherd turned out the last of the four screws that had been revealed when she'd rolled back the edges of the carpet.

A flat handle was set in flush at the center of the panel and folded out so the panel could be moved.

Rose Shepherd reached out, took the handle, drew it and the panel upward, then set the panel against the lower bunk's edge.

She flopped back the blanket that lay across the interior of the compartment. To either side of the opening, clamped securely in place, were two full-sized 9mm Uzi carbines, with full-length barrels and retracted folding stocks. Up the magazine well of each was a twenty-five-round stick. She recognized these as Israeli Defense Forces surplus by their finish. A dozen more twenty-five-round magazines, all of them looking to be fully loaded, were clamped in place at the nearer portion of the compartment, between the two Uzi carbines. "Realize the deep shit you'd get into for having these?" Rosie laughed. Occupying the rest of the compartment were two SIG-Sauer P-226 pistols, a dozen loaded fifteen-round magazines for them, and two peculiar-looking knives.

The knives seemed to combine the familiar lines of the American Bowie recurve and the point of the Oriental *tanto*. The blades were approximately six inches long. She took one out of the clamps. The stock was a full quarter inch thick, the double quillon brass guard a quarter inch thick as well and extending well above and below the flat ground blade. The handle was full tang, slabs of what looked like black linen Micarta brass-riveted on either side of it, the hilt drilled through with a brass grommet and rounded at the butt. Inscribed on the blade in the only letters large enough to see in the poor illumination from the meager overhead lights were the words *Big Ugly One*.

"I'm going into the turnoff, Rosie."

Rose Shepherd grabbed up one of the Uzi carbines and three spare magazines, dropping the magazines into the side slash pockets of her denim skirt. She put the knife back into its clamps. "There were two of you," Rose began as she slipped in beside Kelly Martine again, "weren't there?"

"And that's none of your business," Kelly Martine almost snapped, her voice suddenly sounding hoarse, tight.

"All right."

Kelly Martine turned the wheel right, the screech of the air brakes drowning out the thrumming of the rain for an instant. As the semi's headlights swept the two-lane county road, past the reverse-facing stop sign, she saw lights. "Slow up," Rose ordered her, working the Uzi's bolt, assuming—correctly, she discovered—that the carbines had been stored chamber empty as she herself would have done.

Rose Shepherd laid the Uzi across her lap and searched with her fingers for the button to power down the window beside her. She activated the door locks instead, tried again, and found it.

What she'd thought she'd heard she had heard: gunfire.

"Stop this sucker, now," Rose almost screamed, rain pouring in on her, soaking her clothes again instantly.

As the truck ground to a halt, Rosie looked at Kelly Martine. "Now, you can split out on me, Kelly. You've got your thing to do. Or you can turn this rig around so it's facing the highway and keep the engine running and help me save the one man who might be able to put this country back together again, someday. I don't have time for an answer. If you're here when I get back, I'll have your answer then."

And Rose Shepherd climbed down into the mud beside the two-lane county road, then broke into a dead run, the Uzi carbine in both fists, the safety slid off. . . .

David Holden, wedged between another boulder and the trunk of one of the big leafless live oaks, raised up the muzzle of the M-16, barely able to handle the weight of the rifle now, firing a too long, too ragged full-auto burst toward the closest of the two-and-a-half-ton trucks. The sound of glass shattering and more darkness than there had been before were his only reassurance that he had hit anything. He tucked down amid a volume of return fire that had to have come from at least two dozen weapons. Bark chips and and rock chips blew everywhere. His eyes squinted against their fury and he raised his left arm to shield his face and head. His cheeks, his neck, his left hand, all felt the impacts as the sharp particles lacerated his flesh. He stabbed the rifle upward again, firing out the thirty-round magazine, then drawing back as more answering fire erupted.

The more answering fire he could generate, the louder the sounds of the battle, the greater chance Rosie would hear it from the highway and drive on.

He was lying to himself, he knew—telling himself that this time she would do the sensible thing that deep inside himself he knew she wouldn't do. But at least she'd be warned.

More gunfire, a machine gun this time. "Don't come for me," he said through clenched teeth into the night. "Don't . . ." He couldn't make his legs respond anymore, which was why he'd picked this notch between the rock and the tree trunk to make his stand, crawled to it through the mud. He turned his head back so his face looked up into the rain. It would help to keep him conscious longer.

A fresh stick up the well of the M-16, Holden returned fire, shouting at them, "Can't hit shit, can you, guys? Come on! Running low on ammo?" There was a volume of fire that was greater than anything they had thrown at him before, whole chunks ripping out of the trunk of the oak, most of the bark already stripped away by the previous fusillades. Holden tucked his head down, punching the muzzle of the M-16 over the rock behind which he knelt, firing short bursts toward the men.

The machine gun started up again, the volume of fire growing rather than diminishing. Holden could no longer return it. As he looked at his rifle, he noticed that the front handguard had been split by a bullet's impact.

He laughed.

The rifle still worked. He confirmed that by flipping the selector to semi, then firing a round into the dirt a dozen or so yards from him. He flipped back to auto.

Two more loaded spares for the rifle remained to him. He had both of his pistols, Rosie's Glock, and plenty of magazines for each of those.

"Come on, you sons of bitches! What's the matter? Only good for shooting defenseless old men on rooftops, huh? Can't cut it against an armed man? That it?"

More automatic-weapons fire caused Holden to tuck back deeper into the crotch between the boulder and the oak tree. He judged he had about another five minutes at the outside before he passed out from loss of blood and never woke up again. . . .

Rose Shepherd stopped a few yards inside the tree line on the southeast edge of the diagonally angling two-lane. There was a line of trucks—she stopped counting after ten when the road took the bend toward the garage where she'd originally left David—and the lead truck, its lights shot out, was itself blocking the roadway, one tire flat in the front. "David," she whispered.

What had transpired was clear to her. The trucks had arrived at the garage, or passed it, and David had judged the time of her return pretty accurately, realizing she'd drive right into the Army convoy. It made her skin crawl even to think about shooting it out with U.S. troops, but . . . She saw the men of the mortar crew as they moved past the headlights of the third truck back, the headlights apparently left on because the truck ahead of them, its lights out, shielded it from David's position. He was evidently wedged in between a boulder of some kind and a big bare-limbed tree just beside the edge of the road about two hundred yards up from the highway.

She noticed the patch on the shoulder of one of the mortar crewmen. At the distance she couldn't see it clearly, but suddenly she felt a sinking feeling in her stomach.

She reached down between her legs, caught up the hem of her skirt at the back, and drew it up between her legs, tucking it into her waistband. The Uzi slung cross body, at high port near her breasts, she worked her way along through the trees. She had to get nearer.

There was a deafening volume of gunfire and there was no answering fire from what she assumed was David's position. But then she heard his voice. "Hey, guys! Guess what! All that ammo? Well, didn't hit me yet, guys!"

"Holden! Surrender. This is you, isn't it?"

The voice came from behind the second truck, well out of range of any stray fire David could return against them, across a battery-operated bullhorn. She could see the man now as he crouched in cover.

"Yeah, it's me. You're the same heroes who murdered the President, aren't you?"

"If you surrender your weapons and come out with your hands over your head—"

"Then you'll murder me, right?"

Rose Shepherd's throat felt tight. David was a fool sometimes, but sometimes he was so brave. This was one of those times.

"You can drag this out, Holden, or end it now. According to what the world thinks, you killed the President, you and your damn Patriots. And that's what everybody's going to keep right on thinking because you won't be alive to tell them anything different. And even if you made it out of here alive, Holden, the whole country'll be ready to kill you on sight. You're through. You and all your lousy Patriots are through."

Rose Shepherd dropped to her knees and settled the metal stock of the Uzi carbine against her shoulder. "Eat shit, motherfucker," she hissed as she squeezed the trigger. It was an easy shot at twenty yards and her bullet must have struck him in the head, just what she'd aimed for, because his head snapped back and away from her, his body almost pulled behind it as he fell, rolled, lay still.

Rose Shepherd swung the muzzle of the Uzi on line with the machine gunner, fired, then fired again, the man, already starting to turn toward the shot, sprawling forward across his gun. She swung the Uzi toward the men huddled beside the forwardmost truck, fired a half dozen rounds without hitting anything besides a driver's side mirror, but pinning them down. She was up, moving, gunfire coming into the trees toward the position she'd just vacated. She angled her run toward the second truck. It was their only chance, and not much of one.

She broke from the tree cover, onto the road, running across the right-hand lane for the cab of the second truck. Two men with M-16's, huddled beneath the truck, turned their rifles toward her. Rose Shepherd fired out the Uzi's magazine, triggering each shot as fast as her finger would move, then broke into a dead run.

"Agh!" Something bit into her right calf and she stumbled, didn't fall, reached out toward the Army truck, grabbed the open door, and pulled herself inside, letting go of the Uzi.

A man raced toward the cab, an M-16 in his hands. As Rose Shepherd stabbed the Detonics .45 toward him, she could see his shoulder patch. "Eat lead!" She shot him in the face, safing the .45, throwing it on the seat beside the empty Uzi as she let out the clutch and the truck lurched forward. She cut the wheel in a sharp left, still not missing the rear end of the first truck entirely, but clearing it despite leaving part of the truck's right front fender behind. The windshield wipers were already running, but they weren't doing much good against the rain.

She didn't know what made her look down, but guessed it was a twinge of pain. Her right calf was bleeding, but since her foot still moved on the gas she deduced that nothing was broken, at least.

A man jumped out at her from the front of the first truck and her right hand left the gear shift, found the butt of the Detonics .45, and she thumbed down the safety. As he clambered onto the Army truck's passenger-side running board, Rose fired. He dodged the first bullet, swung open the door, reached for her. She fired twice again and blew him back through the open doorway and onto the hood of the first truck.

David would see her, have to see her, be ready to jump aboard.

"David!"

She was nearly even with the boulder and the big tree. "David!" She began hitting the horn button, pounding on it furiously.

"David!"

No David. Maybe he'd taken off into the trees or— she hit the brakes as hard as she could, the truck skidding, nearly pitching her upper body over the steering wheel and through the windshield.

The truck went into a lateral skid as she fought the

wheel, the vehicle's bulk lurching into the skid, almost overturning, settling.

Rose Shepherd grabbed up the Uzi from the floor, her .45 still in her fist as she slid across the seat out the open passenger-side door and dropped to the road surface. David lay motionless behind the rock. She ran toward him, gunfire coming at her from back by the trucks. She dropped to her knees beside him, her right calf paining her badly. David was pale. "Oh, my God!" She shook him, touched her fingers to his face.

More gunfire.

She tucked down, firing out the Servicemaster, not bothering to look for more spare magazines from the purse slung to her left side, just dumping the pistol there. She grabbed up David's M-16, buttoning out the magazine, taking one of the two fresh ones from the mud beside him, ramming it up the magazine well. She fired a burst over the top of the rock, then ducked. Answering fire tore into the rock and the tree trunk.

Rose Shepherd put down the assault rifle, touched her fingers to David's neck. There was no detectable pulse. Her eyes filled with tears. His head sank to her chest, her hands touching at his face.

Against her cheek, she felt a wisp of breath.

"David!"

Rose Shepherd looked up. She looked back, toward the truck, the engine still running. If she could get him into it. That was no good.

Something she had noticed on the truck. It was the same with all Army trucks. "Spare gas."

Rose Shepherd grabbed up David's M-16 and the

one remaining spare magazine, fired a burst, waited
for the answering fire from the trucks, then, as it
subsided, she ran, keeping to a low crouch, gunfire
tearing into the road surface beside her feet, bullets
ricocheting off the bodywork of the truck. She made
it around the front end of the truck, the windshield
spiderwebbing, then shattering out as she pulled herself into the cab and behind the wheel, her head
down below the dashboard.

The Uzi was slung to her body. She thought to
change magazines, stashing the empty in her purse.

Her right hand moved the transmission. "Where
the hell's reverse on this thing!" She found reverse,
the truck grinding back across the width of the road.
Neutral. Then first, she hoped.

Her hands fought the wheel now as the truck
started forward. She turned the wheel into the tightest right she could make, her right hand leaving the
wheel for an instant, upshifting the long throw gear-
shift into second, her right leg stiffening as she
stomped the accelerator again.

She had the front of the truck almost dead even
with David's position now, gunfire hammering into
the vehicle, what little windshield glass remained
spraying into the cab as she found neutral and
worked the emergency brake. She told herself not to
worry about the glass particles in her hair.

Rose Shepherd threw open the driver's side door,
the Uzi and her purse still slung to her body, the
M-16 in her right hand. Gunfire tore into the pavement near her feet. She slipped in a muddy tire track,
fell to her knees. She looked back over her shoulder,

snarled, "You're gettin' yours, guys," then hauled herself to her feet.

She limped rearward along the side of the truck bed, at the back of the truck stopping, leaning against it. A five-gallon gasoline can. She looked at it for a second, wondering just how far she could throw it, praying it was full.

Rose Shepherd leaned the M-16 against the rear bumper and started working to free the jerican. David—he seemed almost dead. But she'd go on fighting, fighting for him. Get every one of—the gas can was free. She broke two of her already short nails getting the cap open, the smell of the gasoline confirming the can was full as much as the weight had. She needed something dry. Nothing was in her purse that would do. Her skirt and her slip were still soaked. She licked her lips, out of reflex looked around to make certain no one was watching, then reached under her clothes for her underpants.

Her panties were the driest thing on her body, and as she stuffed them down into the can to saturate them with the gasoline, she bent well over the can to keep as much water away as possible. She drew the panties out of the can, heavy with gasoline now, dripping with it. She stuffed half into the opening for the cap, using her slip to wedge them in place, stuffing part of that down into the opening as well.

The gunfire was slacking off.

They were either closing, or getting ready to.

She gave the can a test heft.

So much for throwing it.

The road was slick with rain and mud and she

could skate the jerican along, at least far enough to cause a little panic and buy some time.

The disposable lighter in her purse. She began hunting for it, then remembered where she'd put it. She searched her left pocket, past the empty magazine, and found it, praying it wasn't too wet to work. She struck the flint. Nothing. "Come on. Come on!" She struck it again. Nothing. It was wet. Too wet? She struck it again, saying, "Please work!"

Flame. She cupped the flame against the wind and the rain within the palms of her hands, the flame burning her. She lit the end of the gasoline-soaked fabric.

Rose drew back as it flared close to her face. She grabbed up the can, holding it as far away from her as she could, the flame nearly to the opening where it would ignite the entire can and explode.

She stuck her head around the far side of the truck bed and flipped the can into the roadway on its side, trails of burning gasoline spilling from it, hissing in the rain as it slid across the blacktop.

The can stopped dead about twenty feet or so past the front of the truck. She pulled back, grabbed for the M-16, and ran. There was a single earsplitting crack. She kept running, looking toward the concentration of men and trucks. There was no gunfire now, as burning gasoline rolled toward the first truck.

Rosie dropped to her knees beside David. "David! Can you walk?" It was a ridiculous question, she realized. He wasn't even conscious, was barely alive.

They'd taught her how to do it in the police academy, the fireman's carry, shown her—by having her do it—that someone, if she knew how, could carry a person over her shoulder who weighed significantly more, was significantly larger.

She fired out the M-16 toward the men running away from the first truck, burning gasoline slewing toward them, but not enough to do any damage, she thought. She threw the M-16 away and grabbed David's right arm at the wrist as she dropped into a crouch. This was the really tough part, she remembered. "Holy—"

She almost fell backward as she stood, her back paining her, her neck muscles spasming. David stood well over six feet and, solid and muscled, had to weigh over two hundred pounds. But she had him up —sort of—and she started toward the truck, praying nobody would open fire on them. "Please, God . . ." She was almost at the truck when she heard the sound of the explosion from behind her. It was only a little louder than the exploding jerican. She couldn't look back.

Another few feet.

No gunfire.

She lurched forward, David slipping from her shoulder onto the front seat, or at least halfway. She pushed his feet up and in, then shoved him across the front seat, pushing in after him, wondering if she'd ever walk again.

She stomped the clutch and found reverse, but the truck wouldn't budge. The emergency brake. She released it; the truck lurched rearward. She cut the wheel hard right, the rear end fishtailing right as she fumbled clutch and transmission into first, then released the clutch, nearly going over the edge of the road into the hopeless morass of red-tinged mud. For the first time she realized the sun had risen. But the rain poured down with such intensity that the morning was only a few shades lighter gray than the night had been. She fought the wheel into a tight left, the truck bumping over something—she hoped one of the enemy personnel—and onto the center of the roadbed. She fought the wheel back right, straightening out.

Rose looked into the shot-away remains of the driver's-side West Coast mirror. Behind her there was fire, one or more of the trucks in flames, but another of the trucks was pushing the lead truck—on fire—over the side of the road, more of the trucks curling around it, starting after her.

She was near the end of the road, no sign of the semitrailer truck. "Wonderful!" As she started into the right, slowing only for the turn, not stopping, she saw the semi dead ahead on the shoulder of the road. She stomped the accelerator, released pressure, worked the clutch down, and let it up as she finished the change into the higher gear. She wasn't certain which gear it was, the truck moving sluggishly. One of the tires was already shot out. She remembered that.

She started hitting the horn button. On the second try the semi's lights blinked. She slewed the Army truck in front of it on the shoulder, rolling on enough yardage that she hoped Kelly Martine would be able to maneuver around her.

Rose jumped from the truck cab, shouting, "Kelly!" But, long blond hair caught up in a blue bandana handkerchief, an Uzi carbine slung to her side, Kelly Martine was already running toward her.

Rose started hauling on David's ankles, drawing him along the seat, half out by the time Kelly Martine reached her. "Help me. He's dying."

"He is cute!"

"Shut up and I'll get you his autograph. Hurry it up!"

Rose hauled on his ankles, Kelly Martine taking David's legs, pulling him nearly out of the cab. Rose reached up and caught his upper body by the armpits, Kelly taking his ankles and they slid him fully clear, his weight sagging down between them. Rose inhaled, gasped, "Come on. We've got plenty of unhappy assholes right on our tail."

They carried him slung between them like a heavy sack, toward the cab of the semi, the rain falling in sheets now. Rose Shepherd could hear the noise of the Army trucks reaching the intersection with the highway. "Hurry!"

With Kelly's help Rose propped David against her, barely holding him upright, his body slumped over her, chin resting on her shoulder, as Kelly opened the cab door, climbed inside, then reached down for him. Rose let David fall back toward Kelly, catching his legs under the knees, lifting as Kelly dragged. "Into the back. We can put him on one of the bunks."

Rose nodded, exhausted, looking behind them as she climbed aboard. "No time. I'll do it! Drive this thing!"

Rose Shepherd slid between the two front buckets, Kelly Martine slipping past her, dropping into the seat. David lay across the floor, over the hidden compartment, its lid replaced but the carpeting still pulled away.

As the truck started rolling, Kelly Martine called out, "They're trying to cut me off!"

Rose looked at David. He was as well off on the floor for a few minutes longer, because if they did get cut off, he'd be murdered assuming he wasn't dead already. She tossed her purse on the lower bunk, scrounged in her pockets for the spent Uzi magazine and flipped it onto the bunk as well, then got onto her knees behind Kelly in the driver's seat. "Roll your window down!"

Rose Shepherd punched the Uzi carbine through the open window at one of the Army trucks that was dead even with them, and trying to slip in front of them. Rain streamed across her face in torrents, but Rose fired, pulling the Uzi's trigger as fast as her finger could move, peppering the passenger-side window of the Army truck, blowing the glass inward. The truck swerved away as Rose heard and felt the grinding of the semi's gears.

"There should be a long downhill a coupla miles ahead. We've got a chance. Hold on!"

Rose didn't have anything to hold on to, so she crouched down lower, changing magazines in the Uzi carbine, then, on hands and knees, crawled behind the seats, not looking at David, afraid she'd cry if his eyes were staring blankly upward. "Get the other window down!" She crawled up into the front passenger seat, shoving the Uzi carbine into the rain, wiping rainwater from her eyes as she looked back. A phalanx of the Army trucks was behind them, a wall filling the highway in all four lanes from side to side. As she watched, the tarp covering of one of the trucks was peeled back, billowing behind the truck in the wind, a machine gun visible at the right side of the vehicle. "This truck got a CB radio?"

"Of course it does," Kelly hollered back.

"Then get on it. We need help. Tell it like it is. Do it!"

And Rose Shepherd heard Kelly Martine's voice as she spoke into the microphone. "Breaker, Breaker, Channel Nineteen. Mayday. I repeat, Mayday. Bright blue semitrailer truck with Florida plates southwest bound on Greenwood Highway, pursued by—" She called to Rosie, "Who the hell are they?"

"The same assholes who murdered the President."

There was silence for an instant, then Kelly Martine's voice returned. ". . . pursued by men disguised in Army uniforms. These are the same men who murdered the President. We're Patriots, just two women, and we've got David Holden with us, injured, maybe dying. We need help fast. Bring lots of guns. Hurry. I repeat"—and she began giving a similar version of the same message again.

Rose's eyes stayed on the truck with the machine gun, the truck starting to speed up, about midway now between the other trucks and the semi. Rose shouldered the Uzi carbine, wishing she had something heavier than a pistol-caliber weapon to use. She leaned half out of the truck's window, trying to get a bead on the windshield of the pursuing truck, realizing it would do no good. "What kind of stuff you got in the back of the truck? Give it to me straight, Kelly."

"It's a load of military weapons the FLNA stole from an armory and our people in Ohio stole back."

"Anything really interesting?"

Kelly seemed to think for a moment, then smiled as Rose looked at her. "LAW rockets?"

Without thinking Rose Shepherd asked her, "How do I get into the back of the truck?"

"No way—not while we're moving. The only way in is through the rear doors."

"Locked?"

"Yeah."

"Gimme the key," Rose snapped. She looked at David. She couldn't tell if he was dead or alive. "And keep repeating that message." She wiped rain from her face. . . .

He had stolen a car, something he had never done in his life. He was an agent of the Federal Bureau of Investigation of the United States Justice Department. But he was a fugitive now, just as wanted as David Holden and Rosie Shepherd and all the rest of them. And Rudolph Cerillia was dead, the director, murdered by agents of the government Rudolph Cerillia had fought throughout his life to protect.

"It doesn't make sense."

"The CB transmission? It is hard to hear."

Luther Steel took his eyes from the road and looked at Bill Runningdeer for a full ten seconds before what Runningdeer had said registered at all. And now Steel heard the CB transmission, too.

Static was heavy, almost as heavy as the rain that had plagued them throughout the night and now into the morning. And the sender had to be almost out of range of the van's CB radio. Bill Runningdeer spoke again. "Did I hear that right? Holden dying? Shit."

Why should a radio transmission make sense,
when nothing else did anymore?

"I don't know," Steel hissed through clenched
teeth as he checked to his left and started edging into
the inside lane. He was looking for a turnaround, saw
none, but saw little traffic either. "Hang on, I was
never good at bootlegger turns," Steel told him, then
cut the wheel as he hit the parking brake and the
Ford van started to skid. . . .

Rose Shepherd's hands slipped and she
started to fall, catching herself at the edge of the forward portion of the semi's trailer, hanging there for
an instant, rain tearing at her face and hair and
goose-pimpled bare arms, the Uzi carbine swinging
at her right side. She got her left arm over the top at
the elbow, her right foot finding something to push
upward against; she wasn't sure what. She pushed,
half falling onto the roof of the semi's trailer, spread-
eagling her arms and legs, the wind and the rain lashing furiously at her, automatic-weapons fire coming
from the pursuing trucks, the machine gun still silent.

She got to her knees, tugging her legs free of her
skirt, crawling back along the trailer's roof. She was
terrified, which she considered only sensible. But in
the right side pocket of her skirt she had the key to
the rear doors. If she could reach the interior of the
trailer, get her hands on one of the rockets . . . She
kept going; the wind of the slipstream almost tore
her from the trailer's roof. Her purse hung at her left
side, its usual contents spilled out onto the lower
bunk beside which David lay, the purse now filled to

capacity with spare magazines for the Uzi carbine. Her eyes darted from the slick, wind-and-rain-swept surface of the roof to the pursuing trucks.

Suddenly she slipped and fell flat on her face, as the semi picked up speed. She raised her head, looked over the side. They were on a downhill. "Ohh, God," Rose Shepherd murmured. Her arms and legs were spread wide for traction. She looked forward, the downgrade seeming to go on forever, twisting and curving, but the semi didn't slow down.

Some of the Army trucks were falling back, but three of them and the fourth truck with the machine gun in its bed were speeding up, coming along the highway in a wedge right behind them, gunfire emanating from the passenger windows of the cabs, more from the the truck beds themselves, ricochets pinging off the semi's coachwork.

Rose Shepherd started to crawl again. . . .

      Luther Steel's fists were bunched tight on the wheel of the Ford van. He glanced to Bill Runningdeer in the seat beside him, as Runningdeer loaded red plastic Federal super slugs up the tubular magazines of the Remington 870 police shotguns. Both guns were muzzle down against the floor, and Runningdeer was taking the rounds with both hands from plastic boxes between his legs. Steel's eyes went back to the road. "If those fake Army guys are after David—"

"What if they're not fake, Bill?"

"I don't wanna deal with that, Luther. God help us. Your people and my people, blacks and Indians, always got the short end of the stick, but I always told myself nobody really wanted it that way, that it just happened that way. If that's a real Army unit that killed the President back in the sanitorium, we don't have any country left at all, Luther."

"Yeah," Steel said, closing his eyes for an instant, opening them, peering down the road ahead. He was looking for a bright blue semi and God only knew what else behind it. . . .

There was a convenient enough way down, at least under normal circumstances, a steel-runged ladder, but everybody was shooting at her, bullets were hitting the rear doors of the truck, zigzagging insanely in every direction as they impacted and ricocheted. Rose Shepherd shouldered the Uzi carbine, lying prone on the roof, nestling the metal butt-plate into the pocket of her shoulder. She sighted on the lead truck's grill, firing short, semiauto bursts, two and three rounds, trying to spot where the bullets impacted. A headlight shattered. A bullet sparked as it skittered across the hood. Two bullets dug into the road surface, another ricocheted off the bumper.

She kept firing, nearly through the twenty-five-round magazine. Then suddenly liquid sprayed out from under the lead truck's engine block, steam rose at the seams of the hood. The truck swerved slightly, slowing, and the truck beside it swerved out of the way.

She rolled onto her back, swapped magazines, pocketing the empty because empty magazines weren't that easily replaced these days. The safety set, she figured now was as good a time as any and better than most. She started for the ladder, her wounded right calf throbbed with pain as she scraped it along the edge of the roofline. A burst of automatic-weapons fire tore into the door beside the top of the ladder and she shrank back from it, squinting her eyes shut.

Rose Shepherd shook her head, hair in her eyes, plastered there by the torrent of rain surrounding her. She started down the ladder, looking for the padlock on the hasp below her, spotting it, continuing to climb downward.

More gunfire hammered into the doors.

Rose was level with the lock now, the key in the wrong pocket. She hung by one hand, grabbing the key, then shifted the key to her left hand. She didn't look back. Knowing someone was about to shoot her off the ladder wouldn't change things. Her left hand left the ladder rung above her and moved toward the padlock. Her right foot slipped and she hung suspended by her right hand for a moment. She felt her bra strap snap. "Shit!" She had both feet firmly planted on the ladder now, as firmly as wet rubber-soled shoes could be planted on rain-slicked rounded metal rungs. The key and the lock kept missing, with every bump and turn in the road, the padlock shifting minutely, the key in the wrong spot. She tried again.

The key. The lock. They mated. She twisted the key and the lock popped. Rose let go of the key, twisted the lock, as more bullets pinged into the door near her. She tore the lock free, dropped it into her skirt's left pocket. As she tugged at the hasp, the door swung open, too suddenly, her body slung outward into the slipstream, both feet slipping from the rung, only her right hand holding her to the ladder now. Rose Shepherd slammed her body toward the flat of the door, her only hope, her fingers groping for the hasp, closing over the slick metal. She had it, then started shifting her weight out and away from the door, then toward it, trying to rock the door back toward the rear of the semi into the closed position. Her right foot found the ladder rung.

She tried again, throwing her weight outward, then inward, for once in her life wishing she weighed more than 122 pounds. The door swung inward and she screamed, her face slamming against the metal, her nose going numb, as if someone had socked her in the face.

Her left hand reached out, caught the other side of the hasp, and the door she was clinging to started to swing outward again. Rose held on, her arms aching with the strain. She had to make her move, she told herself. Clenching the fingers of her left hand tight, then releasing her right hand from the ladder, she started to fall, her right hand catching on the wide black rubberized gasket.

She could feel the tips of her fingernails blunting as she clenched tight to the rubber, inhaled, then loosed the grip of her right hand on the ladder rung, flinging herself through the opening, the door swinging closed after her, beating against her wounded calf, bullets impacting the door, tearing through into some of the wooden crates closest to the doors. She stared at the crates. They were marked APPLES.

She pushed herself to her feet, sagging against them. From the smell she could tell they really were apples. She shoved one of the crates off the pile, then another, then another, afraid that the load might shift at any moment. She began to climb over the crates now, toward the front end of the trailer.

More apples; she picked a spot and started digging, pulling up a box, her muscles straining with the weight, shoving the box aside end over end, then digging deeper. At last she hit the lower layer of wooden crates with U.S. military markings on them. Grenades. "Hell with the rockets," Rose Shepherd said under her breath.

These were long-dated fragmentation grenades, but they'd do the trick.

Stuffing one into each pocket of her skirt, she looked around for something to carry more of them in. Her purse was already packed with spare magazines for the 9mm Uzi carbine. But there was nothing else. She caught up the front of her skirt, making it into a sack, as she'd seen her mother do with an apron and had done sometimes herself. She started emptying the box of grenades into the front of her skirt, her left fist bunched into the fabric.

Now the trick was to climb out of the maze of wooden apple crates without spilling anything. She started crawling over the crates, skinning her knee on the rough wood, the trailer swaying sickeningly from side to side, the intensity of the gunfire from the Army trucks somehow greater, louder. She half stumbled, half climbed to the floor of the trailer, keeping close to the wall now to avoid being shot.

The trucks were closer, and the machine gun had opened up.

She dropped to her bare knees, the basket she'd made of her skirt clutched to her abdomen, her right hand snatching one of the grenades from it. She hooked the split ring on the thumb of her left hand, the fingers of her left hand still bunching together the material to keep the grenades from spilling out. She flexed her thumb tight to her fingers, as if she were making a fist, then pulled, freeing the pin. She made a mental note to keep at least one pin just in case. She dodged her head slightly to the right, to see past the constantly flapping door, then bowled the grenade out through the opening. The spoon flipped off the grenade as it rolled toward the lead truck and skittered off the driver's-side front wheel, exploding. The damaged truck swerved away, going half up the embankment along the side of the road, bounced away from it, and recovered. A small fireball rose in the distance where the first grenade had exploded. She pulled the pin on the second, aiming for the same truck, bowling the grenade out through the opening. The truck swerved to avoid it. The grenade exploded; the truck seemed to rise a foot or so off the ground, then drop, swerving half into the incoming lane, skidding laterally, then flipping over.

The truck with the machine gun was coming up fast. Rose flipped another grenade, missing the truck, ripping chunks of road surface up instead, a massive slice of macadam pavement flying through the window of the second of the three trucks that was in close pursuit. The truck swerved, cutting across the oncoming lanes. Rose Shepherd's eyes opened wide in alarm as she saw the truck, its windshield shattered, career over the edge of the road and crash from sight. In the next instant there was an explosion, the noise like a clap of thunder, a fireball, orange and black, belching upward through the rain.

The last of the three trucks that had kept behind the semi on the downgrade was the one with the machine gun. It was speeding up now, swerving right and left across the road to keep control, the gun in its bed firing, brass flying in a tiny whirlwind in its wake. Rose threw another grenade, missing almost entirely, part of the explosive charge blackening the passenger side window, the machine gun missing just a beat, then resuming fire. Bullets tore through the side of the trailer now and she buried her head against her knees, rolling another grenade into the road surface, the grenade exploding as she sneaked a peek after it, the canvas covering that flapped in the slipstream of the Army truck's wake now aflame.

But the machine gun was still firing, tearing through the walls of the trailer now, bullets whining everywhere about her like a swarm of angry bees. . . .

David Holden's eyes opened. There was gunfire. Movement. He could hear a woman's voice. "This is the Patriot truck. We have David Holden with us. Wounded seriously." Was that it, Holden wondered. Wounded seriously. He felt very light headed, very weak, but tried to remember how he'd been wounded. "We need assistance, now traveling southwest on Greenwood Highway with fake Army personnel in pursuit. We need Patriot assistance."

He could hear machine-gun fire and realized the vehicle he was in—a truck?—was moving rapidly. Where was Rosie? He reached to his abdomen, finding the Beretta 92F 9mm there. He was lying on the floor.

He looked to his left, straining to see. Yellow hair, a high seat-back masking it so he could only see a little of the hair. He was trying to figure out to whom the voice belonged, aside from the fact that the voice was obviously female. More gunfire. It was still raining. . . .

Rose Shepherd couldn't risk another grenade; the third and last of the trucks was too close. She packed the grenades from the front of her skirt into a nest made by some of the apple boxes, then swung the Uzi carbine forward on its sling. Machine-gun fire and assault-rifle fire punched through the walls of the trailer, but farther forward now than before. She stood, grabbed a fabric cargo strap, tested that it was fixed to the wall, then wound it around her left arm. She edged toward the doors, just able to see the rear of the third truck.

"Oh, boy," Rose Shepherd kicked the still unopened door outward and it swung away. The Uzi carbine came to her shoulder and she opened fire, aiming for the Army truck's tires.

And from the cab of the semi she heard gunfire. . . .

Glass sprayed over him and he heard a woman's scream. His eyes had come open again without his being conscious of it. Whatever he was riding in was swaying maddeningly. He looked forward. The windshield—it had to be some kind of truck or bus—was partially shot out and he could see more of the blond hair now, a streak of blue bandana, a woman's arms struggling. He shook his head to clear it and almost passed out again.

The blond-haired woman he'd seen the last time he'd opened his eyes—she was pretty, but nobody was prettier than Rosie or Elizabeth had been, or his two daughters had been; that idea warmed him, invigorated him—the blond-haired woman was fighting with a man in green BDUs. The door of the truck or bus—had to be a truck because buses didn't have doors on both sides—was open, the man in the green BDUs trying to throw the blond-haired woman out the door. There weren't any hands on the steering wheel.

David Holden looked down to his right hand. It held the Beretta 92F military pistol. He tried to raise his hand and it worked. He was pleasantly surprised.

He had to roll onto his left side to do it, tried it, almost lost it again in a spasm of pain beneath his right rib cage. Holden blinked, shaking his head. A wave of nausea came and passed.

The woman was being choked with her seat belt. The man in green fatigues or BDUs was holding one hand on the wheel, his knee braced against the woman's head, his other hand twisted into the seat belt, crushing her larynx.

Holden took a deep breath. If he sounded right, the man would look up, give him a clear target. He tried another deep breath, almost passing out. "Hey, asshole!"

The man looked up and David Holden, the pistol already raised to eye level, shot him five or six times in the head, losing count when the windshield was

hit and blew outward and the blond-haired woman
screamed. . . .

For some reason she couldn't understand, the
truck with the machine gun was falling back.

The Uzi carbine was empty and Rose Shepherd
reached into her skirt for a spare, saving the ones in
her purse until—and she found one of the two grenades she'd put into her pockets.

The truck was still falling back.

Rose Shepherd let the empty Uzi carbine fall to her
side on its sling, taking out both grenades. Growing
up a girl, except for Wonder Woman comics and the
occasional spunky frontier wife who shot a ma-
rauding outlaw, there weren't a lot of John Wayne–
like role models, such as boys had. So she didn't try
pulling the pins with her teeth, merely pulled each
with the thumb of the opposite hand and then
shrieked into the slipstream as she lobbed them both
into the bed of the truck, "Die!"

Something slammed her down to the floor of the
trailer like a giant slap. . . .

Luther Steel held the Remington 870 beside
his leg as he approached the wreckage of the truck.
He couldn't show his shield and shout, "FBI!" because it might have gotten him shot.

The government was no longer the protector of the
American people, but the enemy, the oppressor.

People—men and women and older children, ordinary looking—were methodically looting boxes out
of the jackknifed trailer of the semi, the boxes
marked variously as apples, grenades, rocket launch-

ers, 5.56mm Ball, and more apples. Perhaps, these days, ammunition and food were of equal value, because without either you were easy prey to death.

Others, like the looters, very orderly, businesslike, were attending to three bodies laid out under a lean-to made of a piece of brown oilcloth that looked snatched from a kitchen table, and set up in the muddy median strip of the four-lane highway.

"That deuce-and-a-half back there had the hell blown out of it," Runningdeer remarked, his Uzi submachine gun out from under his raincoat, but not held in any way that could be considered threatening by anyone but the weapons paranoid. There were occasional looks as Steel and Runningdeer approached the lean-to, but Steel assumed the looks were probably because he and Bill Runningdeer, despite their rumpled suits and the fact that neither of them had shaved in better than a day and a half, looked like cops. And it wasn't because he and Runningdeer were armed—a good fifty percent of the four dozen or so people who'd congregated here, their pickup trucks, sedans, Broncos, Suburbans, and even another semi parked along the sides of the road, were armed as well.

As Steel stepped onto the muddy median, one of the people gathered around the three bodies looked up at him, as if somehow an alarm had been sounded. "Who are you?"

"Ex-Feds. We're Patriots."

The man smiled. "All three of 'em, God knows how, they're alive. The man's s'posed to be David Holden himself."

"Amen, brother." Luther Steel nodded.

Chapter
1

"**P**ublic outcry against the so-called Patriots persists, sometimes carrying righteous outrage into the realm of the very lawless violence for which the American people have so come to despise the Patriots themselves," said the pretty blond-haired woman in the expensive-looking suit, her smile meticulously absent as she looked meaningfully into the eye of the camera. "We switch now to Darren Loque in upstate New York."

The television screen was filled with the image of a tree, the angle on the video such that the tree looked disproportionately sinister in its height. The sturdy old oak, as befit the season, was entirely barren of leaves and stood out against a heavy-laden gray sky, the limbs splotched with patches of dirty-looking snow. There was a fast cutaway to a thick rope, one end twisted into a clumsily knotted hangman's noose. The only thing missing, David Holden thought bitterly, was someone whistling a lonely-sounding Dimitri Tiomkin film score as Frankie Laine began to croon a western ballad.

"There is anger in these woods and the hamlets dotted in and near them, and that anger took the form of mob violence sometime last night when a man local residents say was long suspected of being a leader among the so-called Patriots was taken from his home, stood up in the bed of a pickup truck"—there was another fast intercut, this to tire treads in mud-laced snow—"and hanged by the neck from this tree behind me, hanged by the neck until dead."

David Holden shut off the television set, feeling a twinge of pain in his right side as he moved. But the pain was more stiffness of new skin than anything else, Holden told himself. He lit a cigarette.

"That's what I like about the news," Rosie said from across the living room, looking at him over the rim of the coffee mug she held in both hands. "Always so cheerful, not to mention unbiased."

"Luther says Clark Pietrowski's almost healed up. Hell, Clark's old enough to be my father. We've holed up in this house long enough. If we don't retake the initiative, the Patriot movement'll be dead and Roman Makowski will be able to get away with anything he wants for the country."

"The doctor hasn't given you the okay yet," Rosie said matter-of-factly.

Holden sat on the arm of the couch. "Would you let a little thing like that stop you?" He smiled at her.

"Not if it were me. But you? Yes. You almost bled to death, and that gunshot wound in your side became infected. You realize how close to death you were? If you don't, I do." She hugged her arms across her chest and visibly shivered.

Holden let himself smile. "If you hadn't hauled me out of there and risked your own life . . ."

She looked uncomfortable as he started to bring it up, and she turned away. "I did what I had to do, that's all. It wasn't any big thing, David."

Holden just looked at her. For two weeks they'd lived together in this house, like man and wife, which they were in all but the legal sense. Of the first few days he remembered very little, except occasionally awakening, in a lot of pain or woozy with pain-killing drugs, to find Rosie dozing in a chair, where she sat watch beside his bed, or the doctor the local Patriots had found for him attending him. And after the first few days he'd been able to stay awake a little longer and even sit up.

Rosie hadn't allowed him to have transfusions, only saline solution, afraid for him that the source of the blood might not be safe and he might become infected. He would have made the same decision for her.

She'd cared for him, fed him when he was too weak to feed himself, bathed him, and dressed his wound. Never once had she told him how she'd rescued him, simply that Kelly Martine, the daughter of the Miami Patriot cell leader, had helped her drag him into the cab of the semi and that the trucks of the fake Army unit had pursued for a while and there'd been some shooting. The Army unit, of course, wasn't fake at all, they learned to their sorrow. Never once had Rosie mentioned the shrapnel wound she'd sustained in her left shoulder when she'd blown up one of the trucks that had been fitted with a machine gun, nor the bullet wound to her right calf. She'd told him how he'd saved the Martine woman's life by shooting the man who'd jumped aboard the cab of the semi and tried killing Kelly.

Holden hadn't really learned the particulars—how she'd literally carried him out of the danger—until he'd been able to piece together bits and snatches of what the Martine woman—a pretty girl with long blond hair and a mouth that would have made a sailor blush—and Luther Steel had told him.

It was two weeks to the day since the assassination of the President, and the little tract house where they'd been given sanctuary almost felt like a home, the bed like their bed, the dishes like their dishes.

"But whatever you want to do, I'm with you," Rosie told him.

"Life wouldn't be worth living if you weren't," David Holden told her honestly. "Get on the phone; see if you can get in touch with Luther."

Rosie nodded, thrusting her hands into the pockets of her dress, walking toward the kitchen wall phone.

Holden stubbed out his cigarette.

Chapter
2

*T*he stream was icy-cold and crystal-clear. Of the survival gear secreted within the Ford, the Katadyn filter had proven exceptionally useful, and the results of the tests Geoffrey Kearney ran revealed no detectable impurities. Still, to be on the safe side they boiled water for drinking and cooking. Kearney did trust the water for bathing. In the last few days the gradually dropping temperatures had finally taken their toll on Linda Effingham. And Kearney had constructed a primitive but effective sun-shower for her.

Bathing together in the stream had been idyllic, fun, but this morning he was alone, and although he hated to admit it, he was uncomfortably cold.

It was as if the weather were signaling them, telling them, *Return to the killing grounds; the honeymoon is over and there's work to be done.*

Geoffrey Kearney could not ignore the imperative, try as he might. He had come to the United States, rather less than legally, to discover the identity of the Front for the Liberation of North America. That accomplished, his next task was to eliminate, terminate, liquidate, eradicate—whatever the euphemism of the moment. The ostensible motive for these orders was to help Canada, which was suffering to a substantial but lesser degree the same FLNA-inspired violence as the United States. But the real reason the British Secret Intelligence Service had sent him would have been obvious to an imbecile. If the economy of the United States collapsed, it would drag all Western allied nations—and quite likely the Eastern Bloc countries—down with it. There would be global depression on an unprecedented and all but irrecoverable scale.

He sat naked on a towel draped over a rock beside the stream, drying himself, his pistol on the rock beside him. His skin was goosefleshed with cold. The towels were courtesy of the motel they'd evacuated so hastily, but the theft of them didn't bother his conscience, since the management would merely add the cost to his credit-card charges. Sturdy towels, he reflected, since they survived washing in the stream each morning and drying over a fire when sunshine wasn't available.

It was interesting to contemplate his own moral boundaries. Had he just stolen the towels with no hope of recompense to the motel, it would have bothered his conscience. If he succeeded and located the leader of the FLNA and then—euphemisms aside—killed the fellow, taking a life in that context wouldn't bother him a bit.

By and large there had been sunshine every day,

and warm happy nights sleeping with Linda. Small game had been plentiful. He'd even had the opportunity of killing a deer, but avoided it since there were no smoking facilities and the bulk of the meat would be wasted by spoilage.

Twice he'd sneaked into the nearest town and purchased cigarettes and a treat or two. The cigarettes had given him pause about his own abilities for long-term survival. Without cigarettes it wouldn't be very pleasant. And Kearney didn't fancy himself smoking ground-up leaves (although, of course, tobacco was ground-up leaves). On those occasions when he'd ventured into the community in the valley, he'd gotten newspapers as well and examined them carefully, at once trying to read between the lines for real news and, with the sole major metropolitan daily, scrutinously pursued the want ads.

It was only two days ago, after returning from one such foray, that he'd found the ad he'd been expecting to appear some time before. *Cherry nine-year-old Rolls-Royce Corniche, right-hand drive, specially equipped. Must see to appreciate. Must sell. Sincere persons only. $42,750, FIRM.*

"What are you thinking about?" Kearney had heard Linda approaching, and now finished toweling himself dry and stood up. She handed him the shirt she'd washed for him yesterday and he slipped it on. There was no reason for her to stare at him as she did, because they slept naked beside each other each night, but she stared at him, at his face. "We're leaving, aren't we?"

"One of the advertisements in the newspaper. It

informed me I'm to keep a rendezvous for new orders and new equipment. It's a must, I'm afraid."

"What will you do with me?"

He finished pulling his pants up and drew her into his arms. "Lots of possibilities, really. I'll simply tell my superiors that you're my native guide. We Brits are fond of using native recruits to assist us. It's an old and time-honored tradition, really. Won't catch any flak about it, darling." And he tipped her chin up, touched his lips to hers, felt her hands touch his skin beneath his open shirt.

"Don't leave me," she breathed into his right ear. "Ever."

Chapter
3

*T*hey slept in the woods away from the car that night, more at home in the open now after their two-week sojourn in the wilds of the mountains, and the car too tough to camouflage at any event.

They arose before dawn, keeping to side roads that were hell on the car, trying to avoid the roadblocks. Kearney told himself he could get through them anyway, but he was reluctant to take the risk with Linda aboard—though eventually he'd have to, he knew.

By midday, topography forced them to return to a main artery as they neared the outskirts of Asheville, North Carolina. They sat in gridlocked traffic that was passing at a snail's pace through an Army road-block. They sat and waited for more than two hours, palms sweating, making nervous small talk. Despite the cold the sunshine was very warm through the dirty glass of the Ford. When at last it was their turn, it was necessary to step out of the car, submit to a search of all luggage, a metal detection search of their persons with the little portable wands like those used in airports, and answer myriad questions. While their papers were checked, the car was gone over with an electronic explosives detector and a sniffer dog.

The dog bothered Kearney a bit. He was confident the items stored in hidden compartments throughout the car were safe from conventional search but had no idea what the eager-looking khaki-and-black German shepherd's keen nose might turn up. And the soldiers were rude. He tried to pass that off as the natural behavior of bored and very tired men performing an unpleasant and stupid task: but it was more than that.

There was a peculiar unit insignia on their uniforms, one he'd never seen before but somehow felt he was destined to see again.

At last, once through the roadblock, they were able to drive on to the city itself. Asheville sat like a jewel of culture and accommodation within the rugged mountainscape of the Smokies. They were stopped only once for a random and rather perfunctorily executed search, then on to one of Asheville's best and largest hotels. Here, although the parking lot was not in the least crowded, there was a sense of tension in the lobby. With gas prices spiraling upward, the cost of places to stay and food to eat enormous, and the dangers and inconveniences along the road at the least discouraging, no one traveled these days unless he must. Nevertheless there remained a refreshing sense of the ordinary as well, despite the travel forms that had to be filled out at the hotel's registration desk. These were in triplicate, white atop blue over yellow, self-duplicating, clearly designed to be a means of tracing travel movements, one form for the local police, one for the Federal government, and one to be maintained at the hotel or motel where the form originated.

Kearney lied glibly on the form, filling it out for himself and his "wife," as was permitted. As a well-practiced liar he almost appreciated the new challenge.

By the time they reached the room, Kearney and Linda Effingham had already agreed to presume that randomly selected rooms within the hotel might be the subject of random sweeps of electronic eavesdropping, so any important matters would be discussed in the shower together with the water running at full power. She'd laughed, saying he just wanted an excuse to rub her body with hot water and soap, and he told her she was clever for seeing through the transparency of his deception.

They undressed, turned on the shower, and readied themselves to "conference" as soon as Geoffrey Kearney had secured the door, ensuring that anyone who tried to enter the room would at least make a considerable amount of noise. His weapons, all of them except for the B & D Trading Company Grande penknife, were concealed within the secret compartments of the car. He felt slightly uncomfortable without a gun around just in case of trouble.

She turned up the water. It was warm, pleasant.

His hands moved to close the shower curtain more securely, and as he turned around, Linda was standing inches from him. His hands stopped at Linda's breasts, lingering there.

"It feels good when you touch me."

"It feels good to me too," he responded honestly.

"So, what's the next step?"

"We could go to bed, I suppose, or would you like dinner first?"

She giggled and Kearney held her close against him, averting his eyes from the spray of water, his lips touching her bare, slick shoulder.

"I have my meeting tomorrow." He hesitated for a moment, then said it anyway. "I could likely arrange for you to get out of this country to safety and—"

"No"—and she hugged her arms around his stomach and touched her lips to his chest. "I want to stay with you, forever."

Kearney just held her.

Chapter
4

David Holden looked at his watch. In a half hour their transportation to get them out of Columbia, South Carolina, would arrive to take them to the New Metro Patriots campsite, about sixty-five miles north of Metro itself. He and Rosie had spoken little since the call came late that afternoon that transport had been arranged; they merely set about the tasks necessary to prepare for departure, with no time or inclination for any real conversation.

Rosie had told him matter-of-factly, "I'll fix your hair," and insisted on doing so. He'd grown a beard and mustache over the two weeks they'd stayed here. But to help to make it possible for them to escape Columbia, it was necessary for them to alter their appearances even more. As she'd begun to wash the dye into his hair, she had assured him, "Now, don't worry, this stuff washes out. At least, it'd better wash out." She was now a redhead, and the look went nicely with her skin tone. With her long hair up she looked different. And she had contact lenses that were designed to make her hazel eyes look blue.

He finished knotting his knit tie and looked down to the dresser top. He picked up the glasses and put them on. They were a mild magnifying prescription —ordinary window glass would have been too obvious—the frames dark and heavy. She'd dyed his hair a dark blond and then applied the same dye to his beard and mustache. With the glasses in place he would have had a hard time recognizing himself.

The closest the couple had come to a discussion was whether or not they should go armed, a subject they'd debated on and off for the last several days.

Unless a vehicle was specially modified, smuggling weapons in it would be like asking to get caught. And according to news broadcasts fed to David and Rosie by the Columbia Patriots, who brought them groceries and newspapers and cigarettes and the like, the military security forces operating the roadblocks were using electronic equipment for body searches. Yet if the two were unarmed and then discovered, arrest (or, more likely, assassination) was inevitable.

In the end, they agreed to opt for avoiding roadblocks and moving cross country, on foot if necessary, rather than risk being weaponless.

Holden slipped into his shoulder holster. With saddle soap he'd cleansed it of blood. Under his left armpit was the Beretta 92F Compact, thirteen rounds in the magazine and one round in the chamber. Under his right armpit were two of the outlawed twenty-round magazines for the Beretta pistols (actually, 93R machine-pistol magazines). Attached behind the double magazine pouch was the inverted sheath for the Defender knife, the butt of which hung down to his waist.

Holden threaded his belt into his pants, stopping as he approached the loops beside his left kidney. Here he threaded in place a double magazine pouch for two fifteen-round-capacity Beretta magazines, then continued, stopping again at the right kidney, where he put the fabric sheath for the Leatherman tool.

He finished with the belt, then picked up the full-sized Beretta 92F military pistol and stuffed it into the waistband of his trousers at the small of his back, between the magazines and the tool, along with cigarettes, a disposable cigarette lighter, handkerchief, and phony ID . . .

David left the room almost the instant she reentered from the bath. He called over his shoulder, "I'm seeing to the papers and maps, Rosie," then disappeared. She was wearing only her white panties, catching up her bra from the bed as she passed it on her way to the full-length mirror on the closet door.

Rose Shepherd slipped her arms into the straps and settled her breasts into the cups, then reached her hands behind her and closed the bra. She looked at herself in the mirror and she didn't like the red hair and the blue eyes she saw, preferring what she'd been born with, but she shrugged and picked up the Null shoulder rig. She snapped the Model 60 Chiefs out of the inverted white plastic holster, confirmed the little .38 Special revolver's loaded condition and reholstered, then slipped the harness over her left shoulder. There was a little scar from the shrapnel wound, but the doctor had told her it would all but disappear in time. She secured the holster under her left arm.

Rose Shepherd hated garter belts because they always looked like something out of a sex movie, but for the next weapon she carried there wasn't any choice, when she intended wearing a dress or skirt. She stepped into the white, lace-trimmed elastic strap and positioned it at her hips. She wore no garters and indeed no stockings; instead, the belt served to secure, by means of a strap on the left side, a sheath for her Cold Steel Mini-Tanto.

She adjusted the position of the sheath, so as to carry the knife on the inside of her thigh.

She walked back to the bed and started to put on her slip. Her eyes moved about the room over the bed, to the closet, the bathroom doorway, the dresser.

Rose Shepherd wondered if ever again there would be a semblance of a home for herself and David. She wanted to cry, really felt like it, but told herself it wouldn't do any good at all anyway. . . .

David Holden took Rose Shepherd into his arms. "We'll have a house, someday. I promise you. And remember I promised you, all right?"

"I'll remember, David."

He kissed her hard on the lips, looked at her, and said, "You're beautiful. But you're right; I like you better as a brunette."

"I like you better as a brunette too." She smiled.

"Right." He crossed the living room to the couch, where he'd laid both their coats, two suitcases, and a backpack with most of their worldly possessions already placed beside the door. He picked up Rosie's coat—a heavy woolen thing that seemed to weigh a ton—and her purse, the purse inordinately heavy, even for her. "What's in this thing?" Holden asked as he started toward her.

"Remember when Kelly left, she left me that Uzi carbine and all the spare magazines, just in case we needed them?"

"Yeah. You couldn't have the Uzi in here; the magazines? Naw."

"No, that knife, remember? 'Big Ugly One'? I really liked it and asked her if I could trade her something for one of them. I didn't have anything to trade, but figured maybe sometime . . . Anyway, she gave it to me. She kept refusing to take anything and I couldn't let her do that, but she said that I could give her something in exchange for it if we ever met again. I needed a good stout knife besides my little sticker here"—and she patted her left thigh.

Holden shrugged. Setting her purse down, he helped her into her coat. As he went for his own coat —about the heaviness and weight of a ski jacket, but hip length—he saw Rosie pulling back the drapes and looking through the living-room window onto the street. "They're here."

David Holden caught up their luggage. They looked at each other, then once more back into the house. She opened the door and walked through, and he followed her into the night.

Chapter
5

Holden held Rosie Shepherd's hand as the station wagon moved through the back streets of Columbia. The driver, a Patriot named Bob Amateau, seemed to be good at his work, Holden thought; the woman beside him in the front seat, also a Patriot, Ruth Leeds, broke the silence that had endured since Holden and Rosie had entered the car. "The word tonight is that President Makowski—"

"Don't use the words *President* and *Makowski* in the same breath, please. Just a quirk on my part, but . . ." Holden let it hang.

Ruth Leeds began again. "Makowski's supposed to announce that because of increased Patriot violence, he's declaring martial law in selected areas."

Bob Amateau, his voice almost stereotypically deep for a black man of his size, added, "That means, of course, he can do away with little inconveniences like habeas corpus, search warrants, even arrest warrants. They have us on the ropes, Dr. Holden."

"David, please, Bob. You said they have us on the ropes. Well, if they think that, maybe we'll have a better chance than we had before. We don't have any choice, really, do we? We can keep fighting for what we know is right or Makowski gets to turn the nation into his own personal fiefdom and we have nothing to look forward to except more of the same forever, or worse."

Ruth said, "If we could just turn public opinion around, David. We need manpower now that Makowski's using those Army units of his. Without manpower we haven't a prayer. And instead of helping in the fight, the American people are actually helping Makowski to enslave them. That's crazy."

Holden asked if he could light a cigarette without bothering anyone. Since no one minded, he cracked a window and did, lighting one for Rosie as well. "Wars aren't won only on the battlefield, as we all know. And modern warfare has become more and more of a public-relations contest. If Makowski can win the hearts and minds of the people by turning them against the Patriots, he doesn't need battlefield victories," Holden said.

"From what we've seen here," Bob Amateau said, "it seems likely that Makowski's people are working off some sort of list of supposed troublemakers, like the Chinese communist hardliners did in the aftermath of the occupation of parts of Beijing by the pro-democracy students, arresting selectively to instill fear in the rest of the population."

"It's working," Rosie interjected.

"Those guys—we're still trying to peg some sort of unit connection, but it looks like it was just created—

those guys are tough," Ruth Leeds told them. "One of our local guys was caught up in a random roadblock search. He should have been more careful. All he had on him was a .22 target pistol in the glove compartment. No warrants were out on him or anything. The official reports read that he attempted to open fire on United States military personnel with an 'assault weapon.' He's dead."

David Holden flicked ashes out the window as Bob stopped the station wagon for a red light. "That's the sort of stuff we have to start documenting, Bob, Ruth, the sort of thing that we can use to our advantage in the world press."

"I'm getting the feeling I know why you asked to see me," Ruth Leeds said, laughing hollowly.

Holden stubbed out his cigarette. "I didn't want you, or Bob for that matter, risking your lives to drive us out of here. We could have taken a car—"

Bob interrupted. "With me as a cop, you've got a chance even if we do get stopped. On your own, without knowing the city and the county, you'd never get out of town alive. And as for Ruthie, here, hell, she may be a prizewinning black female journalist, but she's also pretty good with a gun. With me behind the wheel and Ruthie in the front seat, anybody with brains is going to think twice about funny business. You see, Ruthie's paper is still honest and prints as much truth as it can get away with."

"How long they'll let us stay in operation is anybody's guess. Makowski's got a conference of the nation's newspaper editors lined up in a few days. I think he's going to let them know—subtly, of course —that if they don't play ball with the administration, they'll get put out of business. And, you think about it, all he has to do is declare martial law in a specific area where an offensive newspaper is being printed, then restrict the supply of paper and ink, restrict distribution, even shut the paper down at the source— using the excuse that the paper is contributing to whatever crisis caused civil authority to be suspended in the first place."

"It's hard to think of that happening here," David Holden said without thinking. He was being naive again, he supposed. He felt Rosie's hand squeeze his in the darkness. "If, Miss Leeds, you can get information out on things like that murdered Patriot you mentioned, that'll help. If the government under Makowski wants to vilify us, then we have to vilify the government. And at least the truth'll be on our side."

"Give him a few more weeks," Ruth Leeds offered, "and Roman Makowski'll have figured out how to restrict entry to the U.S. by foreign press, or at least restrict movement on the grounds of protecting the safety of the correspondents. But until then, I can get stuff out. After that happens, it'll be a lot harder, but I still have ways."

"I admire you a great deal, Ruth," Rosie Shepherd said, as if that opinion had been on the tip of her tongue for a long time and she were finally just now saying it. "I've always had to do things in a direct way. You know, there's a door and there's no key, so you break down the damn door, like that. But you can do more with a few words than I can do with a case of ammunition. I respect that a lot."

"We're both fighting for the same thing in our own

way, aren't we, Detective Shepherd? Both ways of fighting are needed."

David Holden started to say something, but then he noticed two things: There was the flashing light of a police car visible in Bob Amateau's rearview mirror and the car they were driving was slowing down drastically, pulling over to the curb.

"Military police. Could be nothing, could be some of the security-force people. Keep your seat belts locked," Bob announced.

David Holden reached to the small of his back for the full-sized Beretta as he heard Rosie Shepherd open her purse and rack the slide on the Glock-17 that she was carrying there along with her .45 and the knife.

Chapter
6

Bob Amateau stepped out of the car. Ruth Leeds looked over the backseat at Holden and Rosie Shepherd and whispered, "If they get past Bob and his badge, we've got trouble in abundant amounts."

A yellow streetlight, common in high crime areas, caged to protect it against anything short of a bullet, shone brilliantly from across the street. Holden looked at Rosie. By now Rosie had her .45 in her right hand and the Glock-17 in her left, both hands beside her thighs, hands and guns covered by the fullness of her dress. "Whatever happens," she said, "if we have to split the car, I need the suitcase with the Uzi in it. It's got most of the spare magazines for these babies too."

David Holden merely nodded, the full-sized Beretta tight in his right fist. If these were ordinary military policeman just doing their job and being curious, a nonviolent solution to the traffic stop had to be found. For him the policy still held: don't kill or injure legally authorized law enforcement or military personnel.

The special unit Makowski's government had been fielding was a different story. They were armed to the hilt—even sporting the brutally effective Monadnock nightstick, among other weapons.

Holden didn't need to turn his head to see what was taking place behind the station wagon. The two military policemen suddenly grabbed for Amateau, jostling him off balance and knocking him to the street. One of them laced him across the neck and shoulder with a Monadnock.

"Ruthie—get behind the wheel," Holden rasped, glancing at Rosie beside him; she was already starting out of the car on her side.

Holden hit the passenger-side rear door and jumped out, Rosie shrieking, "Freeze, assholes!" Both pistols were held at almost full extension of her arms, at chest level, pointed toward the two MPs.

"You heard the lady, freeze—and she's a better shot than I am; and I know she's a better shot than either of you guys." David Holden started to advance, the full-sized Beretta tight in his right fist, his left hand curling under the left side of his jacket, breaking the smaller of the two Berettas from the leather, his left thumb hitting the ambidextrous safety up.

The MP with the drawn club stood as if he were playing statue, the club still raised to strike Amateau another blow. The second MP's hands were at his side. As Holden drew closer—he could hear the clicking of Rosie's heels on the pavement as she advanced as well—he could see that the flap on the

MP's hip holster was open. "Don't go for that gun, pal—just a friendly reminder."

Holden approached from the far left in a tight arc, Rosie doing the same from the right. She'd taught all of them in Metro Patriots the safest ways to approach an armed subject, and in something like this, Holden followed her lead, as she followed his in military matters.

"You with the club!" Rosie commanded. "I want you to reach up with your left hand very slowly and grasp the club, tight. Then hold it as high as you can over your head with both hands. Twitch and you're dead."

"We've got backup—"

"Shut the fuck up, Charlie!"

Holden held his pistols on both men. In the yellow light of the lamp from across the street, Holden could see the unit insignia patch each man wore. It was the same as the patch worn by the men of the unit that had attacked the sanitorium to kill the President, the same as that worn by the men who'd almost finished him at the garage.

Rosie ordered, "All right, you, mouthman"—and she gestured with one of the pistols toward the one who'd just told Charlie to shut up. "With your left hand reach down to your gun belt and very slowly open the buckle, then let the gun belt fall slowly to the pavement. Move too fast and you'll never move again. Go for it."

The second MP started to move his left hand, fumbled with the buckle of the belt, released it, and let gun, holster, and belt fall to the street.

"Now—take two giant steps back, then down on

your knees and get your hands clasped on top of your head. Nice and easy. Hey, baby."

It took Holden a minute, but he realized Rosie was addressing him. "Yeah?"

"Use his cuffs just like you learned how."

"Yes, Mother." Holden grinned. He circled the MP as the man finished his two giant steps and knelt, hands locking on top of his head. Holden shoved one pistol into his belt, grabbed up the gun belt, and dropped into a crouch. He pulled the M-9, the military-issue version of the same gun Holden held on the man, from the holster, shoving the pistol under his coat at the small of his back. He opened the cuff case and took out the cuffs, then rose to his full height and continued the arc to get behind the man.

Rosie was already working on the one with the club. "Now, turn around real slow so I don't think you're up to something and kill you."

Holden kept half an eye on the proceedings until he was close enough to cuff the kneeling man. His pistol still in his right hand, he snapped one bracelet over the kneeling man's right wrist, then twisted the arm down, applying some upward pressure, like a modified hammerlock. "Lower your other hand, behind your back." The kneeling man obeyed and Holden clamped the second bracelet on. "Lean your head forward," Holden told him, his left hand going onto the man's shoulder so if he tried something, Holden could push him off balance. Holden rammed the full-sized Beretta into his trouser band—it was getting awfully tight—while he quickly patted down the MP, not so much for a weapon as for a hidden cuff key in a belt keeper. There was none.

Holden stepped back as he redrew both his pistols.

Rosie took the club out of their second prisoner's upraised hands, and rested it on his neck. "Clasp 'em on top of the head," she ordered. As she tucked the club under her right arm—her right hand still held the .45—she reached her left hand toward his belt and relieved him of the holstered Beretta. It went into her pocket, making the coat hang oddly on her. Then she grabbed for the cuffs, much more professionally than Holden had, securing one wrist, twisting it down, then clamping the second bracelet on.

"Turn around, Hortense," Rosie snapped.

Holden laughed.

The standing man turned around.

"So, Mabel, what's the scam, why you lumpin' the man here?"

"Stop it."

"What? What's that, Betty?"

"I said stop it with the girls' names, all right?"

"Look, Beatrice, you tell me what I want to know or you'll get worse than a coupla names. So—why the routine on my man here?"

"He asked for it."

Rosie smiled very sweetly. Then the Monadnock began to move in her left hand as if it were something with a mind of its own, and in the blink of an eye the short end had jabbed into his abdomen and he dropped to his knees. "Look, Gloria, you answer me wise again and you'll need a girl's name, 'cause the next shot goes for the jewels, understand?"

He nodded his head.

"Can't hear you, Petunia."

"Yes, ma'am!"

Rosie took a half step back. "What are your orders?"

"We were to—"

"Charlie—"

Holden took a step forward and placed the muzzle of his pistol against the side of the other man's neck. The man fell silent.

"That's it." Rosie laughed. "That's right; Charlie, huh? Short for Charlotte or Charlene?"

"Neither one."

"Pick one, then—I'm renaming you."

He didn't answer.

"Pick one, asshole; I'm runnin' out of time and so are you!"

The kneeling man, his voice a hoarse whisper, said, "Charlotte."

"I can't hear you!"

"Charlotte!"

Rosie laughed again. The kneeling man was crying. "All right, Charlotte, gimme the orders."

"We were told that Detective Amateau was a Patriot leader. We were to follow him until we found a quiet place and pull him over, then kill him. We lost him when he left his house, then picked him up again a coupla blocks back."

Ruth Leeds had exited the car and had knelt beside Bob Amateau, lifting his head into her lap. Amateau's face was bloodied and now, as he tried to stand, he looked weak in the knees. "You're the same guys that killed my lieutenant, aren't you? Aren't you?" Amateau drew his revolver from under his coat, but Ruth Leeds held his right forearm, trying to restrain him.

"You call for backup, Charlotte?" Rosie snapped.

"No, ma'am."

"Who told you to kill him, Charlotte?"

"The captain."

"What's the captain's name, girlie?"

"He's Captain Steven Kowalski."

"What's your unit insignia mean, Charlotte?"

"The Presidential Strike Force."

"Who's the overall boss, aside from that schmuck pretending to be President?"

"Mr. Hobart Townes, ma'am."

"How can a civilian run an Army unit, Charlotte?"

"I don't know."

Rosie rested the club on the top of his head.

He shouted, "I just don't know!"

"Where'd he get you sissies from?"

The man didn't answer right away and Rosie bent over, staring him straight in the eye. "Where's he get you sissies from, Charlotte?"

"Prisons."

"Prisons?"

Holden felt his jaw drop.

"Yes, ma'am."

"What were you in prison for?"

"Ahh . . . it was a mistake—"

"What?!"

"Rape."

Holden shouted to Rosie, "Don't—"

Rosie Shepherd wheeled the nightstick in her hand and caught the L shape that made the handle under the man's chin, snapping his head back, stopping just short of breaking his neck. "How about him, the other guy?" Rosie snarled.

"Coupla counts of armed robbery, he says."

"What about your captain, this Steven Kowalski creep?"

"Don't know for sure."

"Gimme the rumors, then."

"They say home-invasion murders and maybe some crack dealin'—I dunno nothin' else."

Rosie took a half step back; and as she flicked the club away, she kicked out with her left foot against his chest and dropped him flat to the pavement. She looked at David. "What the hell do I do? Kill him? I mean, I can't, for God's sake."

"God, lady—don't . . ." He hauled himself up to his knees, losing his balance, falling forward, his lips kissing the pavement. "Aww, please?"

Holden asked a question. "What kind of prisons?"

"Fe-Fe-Federal."

"Were you military?"

"All of us, I guess, one time—look, man, don't let this crazy bitch—"

Holden closed his eyes. He heard the man scream. As he opened his eyes, he could see Rosie pressing down with the nightstick, the L shape's apex at the base of the man's neck, the pressure of her left hand shoving his face harder against the pavement.

"What happened to the real military?" Holden looked at Rosie as she asked the question, then at the man, waiting for his answer.

"I dunno for sure."

"Gimme what you do know, Charlotte."

"Some guys say . . . they say the top officers got arrested 'cause they wouldn't do what they was told. Some generals and shit, and some of the others."

"What others?" Holden asked softly.

"Special Warfare guys. Like SEALs and Special Forces and them."

"What else do you know?" Holden asked.

"Nothin'—so help me God! Nothin'!"

Holden looked at Rosie.

The yellow light made her red hair look unreal. All of this was unreal, he realized. It was a nightmare. It had to be. Elizabeth and the children killed in an FLNA terror raid that day at the commencement exercises, the President of the United States assassinated by men in United States military uniforms who were really killers and drug dealers and rapists set loose to be Roman Makowski's private army, his own private SS.

When he woke from the nightmare—and it had been going on so long, David Holden wanted to cry —he'd miss some of the people: Rufus Burroughs, who'd made him a Patriot, given him a purpose; some of the Metro Patriots like Patsy Alfredi, Mitch Diamond, the CB whiz, all of them really. The dead, after Elizabeth and the children, Rufus chief among them, then Pete, who'd died in the gas chamber where the FLNA had set the trap he—Holden— hadn't walked, but run into. But if he woke up, then Elizabeth and the children wouldn't be dead anymore and the only real emptiness except for the void left by his dead friends—had they ever existed?— would be the emptiness of Rosie's absence. And nothing would ever fill that emptiness.

It was then that David Holden realized he would never win. If this was real, then even if, by some miracle and a lot of lives lost, they got the country back, Elizabeth and the children would never return. And if it was only a dream, Rosie Shepherd had never really lived, not as this Rosie Shepherd anyway, never loved him, fought beside him, nursed his wounds, listened to his dreams and his nightmares.

"What'll we do?"

David Holden looked at the man whom he had cuffed. "Did you guys kill Detective Amateau's lieutenant?"

"One nigger looks—" Amateau screamed an obscenity and the man fell silent.

Holden looked at the man Rosie had forced to talk, Charlie. "Charlie. Tell me the truth. Have you and this man followed Captain Kowalski's orders before and just murdered other people because they were suspected Patriots?"

"I didn't wanna, but we hadda, man!"

"How many? Now, be honest with me."

"It ain't many. Three guys, and they was all—"

"Black? Cops? Alone? All of the above?"

Charlie didn't say anything. Rosie let go of his neck with the club and he raised himself up a little, tears rolling from his eyes.

"Whatchya gonna do about it?" It was the man beside David Holden who spoke, sneering. "Get us arrested? Grow up."

That was, of course, the problem. Being grown up meant there were many decisions to make and the only one responsible for those decisions and their outcomes was yourself.

David Holden looked at Rosie Shepherd. If it was a nightmare, it wasn't a sin because these men didn't exist. If it was reality and his soul was not beyond redemption already, or even if it should be, there had to be something left of justice.

Holden shifted the full-sized Beretta to his left hand, drawing the liberated pistol from under his coat.

"You guys carry chamber loaded these days, don't you, pal?"

The man just looked at him.

Holden heard what sounded like the longest flatulence ever, and there was a foul, rotten-eggs smell.

"God help us all. You're a self-proclaimed murderer, and so is he."

"God Almighty, no, man! Please, aww . . ." Charlie was screaming.

Holden didn't glance at Charlie.

He had eye contact with the man who'd just soiled himself.

Holden pointed the muzzle of the man's pistol, settling it between the man's eyes.

"You can't; you got no right! I got a right to a trial, and a—"

"Martial law, remember?" David Holden pulled the trigger.

Rosie Shepherd screamed.

David Holden couldn't see for an instant, and then he felt tears rolling down his cheeks and he could hardly breathe. "Step away," Holden stammered.

Rosie turned away.

David Holden walked a few paces, so it would be a clean shot, and as Charlie screamed, Holden fired.

As the sound of the shot died, Holden safed the pistol, just holding it in his hand, not knowing what to do with it really now.

Rosie came up to stand beside him, gently taking the pistol from his hand. "Whatever happens to us, I'll love you forever, even if we're in hell together," Rosie whispered, her eyes filled with tears as Holden stared at her.

He guessed it really wasn't a dream, and he held Rosie and she held him.

Chapter
7

*T*he morning was crisp, cool, so beautiful it was hard to imagine there was ugliness anywhere.

Geoffrey Kearney stepped from his car and walked a few paces to have a better view.

The house and grounds here were the city's principal attraction, a baronial manor in the grand tradition, something that had survived from a gentler era.

Kearney was suddenly reminded of home, although he had never lived in such a place, to be sure, nor often visited one, but the air almost smelled English this morning.

Kearney snapped up the collar of his jacket and then looked at the Rolex on his wrist. Three minutes until the meeting. He oriented himself and walked out of the parking lot onto the grounds proper. There was an arbor at the base of a half-dozen low stone steps, the trellis and the bare vines all that there was of it now in winter.

A woman, very pretty, sat perched on the edge of a

stone bench atop a Scottish tartan afghan. She had auburn hair caught up at the nape of her neck in a deep red bow of rather large proportions. His contact was to be wearing red. She was swathed in a heavy-looking gray tweed coat, the tops of black leather medium-heeled boots disappearing beneath its hem.

Kearney kept his hands where she could see them as he approached. She looked away from the great house and up at him. "I come here a great deal just for the quiet."

Kearney answered, "My first time."

"The first time is always the best."

"With many things."

"Do you have a cigarette?"

"Yes. But my lighter's gone bad." It hadn't, of course, although lighter fluid was now as outrageously expensive as everything else.

"I have a lighter."

Kearney perfunctorily offered her a cigarette from his pack. He was almost surprised that she took it. "Kearney," she said.

"Yes. And what should I call you?"

"Anything you want." He thought she might be a Scotswoman, even in spite of the afghan. They began to walk beneath the winter-dead arbor.

"Oh, well"—and he thought hard for a moment. "How about Lady Elaine?"

She smiled a little, then actually laughed. She had a pretty smile and even prettier green eyes. "We might sound a bit conspicuous if someone overhears."

"My whole body's a weapon, trust me, m'lady."

He lit her cigarette and his. "Hello! My lighter works."

She laughed. "You're the charmer, aren't you?" Then her voice changed a little, became a bit more professional, more matter-of-fact. "I've got new orders and a new car and a new load of equipment for you, more like the stuff you originally asked for but that we couldn't put together on such short notice for you here."

"What and where, m'lady?"

"Quit that, will you? It's . . ."

"What?"

"Never mind," she said, smiling as she exhaled, shaking her head. "You're car is hot, as they say, so we got you something else."

"If it doesn't have off-road capabilities, there's no sense changing. The car's not that hot—not yet, at least."

She dropped the cigarette to the cement, crushed it under her boot, then walked on, hands thrusting into her pockets. "It's just what you requested in your last report, set up just as you asked—except for that silly business about rockets and lasers and whatnot."

"It was the whatnot I'd really had my heart set on too. More's the pity, I suppose. Has it been supplied?"

"Yes. What you asked for there, too, I'm told. What's this about a woman? With you I'm just sure she's part of the job."

Kearney felt himself smile. "Well, she was actually, but you're right. She's more than that now. She's helping me, any event. It's none of the office's concern."

"They were concerned about one thing, Kearney"
—and she stopped dead in her tracks and stared up at
him. Kearney snapped his cigarette butt to the walkway, crushed it, looked at her. "They think you're
getting involved."

"What? The idiots in psych reading between my
encrypted lines?"

"They think you're taking this personally. This is
an American problem. You're only here for one
thing."

"Let me guess: Lots of sex and a big chit at the end
of the month on my American Express card? No—
that wasn't it, was it? Hmm."

"Don't be funny, Kearney. Find the bloody bastard and kill him. If it's this Borsoi or whoever. Kill
him."

Kearney lit another cigarette, tossed the tarnished
brass Zippo into his right palm, then pocketed it. "If
it's so damned easy, why don't you find Borsoi? Or
why doesn't one of the chaps round the office dash
over here on the Concorde some Friday after work?
He could be home for tea on Sunday, couldn't he?"

"Some say you're biding your time because of this
girl. It's the general consensus you should drop her,
unless she's learned too much. Then—"

Kearney had turned away, but now he turned
around and looked at her hard. "Don't you dare tell
me that, and don't you dare let anyone else try that.
Because then I might just bloody well forget we're on
the side of the angels and they'd see me back home
faster than anybody wants. But not until it was too
late."

She was staring down at her shoes. She raised her

face, smiling, but the smile faded as their eyes met. "You're serious."

"You're clever, Lady Elaine. Fast on the uptake. Quick witted. Hot stuff. Yes."

She didn't say anything.

Kearney looked away from her, studying the orange glow from the tip of his cigarette instead. "Tell my wonderful and all-knowing superiors that I'm getting the job done as fast as I can. And tell them the girl is off limits. And tell them—tell them— bloody hell, you think of what to tell them. Make it up." And he looked at Lady Elaine. "Just tell them I was sincere when I said it. Where do I get the car?"

She looked down at her hands for several seconds, then told him. . . .

The car was, in fact, just as Kearney had ordered it, a dark battleship-gray Chevrolet Suburban with midnight-blue trim (he'd left colors optional, of course, but was esthetically pleased with the selection). Fitted with the heavy-duty suspension, the Suburban had the complete towing package (transmission and oil cooler, heavy-duty battery), front and rear air conditioners, thirty-five-gallon main fuel tank, and thirty-five gallon auxiliary tank (for gasoline, not diesel), and the 451-cubic-inch eight-cylinder engine beneath the bonnet. He'd opted for four-wheel drive and a two-thousand-pound capacity winch, the winch portable and mountable to the two-and-a-quarter-inch-diameter ball locked into the hitch assembly anchored beneath the rear of the undercarriage.

Merely by turning down the center seat, it was large enough to sleep in, comfortably.

He'd needed greater accessibility to a weapon and the Suburban provided him with that; it's center console, between the two fully-adjustable front buckets, was fitted with an all-but-impossible-to-discern and electromagnetically shielded false inner bottom. Within this compartment he concealed the Smith & Wesson 5904, the Cold Steel Bowie, the Cold Steel Terminator push dagger, and spare magazines for the pistol—something he could get at in a hurry when he had to.

In various other locations within and under the car there were hidden compartments to accommodate additional requirements. He found the Colt CAR-15 satisfactory enough, but also found that he needed something that could speak with greater authority when required. Hence the CAR-15 in 5.56mm was gone, replaced by the Heckler & Koch Model 91 with fixed buttstock. In 7.62mm NATO (.308 Winchester), it would also make a much better medium and large game rifle should a protracted stay away from civilization be required, and have better terminal ballistics than the Colt in the antipersonnel context.

Once again he'd opted for semiautomatics only, since he could not possibly carry a sufficient ammunition supply to satiate the ravenous appetite of a selective-fire weapon, and under most circumstances, he wouldn't require full-auto capability at any event. Using that same rationale, and to better fill the portable high-firepower requirements for which the Colt had come in handy, he now had secreted within the new vehicle one of the Uzi 9mm carbines. With folding stock collapsed it was quite portable, yet capable of excellent accuracy out to considerable ranges with the stock extended. It had been a choice between the Uzi and the H & K 91, for his purposes more or less equal as semiautomatics since, perforce, the semi Uzi fired from a closed bolt, unlike its full-auto variant. Kearney had decided on the Uzi carbine because semiauto Uzis were more widely encountered— hence, should his own supply dwindle, spare magazines would be more easily obtained for it than for the H & K 91.

There were two additional handguns. These were to be his primary carry firearms; the 5904 he retired to the hidden compartment within the midseat console for fast-breaking emergencies. The new pistols were the Smith & Wesson Models 5906 and 6906— both stainless steel, although the latter handgun had an alloy frame. The 5906 was the same size as the 5904 he had been using, but a little heavier because of its steel frame. The 6906 was smaller and more easily concealed. All three Smith & Wesson pistols had a commonality of magazines (with the exception of the short magazines that were only for the smaller 6906) and used the same ammunition as the Uzi: Federal 115-grain 9mm JHPs, the 9 BP round.

This greatly simplified stocking and, if necessary, resupply. The only odd caliber in the lot was for the H & K 91 rifle, yet even this had been a widely used sporting round before the United States government under Roman Makowski had begun the wholesale confiscation of privately-held firearms. By comparison, within a short space of time Great Britain, with its historically tough (and rather stupid, he thought) firearms laws, was virtually an armed camp.

Beyond armament, the Suburban secreted other treasures of considerable potential. The CB radio was specially designed so the signal and reception capabilities could be boosted, thus increasing sending and receiving range. The scanning monitor was similarly equipped for boosting and covered the widest possible range of signals, enabling the operator to listen in on virtually any radio transmission. When the glove box was opened a certain way, the actual compartment could be folded out; behind it was a small personal computer with which Kearney could encrypt and decrypt and perform various other functions, including balancing his expense account. But the real virtue of the computer was the library of material on disc into which he could tap and the potential of using the receiver as a modem or fax machine, in conjunction with a radio telephone wired into any conventional telephone line.

The front end of the Suburban was specially reinforced, but only the engine compartment and gasoline tanks were armored. Rather than a single spare tire, two were mounted on opposing sides inside the rearmost portion of the vehicle, as were armored five-gallon gasoline cans, which could further extend his driving range if need be. There was a full tool kit and spare-parts kit and, in the engine compartment, two batteries. The shop manuals for the Suburban were committed to disc and available for him by means of the computer.

The girl who'd told him where to locate the car had informed him that it had been purchased stock with the trailering package, then taken over the border from Detroit into Windsor, where the refinements were added. Approximately eighteen hundred miles were on the odometer.

With Linda helping him Kearney inspected the various systems, familiarizing himself, as well as his companion, with them. He paid special attention to the license plates, both individual and in sets (dependent on the requirement of the specific state) and the proofs of registration and ownership that went with each identity package. All the materials were in order. They transfered their luggage. He ordered some additional things for both of them, cold weather gear like sweaters and heavier coats and gloves—and took a last look at the Ford.

"It served us well." Kearney smiled as he helped Linda into the front passenger seat, then slammed the door.

There was business to which he had to attend.

Chapter 8

*T*he dampness and cold of oncoming winter aggravated his discomfort, contributing to the slight limp that habitually plagued him in the early hours of the morning. But each day he was feeling better, his legs stronger, his energy returning.

He would walk, using a cane to lean on until he had limbered up sufficiently merely to carry the cane. As he moved through the park—it was midday and fair, but there were few people about—no one gave a second glance to the brass-headed walking stick. Sticks were about the only things anyone could carry these days for a weapon. In some areas, in addition to human predators, feral dogs were becoming an increasing problem because of the mounting numbers of jobless; pets were the first dependents to be jettisoned. People released them on rural roadways or in parks, and the dogs that survived—usually the larger, more powerful ones—moved in packs. With police departments across the nation otherwise engaged, to the point that twelve-hour shifts were the rule at least six days each week, little help was to be expected for the hapless walker (whose ranks had been swelled by unemployment and rising gasoline prices) should he encounter such a pack.

Self-defense of any kind was now, for practical purposes, illegal.

Legislation was being called for by "President" Makowski that would ban the sale, transportation, or possession of fixed-blade knives, other than kitchen utensils and various specified tools, with blades in excess of two and one quarter inches or any double-edged knives, regardless of size; and, of course, lock-blade knives of any size or description. Sticks, as yet, could not be banned, but in many areas they were already classified as offensive weapons, as bludgeons or clubs.

The regular military Reserve and National Guard units (as opposed to Makowski's private Presidential Strike Force), in conjunction with Federal, state, and local authorities, were still going about the business of assiduously tracking down firearms as yet unconfiscated or not already surrendered, by using the yellow Form 4473s that, on executive order, had been confiscated from Federal firearms license holders. Their licenses had been revoked because traffic in firearms of all sorts was strictly prohibited.

Meanwhile, the value of the dollar was dropping, and ordinary street and personal crime soared, further crippling law-enforcement efforts.

The Front for the Liberation of North America was gaining new strength every day and the white Patriot organization was crumbling. Ordinary Americans hunted Patriots down and to mete out mob justice or turned in suspected Patriots to the soldiers of the Presidential Strike Force. The Strike Force's power base grew exponentially.

In short, Dimitri Borsoi was pleased and reveled in his thoughts as he enjoyed the crisp late-autumn midday. The only blot was that Professor David Holden, Detective Rose Shepherd (who had, unexpectedly to him, proven herself quite formidable as a Patriot leader in her own right), and Luther Steel and the Metro FBI Strike Force members were still alive and at large.

His car awaited him at the edge of the park.

It was old and locked up, so he had little fear of theft or wanton vandalism. As he neared it, he saw that, in fact, it was just as he had left it.

He took the keys from the pocket of his slacks and opened the door, slid inside after checking the rear seat compartment, and closed and locked the door after himself.

His cane resting on the seat beside him, he turned the key in the ignition.

As he did, the radio came on. It was tuned to an all-news channel. ". . . say that the two murdered military policemen, members of the President's hand-picked Strike Force of elite personnel from all military services, may have encountered more than they bargained for while making an innocent traffic stop for a curfew violation. They may have driven into a death trap. Tire marks at the scene in a rundown area of Columbia, South Carolina, police officials disclosed, indicate that the two murdered men stopped a passenger vehicle, and while they were conducting a routine check for identity papers and issuing a citation for the curfew violation, a second and third vehicle pulled onto the scene. Both corpses showed signs of having been beaten. One source, who refused to be identified, indicated that at least one of the men may have been tortured with electrical cables powered by the battery of one of the vehicles; burns had been sustained in various parts of the man's body. Both were killed by a single shot fired at extremely close range into the brain from a high-powered deadly assault-type weapon of the kind favored by the so-called Patriots. Meanwhile, confidential sources within the recently reorganized Justice Department, although refusing to confirm or deny the allegation of mutilation and torture of the two murder victims, state that preliminary evidence uncovered in the early hours of the investigation may link the notorious Professor David Holden directly to the double murder. Holden, and his accomplice and mistress, Rose Shepherd, a former Metro police officer discharged from the force for excessive use of violence in her position as a youth officer, are the subjects of a nationwide manhunt at this hour.

"The White House sources close to chief presidential security advisor Hobart Townes today confirmed that President Roman Makowski had, indeed, undertaken to get leaders of the Front for the Liberation of North America to the conference table since the early hours of his administration. And the effort has finally paid off. Representatives of President Makowski, headed by Townes, will meet with FLNA delegates at an undisclosed site within the next few weeks. The purpose of the meeting is to discuss

FLNA demands in the hope of reaching a compromise agreement that will, in Hobart Townes's own
words, 'restore "domestic tranquility" to the United
States.' In a prepared statement read by a Townes
aid, Townes called for the prayers and active cooperation of the American people in apprehending what
Townes terms 'Patriot gunslingers' whose sole objective is to prolong the violence.

"Meanwhile, in Paris today, French President—"

Dimitri Borsoi killed the radio as he left the park
and turned his car into the sparse midday traffic.

Chapter
9

By ten that morning, faced with road-blocks that could not be evaded, there had been no choice but to "go to Plan B" and abandon the car they'd been given by Bob Amateau and the Leeds woman and hike cross country to the alternative rendezvous. Rose Shepherd had changed from the dress and heels she'd worn to a sweater, blue jeans, and track shoes. They had walked in all but total silence for several hours punctuated by short rest stops and the occasional shifting of a piece of luggage from one hand to the other.

By early afternoon Rose, at once exhilarated from the walk and depressed by David's silence, suggested, "Why don't we stop for a few minutes and have something to eat? I've got the sandwiches Ruth Leeds gave us in my purse."

"I wouldn't have thought there'd be any room."

She laughed, a little more loudly than the remark called for, but happy that David had made the attempt at humor. Since the deaths of the two men from the Strike Force—call a spade a spade, she told herself; they'd been executed—David had said next to nothing. She wanted to tell him to stop blaming himself, but didn't want to break the mood if he was at all brightening in spirits. "Yeah," she said instead, "got 'em tucked away in my purse right beside my bowling ball."

"You're going to get round-shouldered," David said, veering off the deer trail they'd been following for the past half hour or so and setting down his gear beside a deadfall pine.

"Will you still love me? I mean, when I get round-shouldered?"

As she set down her things, he took her in his arms and just held her. Rose closed her eyes for a time, and when she reopened them, her head resting against David's chest, she looked out across the valley below them. A soft, smoky haze floated in ribbons of purplish gray between the softly rising peaks in the distance beyond the valley, which was dotted by winter-dead checkerboarded fields and white houses that looked like perfect miniatures from some rich kid's model train set. In fact, there were train tracks on the far side of the valley.

She told herself it wasn't real.

The train, when it came, would whistle and throw gray smoke from a chemical pellet and whir over the electrified tracks at the whim of this rich little boy. He could stop it and start it at will. And one of the toy cars that moved along the interlacing two-lane roads—some dirt, some blacktopped—might stop on the tracks and be unable to get over them.

And then it would be in the hands of the little boy to determine if the imaginary occupants of the car lived or died. The occupants of the car would have been created in the little boy's imagination and could just as easily be sacrificed. After all, there were plenty more lives to imagine, to create.

Or they could be spared. The train could be stopped—although it was unlikely that the little boy would go to all of that trouble. But a nudge of his hand against the car and the car would be free of the tracks and the occupants inside would have a chance to go on living their imaginary lives.

He could blot them out of his mind forever or let them go on living in the little valley and be together forever.

Chapter 10

Disguises were something that had never interested him. At Halloween, while his friends would be dressing up like ghosts or Frankenstein's monsters or white television cowboys, he would not. It wasn't that he didn't like the candy and the apples, but he consciously rejected the idea of pretending to be something he wasn't, even in good fun.

But for the second time in his life Luther Steel was now forced to break his own rule against altered identities. The first time had been for an adult Halloween party his wife (whom he missed a great deal now that she and the children were in hiding under Rocky Saddler's protection) had insisted he attend. There were men there dressed as everything from Zorro to the Incredible Hulk to panty-hosed and blond-wigged cheerleaders. Steel, on the other hand, had worn an old dark suit, added a little gray to his hair (baby powder), and stuffed his pockets with peanuts, proceeding throughout the evening's silliness to tell the other party guests he was dressed as George Washington Carver.

Today he was disguised as well. No talcum powder, no peanuts, but simply three days' worth of stubble, the oldest clothes he could scrounge from the Patriot cell camp northeast of Metro, and a pushcart with a broom, mops, and various cleaning supplies. Instead of a scientist at a party, he was a substitute janitor at a scientific laboratory.

The real janitor was a friend of another of the Patriots in the Metro cell, and getting the man to call in sick and say that his cousin would be substituting for him this evening was no big deal. Men willing to work evenings these days were few and far between and the laboratory, which processed blood tests for several of the major hospitals in the area, readily agreed.

Security around the facility was minimal, since few criminals would know how or where to fence medical equipment and the few drugs stored there were nothing anyone used for getting high.

Luther Steel showed his driver's licence and curfew permit—all evening workers needed curfew permits in areas where martial law had been declared—and was freely admitted.

To keep the real janitor from any hardships, Luther Steel made a conscientious effort to empty wastebaskets, and to dust and vacuum. It wasn't the first time in his life he'd pushed a broom. College graduation had required considerable sacrifice on his own part and on the part of his family, and he'd accepted the idea as gospel from an early age that no type of honest work was ever to be considered so unimportant that it didn't require one's best.

By eleven at night he had the facility all but cleaned, leaving the front entrance and reception area still to be finished. Throughout the early evening he had catalogued and timed the movements of the lone security guard. Although that schedule, which seemed reasonably rigid, suggested fifteen minutes totally clear, Steel allowed himself only ten. He'd left the reception area unfinished for a purpose, so that if he should encounter the security guard there would be an obvious reason for him to still be found inside the building.

Luther Steel pushed his janitorial cart with him toward the entrance to the main lab. Inside the lab was what he sought.

He entered, turning on the overhead lights. He was to clean here as well and would, but here was the reason for his coming. He half-exited the double doors and pulled his cart inside, set out the mop and pail, quickly wet down part of the floor, and laid the mop aside.

He approached the nearest of the two long, narrow lab tables. The tops were of stainless steel or some type of alloy, gleaming bright. He was almost reassured concerning the medical charts just by the neatness of the facility. On each of the counters were set, one near each end, powerful-looking optical microscopes. He went to the nearest one of these and reached into his pocket. From the faded blue washpants he took a matchbook. Across the front was printed *For Those Matchless Folks Who Eat Here.*

He opened the matchbook and carefully ripped out

the first match, then searched his pockets and found
the glass slide he'd brought for just this purpose. He
set the match on the slide, then placed the slide beneath the objective lens. He flicked on the observa-
tion light. It had been years since he'd used a microscope at the FBI Academy, but he still remembered
how.

He began adjusting the focus. How Rudolph Cerillia, God bless his soul, had ever gotten the data onto
the matchsticks was something Steel could only
guess at, perhaps by using a similar microscope in the
FBI labs in the Hoover Building. As the first name
began to come into focus, Steel realized that indeed
some more sophisticated process had to have been
employed. The writing was too small for the human
hand. It would have been necessary to copy the material onto ordinary paper, then photograph it and
reduce the size to nearly the proportions of a
microdot.

From another pocket Steel took a small notebook
and a Bic pen.

He began to copy. *Trust the following people, only them:
Arthur Harrington Richards, New York City.* There was a
residential and business phone number and an address. *Achmed Saud, Cheyenne, Wyoming.* He changed
matchsticks. *Arline Costigan-Delaney, Seattle, Washington.*
The next cardboard stick read: *Jules Hyde, San Francisco,
California.* There was a short note appending the entry. *Remember not to prejudge people. Hyde is a homosexual, but
he's a brave man and a loyal American."* Steel smiled; Rudolph Cerillia had known Steel's prejudices quite
well. There were names of men and women from
across the country, some of them, like the Hyde en-

try, with little notations, some political, some about drinking habits, some about nonviolence.

The third-from-last matchstick surprised him. *If you are reading this, it is likely I am dead. If my death resulted from other than natural causes, it is likely you are in trouble. The names listed elsewhere within this matchbook will serve to assist you. But other, more immediate assistance might be required. If I was the victim of—* Steel changed matchsticks *—foul play, the source should be obvious to both of us. There is a secret compartment I personally built into the chimney of the fireplace mantel in my living room. If I was able to leave evidence behind, it will be there (see diagram).* And there was a crude, tiny drawing of a fireplace with an arrow denoting the approximate location of the compartment within the fireplace. *I have no one else I wish to leave anything to, and no one who has been more like a son to me—*

Luther Steel's hand trembled as he set the final match onto the slide. He was having a hard time seeing now.*—than you, Luther. Remember my farm in Virginia? Well, twenty paces due west off the back porch, about two feet down, you'll find my bequest to you. Be true to yourself and you'll never go wrong. If there is a life after death—*and the words were scrunched together at the end of the line and Steel had to refocus to read them clearly—*I'll be pulling for you. Remember, I believe you're the best.*

Luther Steel sat there perched on the stool, staring at nothing for a moment.

There were tears in his eyes, because Rudolph Cerillia had been more like a father to him than he had ever realized while the man lived.

Steel sniffed back his tears, looked at the purposely cheap watch on his wrist, the digital readout showing that nine minutes of the allotted ten had passed.

One at a time, until he had several of them going, he struck the matches and dropped the rest, as well as the cover, into the sink beside the microscope, setting all of them afire. He let them burn, stirring them until what remained could be washed down the sink drain.

He shut off the light for the microscope and turned on the water, then pocketed his notebook and pen.

He looked upward and nodded. "Okay."

Then Luther Steel went to grab his mop.

Chapter
11

Of course, everyone had seen this sort of thing occur in western movies set a century ago. And anyone who had watched the news recently would have seen the aftermath, some of the news broadcasters at least apparently reveling in the gore as a ratings booster.

But it wasn't the same in reality.

"Evidently, the Lone Ranger isn't going to ride up and shoot the rope in two," Geoffrey Kearney whispered into Linda Effingham's left ear.

She started to speak and Kearney held his index finger to his lips in the universal gesture for silence.

Linda nodded.

On one level he had regretted their stopping, almost from the moment they'd left the massive Chevy Suburban parked the equivalent of two city blocks down the road, its intruder alarms set. He had a job to do, and to do it he had to investigate the connection between a country county sheriff and the

FLNA. What was happening here had nothing to do with that, but it was because of the FLNA that a man was about to be hanged.

The man, some sort of bag over his head, was shakily standing on the platformlike bed of a large green truck, the truck's engine compartment roughly similar in size to that of the Suburban but the rear end disproportionately elongated. The fellow's hands were tied behind his back and one of the people in the lynch mob was either imaginative or sadistic, perhaps a little of both, because the man was also bound around the knees of his blue jeans, forcing him to stand even more perfectly erect than the presence of the rope around his neck might have induced him to do. And the way the noose was set, it wouldn't do the job right at any event, merely slowly strangle the victim rather than snap the neck in the instant the truck was pulled away from under the poor unfortunate. Or perhaps that was part of the reasoning behind the bag, because watching someone being strangled wasn't a pretty sight at all.

Kearney and Linda Effingham had seen the lights from the roadside—a half-dozen pairs at least, it had seemed from there—and upon working their way into the clearing about two hundred yards off from the road (the clearing shielded from the roadway only partially by a double row of evenly planted, tall-reaching pines), they found exactly eight trucks, all or most with their motors running. All seven had their high-beam headlights on.

Because of the number of lights and the distance from any sort of town or village, Kearney had, upon leaving the truck, taken the extra few moments nec-

essary to unlimber the Heckler & Koch rifle. The
H & K 91 needed a testing, he supposed clinically. At
an earlier stop well off road during the day, he'd
field-stripped and cleaned the weapon and was as
confident as he could be without a test firing that it
worked as it should.

There was a twenty-round magazine up the well at
the rough balance-point of the rifle, clamped to it
with what Kearney called a "jungle clip," a second
upright twenty-round box, both magazines loaded
with Federal Boat Tails, one round already
chambered. Kearney started to set the safety from
0 to 1, the fire position.

The apparent leader of the lynch mob was still
talking. ". . . damn Patriots are gonna learn. You got
anything to say before we do it, Marcie?"

Kearney shook his head. A woman up there?

It was a woman's voice, somewhat muffled by the
head-covering bag, that responded, sounding a bit
nervous. That was forgivable under the circumstances. "Yeah, I do. You men are crazy if you think
the Patriots had anything to do with killing the President. We're the only thing that stands between the
FLNA and your wives and kids. The government
sure hasn't been able to stop—"

"Shut up, Marcie. It's gettin' late."

"Go to hell, Nelson Kilrooney!"

"Maybe, but looks like, 'less a lightnin' bolt
strikes, you'll beat me to hell by a damn sight."

Geoffrey Kearney, his cheek to the butt of the
H & K 91, shouted, "Will this 7.62mm I've got
trained on your head do? I mean, instead of a light-
ning bolt?" he said crouched in a firing position.

There was no movement and no answer for a long beat. Then the man named Kilrooney started to turn around toward Kearney's direction. "Another damn Patriot?"

"No, thanks, my friend, just someone who doesn't care for rough justice. Have her cut down. Don't you do it, because if you move again, even just a little, this gun goes off."

"Fuck you."

Kearney raised his eyebrows in a shrug and touched the trigger of the H & K. The lovely thing about the H & K 91 or its military counterpart, the G-3, was its heaviness. If the shooter did his part when firing, the gun did its part and didn't beat the firer's shoulder to death, nor rise so much out of alignment that a second shot's sight-picture took forever. The headlight on the truck nearest Nelson Kilrooney exploded and Kilrooney started to take flight.

"Don't move again!"

Kilrooney stood stock-still.

"Order her cut down. And if anything happens, you die first. My promise, old man."

Kilrooney didn't answer for a second and Kearney was about to speak again, but then: "Set her loose, Tom, Jed."

"But—there's one of him and twelve of us."

There were actually thirteen, but as Kearney understood from the popular press, math skills in some areas of the United States weren't that well taught.

"Let her go, dammit. We'll get her again."

"What about the headlamp on my truck?"

Kearney shrugged his eyebrows again and fired at

the same truck, this time disabling a tire. As he snapped the sights back on Kilrooney, the man's legs were visibly shaking.

"Cut her free, Jed! Now, or so help me—"

Jed—a rather dirty-looking, tall, thin man with short dark hair—climbed up into the bed of the truck. A second man, a hat pulled down low over the eyes, jumped up beside him. This was evidently the one Kilrooney had called Tom.

"Be ready to run. I'll call the girl over here," Kearney hissed to Linda, still crouched beside him in the pines, "and the two of you run like anything for the Suburban. You've got keys."

"I left my purse in the car."

"Marvelous. Here"—and Kearney shifted his left hand and arm so the rifle rested in the crook of his elbow and dug into the outside patch pocket of the A-2 jacket, finding the car keys. "Don't forget to disable the alarm systems."

"Thirty-six, twenty-four, thirty-six and thirty-two, forty-eight, forty-six."

"Some fellow in Toronto's idea of humor, I suppose, but those are the numbers. Watch out, she's ready."

The girl—Marcie—stood on the rear of the truck bed, rubbing her wrists, the bag and the short lengths of rope on the bed beside her, the noose swaying from the tree limb just behind her.

"Miss—on the truck!"

"Who are you?"

"I've always appreciated a graceful throat on a woman, but there are some lengths a woman shouldn't go to in the quest for beauty. Off the truck and toward the sound of my voice. We'll get you out of here," Kearney shouted. She was pretty enough, but to Kearney's thinking she couldn't hold the proverbial candle to Linda Efffingham's good looks. The girl obeyed, jumped down from the truck's rear, and started—hesitantly—toward where Kearney and Linda waited. "Remember," Kearney reminded Linda, "a girl with the kind of figure dreams are made of and one that's the stuff of nightmares, right?"

Linda laughed softly. "I'll remember. Which one reminds you more of mine?"

"I can tell you've been away from a good mirror too long that you should even have to ask. Be set."

Marcie stopped a few feet in front of them, Kearney ordering, "Step to your right. I need a clear field of fire on Kilrooney."

"Who are you, mister?" she asked.

It took Kearney a heartbeat to remember the name he was currently using. "Harry Lord. I'm Canadian. This is my wife, Julie. Go with Julie to the car, right now. Run for it. I'll be right behind as soon as I'm done here."

"What's a Canadian doing with a gun?"

"Ahh, we're very broad-minded in Canada, you see. When your country enacted all those silly gun laws, it got our people thinking just how silly our own—"

"I never heard about that."

Kearney shrugged his eyebrows again. This Marcie wasn't terribly bright. Perhaps cutting off the oxygen supply to her brain wouldn't have done that much damage after all.

"I was joking, all right? Look, go with my wife." And Kearney realized, as he said it, that he was starting subconsciously to think of Linda Effingham as his wife. Under the circumstances, although it seemed emotionally and biologically correct, it wasn't much brighter than something this Marcie woman would have said. "Go on."

Marcie walked past him. He heard and felt Linda moving off.

The men beside the trucks were looking restless.

Kearney stood up—silly if anyone had a bead on his position, but necessary, and the likelihood that he'd totally missed someone's presence who hadn't shot at him already was very remote. None of the thirteen was visibly armed, which labeled them as good citizens these days, and even less bright than Marcie. "All of you, down flat on your faces, hands and arms outstretched. I won't repeat myself with words, just a bullet."

Kilrooney hesitated. Jed took a defiant half step forward. Kearney snapped the rifle toward another of the trucks, snapped off a shot that sent another tire to radial heaven, then brought the muzzle back to settle on Kilrooney.

Kilrooney dropped to his knees and the others, except for Jed, followed. "Let's rush him!" Jed shouted. No one started to get up.

"You're a fool, you know that?" The light was just good enough and the range short enough, the rifle accurate enough. Kearney shot Jed in the fleshy part of the left thigh. It was almost inevitable he'd have to shoot one of them, and Jed was certainly a prime candidate. Jed fell, both legs whipping out from under him. He rolled onto his back, both hands to the wound. "Next bullet kills. Ammunition's quite costly. No sense wasting it, is there?"

No one moved.

He could have shot out more tires, but the two trucks he'd already targeted partially blocked egress from the clearing and the vehicles were large enough that, with a little effort, he'd have to shoot out at least two tires apiece to make it impossible for them to be moved.

Kearney glanced behind him, saw no impediment to his moving, then started edging back through the trees, bringing the rifle into a half-high-port position, his finger out of the trigger guard lest he should trip on some obstacle on the ground.

None of the men moved.

Kearney had put almost another twenty-five yards between him and them and judged the two women had had ample time to reach the Suburban, or nearly so.

He started to turn around.

"Freeze!"

Kearney was already too much in motion to do that and not inclined that way anyway. He saw a blur of someone in a policeman's uniform with a revolver held in both hands in the point-shoulder position, the man about fifteen feet back. Kearney threw himself left, into the trees, as the first shot tore into the ground inches from his face. Kearney rolled, up to his knees, the H & K already firing, but held high to frighten the policeman off rather than kill him.

The man would have been an idiot not to realize

he was outgunned, and Kearney didn't want to shoot an innocent.

Branches and pine needles swirled downward, Kearney's bullets having impacted with the pine boughs above and on either side of the revolver-armed policeman. The policeman fired two more shots, both of them wild, stepped back, tripped on something, and fell, a fourth round discharging straight up.

Kearney was to his feet, glancing right. The hanging-party participants were in motion, some of them going for their trucks, others heading toward the sound of the gunfire, still others dashing into the woods.

Kearney thought it time to dash himself.

As he ran, he punched the magazine release and pulled the partially spent twenty-round magazine free, then, shifting, rammed the second magazine in the jungle clip into position.

He reached the roadway, quickening his pace now because the terrain beneath his feet was regular and there was less likelihood of snapping an ankle.

He could see the Suburban. It was in motion, reversing toward him.

He threw himself into a dead run, the H & K 91 at high port against his chest.

Kearney heard a shot and, the next instant, the supersonic crack of the bullet as it sped past him. He would have run faster if he could. The Suburban fishtailed a little as it slowed to a stop from the high-speed reverse. Kearney ran to the driver's side and shouted, "Slide over!"

He could already hear engine noises from a yet

unseen police car two blocks away, which could catch him if he lay about instead of driving like a bat out of hell. Kearney jumped into the front seat, the H & K on safe as he handed it across to Linda. "Here, darling, hold this."

"Thanks, you son of a bitch."

Kearney swiveled his head. To his amazement a policeman was sitting in the front passenger seat next to him, his service revolver on a level with Kearney's right eye.

Kearney's right hand was already on the selector and he gambled that the policeman, before sliding over to the passenger seat, hadn't set the parking brake. Kearney stomped his right foot all the way down to the floor, simultaneously dodging at the policeman. The revolver discharged, the muzzle deflected just inches from Kearney's face, his eyes closed in the instant against the powder residue. As the Suburban was lurching forward, Kearney stomped the brake with his left foot, throwing the cop off balance.

Kearney's hands were already in motion, his left hand closing over the cop's gun-hand wrist, his right hammering upward with all the force and leverage he could muster, impacting the gun-hand elbow as he brought his left shoulder up onto the policeman's face. The revolver discharged again, Kearney averting his eyes, using his legs to ram the elbow upward, slamming the policeman's head and elbow into the roof. The revolver toppled from numbed fingers. Kearney snapped his right elbow back, intentionally missing the policeman's nose out of the compelling desire not to kill unnecessarily and the admittedly lower-priority desire not to get blood all over the new car's gray upholstery.

He impacted the neck instead, missing the base of the jaw. The policeman rocked back, both hands to his throat. "Dammit," Kearney snapped. He picked up the revolver as he glanced into the rearview. It was knocked out of alignment.

He stomped the gas pedal, and the car, already rolling, started forward more quickly. He was counting seconds until the policeman died, something he didn't want on his conscience. The man had only been doing his job.

Kearney looked back. A police car was fewer than twenty feet behind the Suburban. Kearney cut the wheel hard right, crossing two lanes, the police car zipping past them. He gave up on trick names. "Linda. You'll have to take the wheel. Count of three. Start getting up here."

Kearney cut the wheel as soon as she was seated on the console, telling her, "Hold on?" then slowed, stomped the emergency brake, and cut the wheel hard left, the Suburban bootlegging around as Kearney released the emergency and stomped the gas pedal. The police car was still going in the other direction. Some of the trucks from the hanging party were on the highway, but pointed in the other direction as well. With any luck enough of them would start turning around to chase him that the police car would be slowed in its pursuit. The police car was the only vehicle with an engine that could catch the Suburban.

The policeman's gagging noises were sounding more urgent.

"One. Two. Three! Behind me! Now!" Kearney moved forward, Linda Effingham sliding under him as he released the wheel. "Make time!"

"Right!"

Kearney knelt over the broad, low drive-shaft hump.

He doubted he'd crushed the police officer's trachea, merely provoked spasming. He reached past the man and twisted him around, shouting, "Don't fight me! I'm trying to save your life!" And Kearney began administering sharp blows against the middle of the cop's back, four of them, then began the abdominal thrusts. As he accomplished those, he noticed three things: Already the policeman's breathing was starting slightly to ease; no glass had been shot out of the car because the driver's side window had been fully down; and the girl he'd just rescued from a hanging—Marcie—had charge of both the H & K rifle and the policeman's revolver.

Chapter
12

*O*nce they were certain the policeman was breathing normally and could survive without assistance, they released him along the highway, pledging to leave his revolver and his radio a half mile or so up the road beside a sign.

"Who the hell are you?"

Kearney told the man, "I've got important business, Officer Kehoe." Kearney'd read the name off the name tag. "If you're the kind of police officer you seem to be, you'd want me to finish it."

"You saved my life back there. After you'd almost killed me."

"I had no reason to kill you, or let you die. Reason is what makes the difference, isn't it? I mean, between humans and animals. Think about that the next time you're trying to put the arm on someone who's just broken up a lynching, essentially doing your job."

"You had a gun."

"And you had to do what you had to do, didn't you? I had to do what I had to do too. So let's leave it at that."

The police officer offered his hand, saying, "I'll tell 'em you went in the other direction."

"Just tell them nothing for as long as you can, that's enough." Kearney took the offered hand, clasped it briefly, then stepped up into the car. As soon as they were away, he'd swap off the Canadian plates and ID for something else. As he closed the door and started to pull out onto the road, he said to Marcie, sitting in the middle seat with the rifle and the policeman's revolver, "Where are you headed? We can drop you off."

"I wanna know who the hell you are."

"Right." He glanced at Linda, then at the odometer so he could verify when they'd reached a half mile. The trip odometer on the Suburban had registered 125.9 miles when he'd entered (reset at the last fill-up of the main tank) and was nearly up to 126.4 as he rounded a bend in the road. He began looking for a road sign beside which he could leave the radio and the revolver. There was one, indicating the speed limit, and he began to slow down.

"What are you doing?" Marcie called from behind him.

"I'm keeping a promise."

"Keep driving."

"No; not until I've stopped and dropped off the revolver and the radio."

"Bullshit."

He heard the clicking sound as the hammer of the revolver was drawn back. "If you shoot me, we'll crash the car and you'll have to walk. I won't, because I'll be dead. Linda might likely go through the front windshield, or she'll try to fight with you and you'll shoot her too. Make up your mind." He stopped the Suburban near to the speed-limit sign. He'd heard on the radio just that afternoon that, because of anticipated shortages in the petrol supply, the Congress was considering emergency legislation sponsored by President Makowski to reduce the speed limit temporarily from sixty-five miles per hour to fifty-five, as it had been some time back. Kearney threw into park, saying, "You can put the revolver and the radio right by the base of the sign and I'll take the H & K up here, please."

"Start driving."

"No." Kearney lit a cigarette. He rarely smoked inside a vehicle, a good way to reduce his consumption, but it had been a long day and promised, if this Marcie didn't shoot him on the spot, to get even longer.

"I'll kill you."

Kearney shrugged his shoulders. "Odd attitude, acting so cavalierly about human life. Had Linda and I felt that way, you'd be stretching a rope right now, wouldn't you? Either shoot me and be done with it or lower the hammer on that L-frame Smith and put it and the radio where I told you to. We're wasting just enough time that the police and your friends from the tree back there might catch up to us."

"Damn you!"

"I may have already done that to myself, but it's a nice sentiment anyway." Kearney smiled into the mirror.

He heard her lowering the hammer on the revolver
—it was rather unprofessional and quite theatrical to
have cocked it in the first place—and she started out
of the car. Linda looked at him, as if saying, *Leave her.*

Kearney shook his head, reached into the middle
seat, and brought the H & K forward. He removed
the magazine, ejected the chambered round, fed it
back into the partially spent of the two magazines,
and handed the rifle to Linda.

Marcie climbed back into the Suburban. "I think
you should meet our people. I owe you one."

"One what? A thank-you or a bullet?"

And for the first time, as he looked at her in the
mirror, Marcie smiled. "I guess that depends."

"Fair enough." Kearney put the transmission into
drive. . . .

He was happy for the Suburban, since the
road wasn't a road at all but a track and terribly
rough. If the ground had been at all wet, the four-
wheel drive would have been mandatory.

At its end there was a great amount of brush. Two
men stepped into the path of the Suburban but on
either side of the headlights. Kearney took it that he
should stop. When he did, Marcie unnecessarily said,
"Wait here," then jumped out.

She conversed with one of the men for several
minutes, Linda saying in hushed tones, "These people are Patriots, aren't they?"

"Yes, I think so. Outlaws in their own country.
Rather reminds one of the Robin Hood legends,
doesn't it? But there's no good King Richard to return and throw Roman Makowski the Usurper down

from his throne. Ahh"—there was movement toward
the Suburban—"the men of the greenwood are coming."

Instead of gray goose shafts and bows they carried
bolt-action rifles. . . .

There had been a walk of a little better than
a quarter mile, Kearney carrying his H & K rifle, otherwise unarmed except for the B & D Grande pen-
shaped folding knife in the breast pocket of his shirt.

There were tents and lean-to structures that gave
the encampment of the Patriots the look of what
were called Hoovervilles during the Great Depression in the United States, a shanty village where people lived because circumstances forced them to and
for no other reason.

There was a modest but warm-looking bonfire at
the center of the camp, and some smaller fires dotted
around its perimeter. As in the outlaw camp of Sher-
wood, at least according to some versions of the leg-
end, there were families living here, women and children, even infants. Life went on, even for outlaws,
Kearney supposed.

A man stood up from beside the fire, a large hunting knife by his left hip and a handgun on his right,
worn almost as though they were somehow badges
of authority.

"You're the man that saved Marcie here from the
hangmen, so they tell me. I'm Devon Dane, the
leader here."

The tall, wiry-looking, whiskey-voiced man extended his right hand. Kearney stepped forward a

pace and took it. "Call me Geoff. My friend's name is Linda."

"Geoff. Sit down. You, too, Linda."

Kearney retook Linda's hand and they sat down at Devon Dane's right beside the fire. Devon Dane was a man above middle age who seemed simultaneously to exude vitality and exhaustion, his accent speaking of the mountains through which Kearney and Linda Effingham had just passed, but with an undeniable elegance. At first guess Kearney pegged the man for a schoolteacher or attorney.

Marcie crouched down between Devon Dane and the fire, almost as a daughter might—and Kearney looked hard at the girl, then at Dane. As he did, Dane smiled. "You note the family resemblance. Only in the eyes; the rest of her is just like her mother, right down to the temper. We'd been out looking for her, then heard someone had rescued her. I thank you again."

"You're very welcome." Kearney nodded. "And you're right about the temper."

"You don't strike me as the sort of man who'd come here without a purpose, nor as the sort of person who'd be interested in eliciting thanks, although you have them. You're British?"

Kearney shrugged his shoulders. "One might say that."

"What do you need?"

"Do you have connections with the Patriots near Harrington, North Carolina?"

Devon Dane paused for a moment, seemed to consider. The firelight gave his face an almost demonic glow, but there was genuine warmth in his eyes. "Some. What do you need?" Dane asked again.

"The county sheriff is somehow tied in with the FLNA. I need to make a connection into the FLNA, for reasons of my own," Kearney added lamely.

"You come here to kill somebody?"

Kearney lit a cigarette. "I might have. Know someone needing it?"

Devon Dane laughed. "Oh, hell, there's a long list. That shit-for-brains dictator we've got in the White House comes to mind, but that wouldn't serve any purpose. Just make a martyr out of him. We have to vote him out."

"You're assuming that'll still be allowed."

Dane lit his pipe with a soft whistling sound. "Maybe I am assuming too much. Probably an election would be too dangerous and he'll have to postpone it—forever." Dane laughed bitterly. "He can't do that under the Constitution."

"I've read your Constitution. Marvelous document, though it seems something of a dead letter these days, things like search and seizure, freedom of speech and press, the right to keep and bear arms, lawful assembly, habeas corpus . . ." Kearney exhaled smoke. "Should I go on?"

"I can get you in with the Patriots over there. Then what?"

"Then I make a connection into the FLNA and start tracking. That's all I can tell you. If I'm successful, it won't do a thing for your problems with the unlikable Mr. Makowski, but at least things with the FLNA might ease a bit. Maybe nothing will come of it at all, on the other hand. Who can say?"

"I'll help you. We have some people who can guide you so you'll miss the roadblocks. How, by the way, do you travel with that thing?" And he pointed to Kearney's H & K rifle.

Kearney laughed. "Well, if you must know, Linda just flashes her winning smile and the Presidential Strike Force people and the police at the roadblocks are so dazzled, they can't see the gun at all. Works every time."

Linda leaned her head against his shoulder, touched his hand.

Devon Dane laughed.

Chapter
13

*T*he van stopped.

David Holden exhaled.

He was stiff, having slept in fits and starts throughout the night, awakening every time there was a change in direction or the van had to slow, expecting to open his eyes to an unsuspected road-block.

He'd been fully awake since a little after five A.M. and Rosie had awakened, too, then dropped off to sleep again with her head on shoulder. As the van stopped, Rosie raised her head. "Are we here?"

"We're here," Holden told her.

The door was worked from the outside and slid open.

He saw faces that smiled at him, were happy to see him, Patsy Alfredi's face, Mitch Diamond's face, a sea of faces from the Metro Patriot cell. At the very back, taller than most of the people in the camp, he saw Luther Steel's face.

"David. Rosie."

As Holden exited the van, then helped Rosie down. He took the hugs, the handshakes, the kisses, moving through the crowd toward Steel, who stood his ground behind everyone else.

Steel and Rosie embraced, and swapped quick, self-conscious kisses on the cheek. Steel extended his hand. Holden took it.

"So. How's Clark Pietrowski?"

"A lot better, last report. He should be up and around soon and helping us."

"Good." Holden nodded. "Ever get to read what was in that matchbook?"

"Yeah. Just yesterday. You look beat. After you guys get some sleep, then let's talk. It's important."

"If it's that important . . ." Rosie began.

"Get some sleep first." And Luther Steel turned and walked away.

The other Patriots were crowded around them again and there was no time to think.

Chapter
14

"Thomas Ashbrooke?" The soft voice, throatily feminine, came out of the sun-bleached brightness. He looked up.

She was a beautifully tall, impossibly long-legged, perfectly tanned girl and the lime-colored bikini she wore was very small, barely covering the traditional parts of the female anatomy such things usually hid, accentuating them in a way that was fetching, seductive, but not at all cheap.

The sky was darkening with heavy gray clouds, as if the island were at the center of a storm and the storm was about to engulf it. A quite cool breeze up from the Med was blowing across the veranda of the hotel bar and Tom Ashbrooke didn't find himself at all uncomfortable with the tropical-weight sport coat, so he wondered how the girl with the almost black hair and flashing dark eyes could just stand there like that, nearly naked. "I'm Tom. Miss . . . ?" Ashbrooke started to stand.

"Please sit down. I'm Electra Dimitropoulous. You know my father. May I join you?" He was standing anyway. Nodding he moved a chair out for her from the little Cinzano umbrella table and she seemed to coil into it, tucking her incredible legs up against one chair leg. He couldn't help but see that her nipples were erect and felt embarrassed noticing it. "It's a little chilly," she remarked.

"Yes." Ashbrooke nodded. She reached into the open-top, double-handled straw bag that had been in her left hand and produced a length of brightly printed lime-green fabric. He imagined it doubled as a skirt, but she cocooned it about her shoulders and over her thighs instead. "Drink, Miss Dimitropoulous?"

"Electra. What are you having?"

"A Schweppes ginger ale, but I was just about to order a glass of something stronger."

"Whatever you have, then." She took a cigarette from inside the straw bag, then apparently went rooting for her lights. Ashbrooke extended his Zippo. "Thank you. Those old lighters really seem to work, don't they?"

"Yes. I've carried mine for better than twenty years." He caught a waiter's eye and signaled for the man to attend them. "I was told by Demosthenes that you were marvelously beautiful, but I naturally thought that a father might be inclined to overstate his daughter's attributes. It appears Demosthenes is not only a world-class smuggler but a master of understatement as well."

She smiled, exhaling smoke through her nostrils. Cigarette smoking was a stupid habit, especially in one so young as she, but at least she really smoked rather than pretending to do so for fashion's sake. The waiter came. Ashbrooke spoke a few words in Greek.

The waiter, in sincere if less than gifted English, repeated, "Two glasses of retsina. Yes, sir."

As the waiter left, Electra Dimitropoulous began to giggle. Ashbrooke smiled. "Your Greek is well pronounced. His English is terrible!"

Ashbrooke smiled, not knowing what to say.

She flicked ashes into the ashtray at the center of the table. The ashes promptly blew off on the breeze and she smiled, looking after them. "I have several bits of information for you, Tom."

"Of what kind?"

"Ohh, Tel Aviv kind, Washington kind, like that. We're too open here After our drink, I know a place. And besides, we shouldn't have much longer before the rain comes."

"All right," Ashbrooke told her. . . .

The sudden rain stabbed downward with such force that it seemed almost like a personal attack, and as they ran along the narrow pathway up toward the little pink house, bright-leafed tropical plants, already heavy laden with water, swatted at them like long, pointed angry fingers from either side.

Electra Dimitropoulous was laughing, screaming with joy, her youthful long-legged stride easily outdistancing Tom Ashbrooke's. The lime-colored fabric that she had taken from her shoulders and wrapped about herself like a half sarong when they'd left the veranda now billowed out above and behind her as she used it like a sort of parachute-shaped umbrella held at arms' length over her head.

She raced up the three steps to the the tiny porch and shrieked, "I win, Tom!"

Tom Ashbrooke stopped at the base of the steps, just standing there in the pouring, icy-feeling rain—her sex, her height, her carefreeness, her youth. "I had a daughter. Your father might have mentioned her."

"Yes," she said, holding the strip of fabric in her graceful pink-nailed fingertips. "Elizabeth Ashbrooke, Elizabeth Holden. The famous Professor David Holden's wife."

"Yes."

"And I know you have a wife, and I promise that I'll sit by the fire with you and only flirt a little, but that's my way. I'm attracted to you, but I think you guessed that." And she laid her left forearm at once consciously and unconsciously across the front of the bikini halter. The cold rain, he supposed, and the way the fabric clung to her were responsible.

"That isn't what I meant."

"I remind you of her, then?"

"Too much. And of her mother a long time ago."

"Should I be happy or sorry, Tom?"

"I don't know." He started up the steps.

"Let me get my key," Electra said. He was almost tempted to ask her where she could possibly keep one, but remembered that women carried everything in their purses. She searched and searched and came up with the latchkey. She handed it to him. "You're still being followed by American agents?"

"Yes. That's why I didn't go to Tel Aviv."

"I understand they can be like witches, melt in the rain."

"Then I hope it rains a lot." He smiled. As he turned the door handle with his left hand, his right hand dipped under his sodden jacket, his right thumb popping the snap, the SIG-Sauer P-226 9mm slipping into his hand from the Galco shoulder rig. "If you don't mind, I'll go in first." Tom Ashbrooke didn't wait for a reply, but entered the darkened bungalow. Thunder rattled and boomed, seeming louder indoors. He flicked on the lights.

There was no one in evidence. He stepped back from the doorway to let Electra pass. From where he stood he could see everywhere in the little house except the bathroom shower, behind the kitchen counter, and the bedroom. He started across the large living/dining area, checked the bathroom, behind the kitchen counter, and then, as Electra came to stand beside him, the bedroom. There was a large closet, wide open, bulging with dresses and blouses and things. As far as the orderliness of her room went, Electra reminded him more of Elizabeth than Diane.

Ashbrooke remembered how amazed he had been when he and Diane first visited Elizabeth after her marriage to David. Here was a girl who couldn't keep her room straightened to save her life, but her house was spotless and perfect.

"Get out of those wet things. Come on," Electra ordered.

Ashbrooke smiled as he holstered his gun. "Did you lock the door?" It was more like a shutter but would provide a moment's warning if someone was breaking in.

"Yes. Now, get out of those wet things."

Ashbrooke peeled out of his coat as he returned to the living room, and kicked out of his shoes. His shirt was soaked and so was the harness of his shoulder holster. The leather would dry by itself if he left it, and he could treat it with something in his gear at the main portion of the hotel. With his handkerchief—only slightly damp—he started to wipe off his pistol.

"Here!" He spun toward her voice. There was a terry-cloth white robe flying toward him. It was a woman's robe, but similar in cut to a man's. It was heavy, and as he held it up, he wondered why she had such a thing that had to be impossibly large on her. "It's unisex."

"Right."

Ashbrooke went to the bathroom to undress. . . .

They sat in front of the white couch on the white woven rug before the fireplace. The logs ignited with a gas jet and getting a fire going had been piteously easy. Ashbrooke sipped at a glass of Scotch whiskey from her cabinet.

Electra Dimitropoulous seemed perfectly at ease with him, her legs crossed under a white crocheted afghan, the pink silk short robe she wore belted tightly around her upper body. "Why do you think they're following you—the American agents, I mean?" She held a cigarette to her lips for him to light. He lit it, then set the Zippo on the couch beside the gun. "To lead them to your son-in-law?"

"David? Maybe. I don't know. But I don't trust

Roman Makowski, so whatever the reason, it isn't for my own good."

"All right. Well, the Mossad people say they've gotten that Peruvian drug dealer your son-in-law captured—"

"Ortega de Vasquez," Ashbrooke supplied.

"Right. They've gotten his information checked and triple-checked—"

"What about double-checked?" Ashbrooke kidded.

Electra studied his face for an instant, then laughed. "Ohh, that too. They corroborate everything he says. President Makowski—"

"Let's just call him 'Mister' or 'Slimy' or something. Okay?"

"Okay. Well, Slimy is sleeping with this woman named Nancy O'Donnell and she's with the People for a Better America, but she's really with the Front for the Liberation of North America just like Ortega de Vasquez has been saying. I bet he's lousy."

"Makowski? At what?" And Tom Ashbrooke was sorry he'd said it the moment the words exited his mouth.

Electra laughed. "He's probably a—"

"Never mind about that."

She nodded, inhaled on her cigarette, exhaled, and said, "It doesn't look like it's any innocent thing, either. I mean, that he doesn't know she's with the FLNA. The Israeli Intell people in Washington have come up with something. They think she's a courier for the FLNA. Seems like Makowski sleeps with somebody different almost every night. But whenever she's in town, it's just her. But she's got a steady lover in Alexandria, across the river from Washington. She leaves the White House and goes directly there. The lover's name is Arturo Guzman."

Tom Ashbrooke thought a moment. "Where do I know that name?" It was one of the things about getting older that was a pain, the added time it took for information retrieval, but he supposed he was better off than a lot of people his age.

"My father says Guzman is one of the largest cocaine smugglers in the world."

"That's where I heard of him." Ashbrooke nodded. The FLNA was, in large part, financed by the drug business, so it wasn't surprising.

"But do you know who he is married to?"

"No," Ashbrooke admitted.

Electra stubbed out her cigarette, sipped at her drink, clutched the drink in both hands against her abdomen as she leaned toward him. "He's married to a Russian emigrée who's the daughter of Alexei Kirovitch."

"Kirovitch would mean 'son of Kirov,' which isn't a Russian name at all. His father must have been an old-time Bolshevik; they loved weird aliases. Like Stalin—'Joe Steel.' This Kirovitch guy. Who is he?"

She laughed. "You must be an honest man these days, Tom. He's the Soviet Union's equivalent of a Cosa Nostra boss, like a *capo de tutti capi* in the Mafia. Because he always procured what everybody in power in the Soviet Union wanted, they kind of left him alone, my father says. But when the current regime came to power, well, I guess there was a wave of honesty and Kirovitch went West."

"How far West?

"Daddy says he lives in a kind of fort on the coast between Rabat and Casablanca on the coast of Morocco. It's a perfect place for a smuggler, Daddy says."

Tom Ashbrooke took one of her cigarettes. It was another thing he liked about her. She smoked real cigarettes, Pall Malls. He lit one with his lighter, closed his eyes, saying as he exhaled, "So it looks like this Kirovitch is controlling Guzman through Guzman's wife, and Guzman is the contact or control for Makowski's girl friend. Guzman's a druggie and Kirovitch's a kind of all-purpose crime czar." He thought about the unintentional irony and laughed. "Shit, I'm too old for this."

"Can I do something?"

He opened his eyes and looked at her. "What?"

She leaned toward him, her arms going around his neck, and kissed him so hard on the mouth that Ashbrooke found himself responding without thinking about it.

Electra drew back.

Ashbrooke stared at her.

"I mean, I know you're married and you're as old as my father, but I wanted to. This way, I thought we'd both know—at least a little . . ."

"Know?"

"What we're missing because you're married and you're my father's friend."

"You're a very beautiful girl, Electra." It was the only response he could think of; and honest though it would have been to say so, it would have sounded stupid at his age to tell her she tasted good.

Tom Ashbrooke leaned his head back against the

seat of the couch and closed his eyes, inhaling the cigarette. He was definitely getting too old for all of this.

He heard the door handle turn and his right hand snapped the butt of the cigarette into the fireplace and reached to cover Electra's mouth before she screamed or something, his left hand grasping the butt of the 226.

He looked into Electra's startled brown eyes for a split second and saw that she truly was her father's daughter. He let go of her mouth, swung the muzzle of the SIG to the door. Out of the corner of his eye he saw her slip his shoulder holster off the chair back and onto the couch beside him as he stood and edged back. He grabbed the holster harness, slung both halves over his left shoulder. There were two loaded spares in the offside magazine pouch.

Electra was in motion, her straw bag in her left hand, her right hand digging into it, reappearing in the next instant with a tiny black semiautomatic pistol.

Ashbrooke wheeled toward the bedroom door as he heard the crashing sounds.

Virtue had paid.

They'd thought he and the girl were in the bedroom.

The front door opened and a man started to step through; the man wore a white suit and had a sawed-off barrel-pump shotgun in his right hand. It wasn't a face that he recognized above the half-mast necktie and open shirt collar, but there wasn't any time for introductions. Ashbrooke, the SIG up to eye level, snapped off two shots.

The shotgun discharged into the parquet floor tiles as the man doubled up like a jacknife and fell back through the open doorway.

Electra Dimitropoulous was beside the bedroom door, the little pistol in both hands.

Ashbrooke started to shout to her.

The shots came through the wall, a submachine gun and inexpensive plaster board combined, chunks of the wallboard spraying across the room as Ashbrooke shouted, "Electra!"

She spun away from the wall, the right side of her chest and abdomen and her right thigh smeared with bright red blood. Ashbrooke threw himself to the floor, submachine-gun fire crackling over his head. He rolled to the left side of the couch, realized he'd just pulled a muscle in his leg—damn age—and fired at the figure in the bedroom doorway, a double tap with the SIG, then another, then a third.

The submachine gun sprayed across the living room floor, the man holding it suddenly rocking back on his heels, bullets sawing through the wallboard above the door frame. The body toppled back out of sight into the bedroom and the submachine gun was silent.

Tom Ashbrooke reached to the Galco holster assembly, drew a fresh spare magazine from it, and swapped for the partially empty magazine up the butt of the SIG.

No one else came through either door.

Ashbrooke struggled to his knees, and then, despite a painful right hamstring, managed to get to his feet. He dropped the partially loaded magazine into one of the pockets of the borrowed robe. Magazines were like a glass of water to a pessimist when they were in a gun and like that same glass to an optimist when they were out, part empty or part full.

Ashbrooke limped across the room, glancing at Electra. If she wasn't dead, she would be. He inspected the body in the bedroom. Dead. He took the submachine gun up and trotted it back across the living room as he went to the porch. The shotgunner was dead too. He took the shotgun.

It was still raining.

Ashbrooke went to Electra.

It was hard to get onto his knees with the pulled muscle—he told himself it was just strained—but he did, setting the Steyr and the pump on the floor. He kept his gun in his hand, although he decocked the hammer, then raised Electra's head. "You were—"

"Stupid." Electra smiled. "Too many movies. People don't shoot through walls in movies."

"I guess you're right, Electra. I'm sorry."

"That people don't shoot through walls in movies?"

Ashbrooke smiled at her. "Yes. That's it."

"Kiss me, Tom?"

"I'd like that very much." Ashbrooke leaned his face over hers, touched his lips to hers. There was a microsecond of response and then she died.

Ashbrooke rested her pretty head on the floor.

He didn't worry what Diane would say if he stayed alive long enough to tell her. Because he knew what she would have told him to do. "Kiss the girl, Tom."

With some difficulty, the muscle spasm in his leg worsening, Ashbrooke stood up. Get his clothes. Get

out. Don't bother to stop back at the hotel room.
Someone could get his things for him.

He looked into the bedroom, at the dead man on
the floor. Neither of them would be carrying ID or
anything else to identify them, he knew, even without looking. But the man lying in the growing pool
of blood on the bedroom's white carpet, like the dead
man on the porch, was unmistakably an American.

The stakes were rising.

Tom Ashbrooke started to get his clothes.

Chapter
15

"**I** still don't know exactly how he did it, but I guess he developed the writing onto the matchsticks like a negative onto photographic stock, the same kind of technique they use in spy novels when they're making microdots." Bill Runningdeer started loading the next Uzi magazine as Luther Steel continued speaking. "It's my bet Mr. Cerillia left us something in the house, in that secret compartment in the fireplace chimney that he indicated in the little diagram." LeFleur and Blumenthal entered the tent, pausing beside the open flap. Steel waved them down onto the cot next to the opening. Both men sat down. "I don't know for sure, but I hope to find out."

"How?" Rosie asked him.

"On my mother's side of the family, there's a cousin. Her daughter works at the White House," Steel noted.

Holden sat back, watched, listened.

"What can she do?" Rosie pressed.

"I'm not sure. But she's on the domestic staff. Be surprised what servants can learn. It's like being invisible, I understand. So, maybe—"

"When'll we know, boss?" Runningdeer asked, looking up from his work.

"I don't know," Steel admitted. "I mean, we could try getting into Mr. Cerillia's home. It's been sealed off. And we may have to do that anyway, but I don't want to unless we have to. But if we can get some confirming clue . . ."

At last David Holden spoke. "If something doesn't happen to give us some evidence to strike back at Makowski with, we're in very heavy trouble. Patriot cells are losing members all across the country, from the information Mitch has been receiving through the network. Even the information network isn't that safe anymore because we're losing so many people it's bound to be compromised. Right now we're one of the few Patriot cells that's anywhere near the strength needed to engage the FLNA."

"That's because of your leadership, Professor Holden," Randy Blumenthal said. He was the youngest of the five men from the now defunct FBI Metro squad Luther Steel had led. "The people trust you and believe in you."

"Not enough people to do the job, Randy. I'm not saying we'll give up, because I don't intend to, and that's the same sentiment I'm getting from everybody around the camp. But this one Patriot cell can't take on the FLNA and the Presidential Strike Force single-handedly."

"The FLNA's been real quiet," Runningdeer opined. "And I really don't wonder why. The lower profile they keep, the more the newspeople are hungry for stuff to talk about—and they talk about us."

"I've studied considerably in the field of counterterrorism," Steel said, leaning back against one of the tent poles. "And logic under these circumstances suggests that the FLNA will shortly start committing acts of violence they can lay at the feet of the Patriots. All that's needed is one real atrocity, and then the fence sitters who weren't happy with what the government was doing to handle the FLNA problem but weren't pro-Patriot either will swing over to the government side and the Patriot movement is done for."

"There's no way we can prevent that either," Holden whispered.

He was getting very tired.

Chapter
16

"*T*urn here," Marcie Dane said peremptorily from the middle seat.

Kearney stomped the brake pedal and started cutting the wheel, slewing the Suburban into the turn, his headlights weaving a crazy zigzagging pattern across a row of darkened houses. This was a side of Harrington, North Carolina, he had never seen during the time he'd spent at the beachside hotel known as Siamese Shoals. Perhaps Linda Effingham was thinking about those happier days they spent together, because she reached out to him in the darkness and rested her hand on his right thigh.

"Why are we coming so close to the town itself?" Kearney asked, glancing over his shoulder a little.

"No choice. All the other roads to the other side of Harrington take us past the sheriff's office and I don't wanna risk that."

"Agreed, Marcie." Kearney nodded.

An all-news station was on the radio and the financial report—rather dismal—had just concluded. "Our top story this hour," the resonant midwestern-accented voice announced, "state and Federal authorities are on the lookout in these predawn hours for the Patriot band responsible for last night's bloodshed in a wooded area near Schuyler's Creek, North Carolina, where authorities say at least a dozen heavily armed gunmen ambushed a group of unarmed citizens who had just apprehended the notorious Patriot terrorist Marcie Dane preparatory to surrendering her to authorities.

"Marcie Dane, wanted in connection with a string of bloody bank robberies throughout the Carolinas and strongly suspected of complicity in last week's bombing of a local tavern, was freed during the unprovoked attack. At least one of the unarmed men was seriously wounded by heavy-caliber assault-rifle fire after his hands were raised and he had surrendered. Several vehicles were also damaged.

"As state police, alerted by the high volume of gunfire, happened on the incident, the fleeing Patriot gunmen attacked them as well. Although neither officer was available for comment, Presidential Strike Force sources indicate that the first officer on the scene was badly beaten after being shot at repeatedly, even after the officer was unable to return fire, while the second state patrolman was kidnapped, also brutally beaten, then left for dead along a deserted stretch of highway near the scene.

"The manhunt for Marcie Dane and the Patriot gunmen responsible reportedly covers the entire southeastern section of the country. Dane and her companions should be considered heavily armed and desperate."

Kearney shut off the radio. "That was very amusing. Do you feel desperate, Linda?"

"No," she answered, a trace of humor in her voice.

"Those son of a bitches," Marcie groaned from the darkness behind them.

"Actually, the plural should be on *sons,* making it sons of what you said. Talk about propaganda, hmm?"

"Whatever you call them, they lie."

"Wars are won with propaganda, as much as with shells and bombs and rockets. If the enemy population can be demoralized—"

"But we're not the enemy, and—" Marcie began.

"Oh, you're definitely the enemy," Kearney interrupted. "But you and your father and the rest of the Patriots aren't the people I was talking about."

Linda said, "If Makowski and his people can convince the rest of the American people that the Patriots are evil, just crazy kill-happy criminals who go around attacking unarmed men, brutalizing police officers, all of that—well, then the American people will be more against the Patriots than they are already. That's what Geoff means. You'll lose. Everyone'll lose. And Makowski and his crowd will win."

"Somebody oughta—" Marcie began again.

"No. Somebody oughtn't," Kearney corrected. "I've said it before and I'd say it again, but making a martyr out of that man would be the worst possible thing anyone could do. There's a certain amount of respect that must be shown for the office, even if the man holding it holds it through deception and murder and is unspeakably vile."

"Then what the hell are we supposed to do—Geoff?"

"Show him up for what he is; force your elected representatives to recall him."

"*Impeach* is the word, Geoff," Linda advised.

"Indeed. Impeach the bloody bastard."

"What if the men and women in Congress won't do that? I mean, a lot of them are probably good people, I guess, but what if there aren't enough of the good ones left? Then what?"

There was a one-word answer to her question that Kearney thought of, but he wouldn't use it. He lit a cigarette as he kept driving.

Chapter
17

*T*he first telephone caller's message was relayed by Mitch Diamond at five-thirty in the morning, the second one a half hour after that.

The first call came from Shawana Tooley.

The second call was from Tom Ashbrooke.

"We've got something" was all that was said after David Holden awakened to the knock at the tent pole.

"With you in five," Holden answered.

"Was that Runningdeer?" asked Rosie Shepherd, lying in the crook of Holden's right arm.

"Yeah. Maybe that message Luther was waiting for from his cousin's niece's sister or whoever it was. Come on."

"David?"

In the darkness of their tent he could just discern the outline of her face. "What's wrong?"

Rosie laughed softly. "Asking someone in our position what's wrong? David! No. A lot of things are wrong, but that's not it. I'm worried about you. You were talking in your sleep."

"What was I saying?" Holden asked her.

"You were talking about executing—executing those two men from the Presidential Strike Force."

"What did I say about it?"

"You weren't making sense, but you sounded like you wanted to cry."

Holden sat fully upright. "I, ahh—"

"You should have let me do it, David. It's the good in you that's bothering you. I mean, if you hadn't killed them, they would have gone on to kill more innocent people. It's like the whole death-penalty argument. Sure, killing anyone is bad, but there's bad and there's worse. When they step outside the human community like that, well, you've gotta fight fire with fire sometimes."

"I know, Rosie"—and Holden folded her into his arms, touched his lips to her hair. . . .

Rosie looked silly in the midcalf-length terry-cloth bathrobe that was tied tight at her waist and the unlaced black combat boots. She sat down and lit a cigarette.

Holden stood beside her there by the entry flap to the administration tent. The radios were there and so were the detailed maps of the entire Metro area and the northern portion of the state, most of those rolled up and filed, some taped onto the canvas walls of the tent.

Luther Steel stood beside the empty chair before the radio assembly. The rest of the people who'd been called for the predawn meeting—Bill Runningdeer, Tom LeFleur, Randy Blumenthal, Patsy Alfredi, and a few others—and the woman who'd been on radio duty were scattered about the tent, either standing, occupying one of the few places to actually sit, or squatting on the tent floor.

"I was here for the first call and I stayed for the second one," Luther Steel began. "Shawana Tooley— she's the relative I told you all about—Shawana is part of the domestic staff at the White House. The night Rudolph Cerillia was murdered, Hobart Townes had Roman Makowski awakened. Makowski wasn't as irritated as Shawana and some of the other staff people were, I guess, because Shawana was told to go in and remake Makowski's bed. Someone had been sleeping in it with him. But the butler on duty noticed that after the meeting with Townes, Makowski seemed furious. Here's the interesting part. They watched a movie on videotape. A comedy. At the end of the tape there was the sign-off with 'The Star Spangled Banner.' That's what infuriated Makowski so. He threw some stuff around the room and shouted at Townes. Then Townes left with a half dozen of his security staff."

"A tape," Patsy Alfredi said quietly. "Cerillia left us a tape."

Steel nodded. "I did some other checking, with some friends in Washington law enforcement. Mr. Cerillia's house had already been searched, ripped apart. Early in the morning following Mr. Cerillia's death—maybe an hour after Townes would have left Makowski—Townes and some of his men went to the house again, ripping cabinets out of walls, prying up floorboards, everything. No electronic stuff was used. And that makes sense, because a strong electro-magnetic field could disturb the tape surface. So if there is a videotape, evidently they want to see it before they destroy it, to find out just how much Mr. Cerillia really did know and if there was any other evidentiary material."

Steel cleared his throat before continuing. "That same friend of mine on DCPD told me something else that was really interesting. There was a personal-articles floater on Mr. Cerillia's homeowner's policy. It covered a gold Rolex watch he'd been given several years ago, a number of other valuables, and a video camcorder. The Rolex, all the other valuables, they were accounted for in the inventory of the house. But no camera. But I had my friend check some more. None of the shops in the metropolitan Washington area that repair camcorders had a unit with this camcorder's serial number in for repair. So somebody stole the camcorder out of the house and the tape that was in it appears to have been this old comedy Makowski and Townes watched with 'The Star Spangled Banner' at the end. And even more damning is the fact that Mr. Cerillia was a big western movie fan. Must have had every one of the big westerns ever made, on videotape. But there was not a single tape in the entire house when the D.C. cops were allowed to enter."

"Then it's in the house, still," Rosie almost whispered.

"In that hidden compartment Cerillia showed you in the diagram on that matchstick." Holden nodded.

"But how do we get at it, boss?" Bill Runningdeer asked.

Luther Steel cocked his eyebrows, shook his head, turned away.

"The place'll be crawling with Townes's men," Rosie said. "He'd figure if Cerillia left a tape and they can't find it, somehow Cerillia alerted us during that telephone call that got disconnected just before Cerillia died. So they'll be expecting someone to go after it, which means they'll leave the security passable—difficult enough to make it look real—on the way in, then close the net once someone's broken into the house and retrieved the tape. What'll we do?"

David Holden looked at his hands. He spoke softly. "I'm reminded of the characters from J.R.R. Tolkein's works. What we need to find is a burglar; a very good one. The second call?"

"Your father-in-law, Tom Ashbrooke. He had a rendezvous with some woman with an unpronounceable last name—Greek, I think," Steel recounted.

"Dimitropoulous?"

"Yeah—that was it. She passed him information, just before there was an attempt on their lives."

Holden looked up. "But he's all right?"

"Yes. I guess so. No mention that he wasn't. The woman was killed. But the Israelis he's been working with came up with this. Ever hear of the group People for a Better America? Well, one of their top people is Nancy O'Donnell. Turns out she's an FLNA courier and having an affair with Roman Makowski."

"Aw, this is like a gossip session," Rosie moaned.

"O'Donnell's also involved, romantically or otherwise, with a man named Arturo Guzman, one of the biggest cocaine smugglers in the world. He's married to the daughter of Alexei Kirovitch, who's living in Morocco now but apparently ran and probably still runs all the rackets in the Soviet Union and worked hand-in-fist with some of the KGB higher-ups. Mr. Ashbrooke thinks—and I agree—that this gives us the link we need between Makowski, Borsoi/Johnson, and the FLNA. But there's no hard evidence. We know, but we can't take it to the American people and prove it."

Rosie said it well. "Shit."

Chapter
18

*T*his was no camp, but a rendezvous only, which meant that the Patriots in the Harrington, North Carolina, area didn't fully trust Devon Dane's Patriot cell to know their true location. But these days the Patriots anywhere were wise to distrust everyone, at least a little. The meeting, instead, was in what seemed once to have been a manufacturing or assembly plant of some considerable size. A falling-down, no longer illuminated plastic sign, otherwise little weathered and new-enough looking, proclaimed the name of a Japanese auto manufacturer.

Many overseas firms had begun to cool their fervor for American investment when the troubles with the Front for the Liberation of North America first began and, since the assumption of the Presidency by Roman Makowski, had, to a considerable degree, bolted, afraid of nationalization of industry to shore up the decaying U.S. economy. The resultant unemployment, the surge in imports—since a sufficient va-

riety of products was not available domestically—
and the subsequent devaluation of the dollar coupled
with the inflationary spiral had doubtless shown any
of the more reluctant among the skittish investors
they'd made the correct decision in the first place.

A misty, cold rain was falling as they walked
across the deserted blacktop parking lot, the yellow
lines that delineated parking slots still bright and
slick looking. Kearney carried the H & K 91, rather
than a handgun of any sort, because he had no desire
to demonstrate to Marcie Dane the location of any of
the hidden compartments within the Suburban nor
any of his additional armament. And, should the predawn meeting go sour, the rifle was his most formidable armament at any event. As before, he had two
magazines clipped together, giving him forty rounds
if needed. A third single magazine was stuffed inside
the waistband of his Levi's.

"Forgive me if I appear ungentlemanly," Kearney
said, stepping through the small doorway built into
the large cargo doors ahead of both of the women.
He'd considered leaving Linda Effingham inside the
Suburban with the alarms turned on and the engine
running, but reasoned she might be safer with him.
At least her presence would give him more control
over the entire situation should something go wrong.

Inside the plant three smallish-looking bare bulbs
illuminated a patch of floor distant about half the
length of the central walkway; between Kearney and
the light source, and beyond it, all was gray darkness.
He saw no one and assumed that the Patriot personnel within the structure were hidden within the
darkness for protection against some sort of trap.

And he wondered about a trap himself. With the Patriot organization seemingly disintegrating, there was danger for all.

Marcie Dane, her voice revealing a mere hint of the trepidation Kearney knew she had to be feeling, called out, "It's me, Marcie Dane! I've got our two friends with us. We're armed. We're coming ahead." And then she turned and looked up at Kearney. "Come on."

"Fine." He smiled, not feeling like smiling at all.

The pistol grip of the H & K's stock was balled tight in his right fist, the rifle tensioned on the multi-position OD fabric sling. The safety was set to 0, but his right thumb was poised near it to bump the lever over into 1, the firing position. There was a round already chambered.

Kearney felt Linda Effingham's right hand reaching out to his left in the darkness, clutching his hand almost desperately. He wanted to speak, tell her something reassuring, but he could honestly think of nothing in that vein that he could say, and his hearing was working overtime to pick up any telltale sounds that might betray the presence of some of the Harrington area Patriots in the darkness surrounding them.

The expected command came out of the darkness. "That's far enough!"

Dutifully, Kearney stopped, the women flanking him stopping as he did.

Marcie Dane spoke again. "That you, Clyde?"

"It's me. What do you want with this meeting?"

Kearney spoke first. "I'm trying to track down the leader of the Front for the Liberation of North America, and I need your help. The sheriff in your county is working with the FLNA. You must know that."

"Bill Homan couldn't lead his way out of the damn bathroom, mister. You English or somethin'?"

"Or something," Kearney responded. "I'm not saying Sheriff Homan is the leader, but he can lead me—lead me into the organization here. And Harrington is a focal point for the FLNA. Since the destruction of Cedar Ridge Islands, everything I can uncover leads me to the conclusion that Siamese Shoals and the entire county are serving as the staging area for a considerable amount of FLNA activity."

"I got bigger problems than those cocksuckin' FLNAers."

Kearney squeezed Linda's hand, as a way of apologizing for the man's mouth. "Listen, Clyde," Kearney began again. "If we can at least partially cripple FLNA activities, the other problems may be easier to solve. If Roman Makowski's excuse for clamping down on the American people disappears, even to a degree, then it may be easier for you and your people to get the truth out and win the hearts and minds of the populace. And even if that never happens, won't you at least feel better knowing the FLNA—who started the whole thing—is crippled? I'm after the man who's their overall leader."

Clyde's voice came back quickly. "What are you gonna do if you find him? Arrest him?"

There was some laughter from the darkness surrounding them.

It was the time for all the truth. "No. I'm under orders—never mind whose orders—that once I'm sure of my target, I'm to kill him. No arrest, no media hype, no expensive lawyers, no amnesties because of hostage takings, any of that. Just make the man who's in charge very dead very quickly. But I can't kill someone I can't find, can I? And, if I am able to find him and kill him, it's going to shake up their organization and make whoever tries replacing him think twice. As long as the head of the FLNA believes that the worst that can happen to him is a public trial and the panic that'd cause, what does he have to worry about? But if the FLNA realizes that even their top leader isn't safe from a knife or a bullet, that's an entirely different matter."

There was no answer for a moment, a long moment. Then a beefy-looking man only about five feet eight inches tall, a pump shotgun lazily held in his right hand, stepped out of the darkness. "You an assassin?"

Kearney looked at him hard. "When I have to be."

Linda's hand went limp in his. . . .

They drove in the Suburban, along a narrow, poorly maintained country road, the grayness from the east spreading inexorably across the sky, but the mist turned to rain. The car's windshield wipers were on half speed, thrumming a soft rhythm. Clyde, the Harrington Patriot leader, sat in the front passenger bucket. Linda, Marcie Dane, and a second Harrington Patriot, named Larry something or other, sat in the middle seat.

A few hundred yards back a double-cab pickup truck and a station wagon, both vehicles loaded with more of the Harrington Patriots, followed.

"Billy Homan's always been a sneak and a liar and a thief and ever'body's always known it for a fact," Clyde said abruptly.

"Not to sound illogical," Kearney interjected, "but if that's such common knowledge, why was he ever elected sheriff to begin with?"

"Billy ran as what you call an 'independent,' and the candidate from the party everybody was gonna vote for—the Democrat—got himself killed in some accident—which probably was murder, lookin' back on it—and it was either vote for Billy or vote for the other fella."

"Did the other fellow have horns, a tail, and a pitchfork?"

Clyde rubbed his stubbled cheek and laughed. "No. Pretty good man, really. Andy Chitwood. Republican. Ain't elected a Republican sheriff in this county since the Reconstruction."

"Better to elect a crook who was probably a murderer? Makes good sense to me." Kearney nodded. He lit a cigarette. "Where exactly are we going?"

"The FLNA has a meeting every week. This morning's the regular meeting."

"Do they play backgammon and serve little sandwiches?"

Clyde laughed. "You're a funny fella, Geoff. Nope. They change the location each week and like that, but we keep pretty good tabs on 'em. Remember the fella we didn't vote for? Name's Andy Chitwood? Reckon Andy was smarter than any of us thought. Andy congratulated Billy after the election and asked Billy for a job as deputy, sayin' it'd show the voters that Billy was a sport and unify the county after the death of the Democratic candidate. Billy hired him on. When Billy started really goin' bad, all of us kinda thought Andy Chitwood was as bad as Billy. But then we learned—some of us, on the zoning board—that Andy was just gettin' the goods on Billy. When the FLNA thing started, ever'body kinda forgot about Billy takin' bribes and stuff to forget about zoning violations and that, but not old Andy. Andy Chitwood stayed on, kept letting Billy dig his hole deeper. Then, when we formed a Patriot cell here, just about the time ever'body with the sense they was born with realized Billy Homan was runnin' with the FLNA, Andy Chitwood—and he was one of our first members in the Patriots round here—he tells us he's gonna stick with Billy and sort of spy from the inside."

"And he hasn't gotten himself killed? Your Deputy Chitwood must either be quite the intrepid operative or this Sheriff Homan is more of a dolt than you paint him to be. Or is it both?"

Cly laughed again. "Hell—but Andy's been after us to bust up the weekly FLNA get-together. Figured we would while we still had the manpower left to try it. You can watch from a distance or be in on it."

Kearney considered his options for a moment, then asked, "Will Sheriff Homan be there?"

"Should be."

That decided Geoffrey Kearney. In one of the compartments within the Suburban, he had a standard medical kit, not to be confused with the rather elaborate first-aid kit he stored openly in the car. The standard medical kit included a variety of prepared syringes, the contents of some as mundane as

B-complex shots for administering in the event of extreme fatigue, the contents of others quite a bit more exotic: what were generically labeled "truth serums," like the old scopolamine injections of the Second World War.

"Can you see to it that, barring extraordinary circumstances, Billy Homan doesn't get killed?"

"So you can follow him?"

"If I have to." Kearney nodded. "But I'd rather capture him. I have a way of getting him to cooperate."

Clyde fell silent for a moment, then simply said, "Agreed."

Chapter
19

*L*em Parrish kept thinking his wife would answer the telephone. And then, somewhere in the fuddle between dreams and wakefulness, he reached for her in the bed beside him and, realizing she wasn't there, sat upright.

The phone had stopped ringing, but he heard his own voice from a distant portion of the house, the answering machine announcing that no one was available to take the call. He picked up the receiver from the table on his wife's side of the bed.

"This is Lem Parrish. Hang on until the message cuts out. Hang on."

He rubbed his eyes, listening to himself speaking over the telephone. He waited for the beep. His wife was still in Canada. He shook his head. The beep came. "Go ahead."

"I dunno what to do, Mr. Parrish."

It was a voice he'd heard before, a woman's voice, frantic sounding, tearful, but he couldn't place the name. "Look, ahh—I'm still half asleep. Who is this?"

"It's me, Jody Greene, Mr. Parrish. Tim's wife."

"Oh, Mrs. Greene." Why was his engineer's wife calling him at . . . He looked at the clock beside the telephone. It was almost seven; he should have been up anyway. "What's wrong?"

"The Army. They came and took Tim away. Said it was 'cause he had a gun. They beat him up when they broke in 'cause he didn't know who they were and wanted to see a warrant."

"What kind of gun, Mrs. Greene? Think. Think hard."

"I dunno!"

"A handgun?"

"Bigger. He hunts for deer with it sometimes. It was his father's. They took him!"

Lem Parrish squinted his eyes tight shut. "Where?"

"They wouldn't tell me! I'm so—"

Parrish cut her off. "Are you and the children okay?"

"We're scared!"

"All right. I'm going to give you a number to call. A man named Mitch or his wife will answer. Tell whoever answers that I said for someone to come over and stay with you. Explain exactly what happened, all right? And I'll check on Tim. As soon as I know something, I'll call your house. If I don't get an answer there, it's because Mitch and his wife didn't think your house was safe to stay at, so I'll know where to reach you anyway because I can reach them. Got it?"

"Yes. But, Tim—he didn't do anythin' bad!"

"I know that, Mrs. Greene. Don't worry," he lied. "I'm going to hang up and start tracking down Tim. Just make that call. Here's the number. You have a pencil?"

He gave her Mitch Diamond's twenty-four-hour number at the garage. Once she contacted Mitch, David Holden's Patriot cell would be informed as well that there was some trouble. If the authorities— it wasn't the Army, but the National Guard people impressed into enforcing Makowski's damned Executive Order number 128946—went after Tim, it could have been because of an anonymous tip from a not-so-neighborly neighbor or it could be a prelude to some new crackdown on free speech.

A prelude to his being arrested himself?

They wouldn't find a gun in his home without tearing the place apart, but a gun could always be planted there. Then another voice could be silenced.

"Shit."

"What?"

"Nothing, Mrs. Greene. Call Mitch. Don't worry." He hung up.

Lem Parrish swung his feet over the edge of the bed, his toes cold on the floor. The first call would have to be the radio station. Twenty-four-hour format—there was always somebody on duty. If Tim had gotten a call, he might have called there.

The telephone rang about five times. Before the voice on the other end could give the routine telephone answering line, Parrish said, "Stu? This is Lem."

"Yo, Lem. Hang on, baby."

The program cut in as Stu activated the hold button. A song was just winding down—good God, Parrish hoped it was a request and not something the station was actually programing—and Stu Shield's voice rolled over it. "That was Trixie and Molly, some mellow morning blues. But, hey, baby, it's rise and shine for the executive rush. And Bix is comin' along with the traffic in five, right after Shelly Hasty and the news. What's the top story at this hour, Shelly?"

Shelly Hasty's voice came back. She was smart, a good newshound and pretty enough to make your eyes water, Parrish thought, smiling. "More violence over night in Metro, Stu. And still no arrests in the mysterious lynching-party shooting in the Carolinas. And staff meteorologist Clint Pritchett promises more cold air flowing down from Canada by tonight on the leading edge of record-breaking lows for the entire week."

The commercial was just starting as Stu's voice came back. "What's up, Lem?"

"My engineer Tim Greene call you?"

"No. Why?"

"He's been busted on a damn gun charge. Snatched him from his house after beating him up. His wife's beside herself."

"Aww, shit. What can I do?"

"If Tim calls in at the station, find out where he is and how he is, in that order. I'm gonna make some calls. Get Shelly on the horn to some of her contacts as soon as she's off the air. Either of you get anything, call me on the private line."

"Yeah, right."

"Bye." Lem Parrish tapped down the carriage buttons and started punching out another number. . . .

A half hour's worth of phone calls netted him nothing but a few people with genuine concern for Tim's well-being. Parrish called back the radio station. There was nothing yet. He told Stu to hold off calling him on the private line and use the other line because he'd be in the shower for the next fifteen minutes. It wasn't that it took him that long to get clean, but Parrish usually defecated first thing in the morning and he needed to now.

That accomplished, he shaved in the shower to save time, not bothering to brush his teeth first. As he was toweling dry, the phone rang. He caught it on the second ring. "Yeah. This is Lem."

It was Shelly Hasty's pretty voice. "I was bumping into a dead end, Lem, but then I figured I'd try the Black Patrolman's Association." Tim had helped out the Association on several occasions with fund-raisers for underprivileged children. "Turns out they'd been monitoring the gun arrests closely, because a disproportionate number of people the local cops have on their good guys' list were getting roughed up. If the National Guard guys have Tim Greene, they'll probably have him locked up with some of the other guys on the list. All of them are people with strong contacts into Metro PD for public-service work, things like that. And all of them are being held incommunicado. The man I talked to at the Patrolman's Association thinks it's because a lot of the people are getting beaten up or injured during the arrests and the authorities don't want word of that getting into the papers, as if the papers printed the truth anymore."

"Some of them do," Parrish advised.

"Yeah, but some of them don't," Shelly said dispir-itedly. "Anyway, they figure Tim'd be out at the county fairgrounds."

"The fairgrounds?" Lem Parrish repeated. "There aren't any sanitary facilities out there, there's no shelter from the elements—"

"Bad times," Shelly observed.

"Bad times," Lem Parrish echoed. "Thanks, kid. And don't put this on the news or you'll be residing at the fairgrounds, too, huh?"

"I'm biding my time. When I go, I'll go with a splash and a bang. Be careful."

The line clicked dead.

Parrish went to brush his teeth while he thought of what he could do.

In the end he came to the same conclusion that had first struck him. He called Tim's wife, Jody. Mitch Diamond's wife was staying with her. He told Mitch's wife, "Get Mrs. Greene and the kids out of there, just in case." Then he left the house. He'd have to drive out to the fairgrounds and fake it.

Chapter
20

*T*he rain was falling in a soft, cold, unrelenting gray-green wave.

Geoffrey Kearney looked back toward the Suburban as he jumped aboard the bed of the double-cab pickup truck. Linda Effingham stood beside the Surburban, watching him, her hands clutched together in the classic movie pose of the woman saying good-bye to her man when she thinks she might never see him again. As if conscious of Kearney's thoughts, Linda Effingham waved, a gentle wave, almost a reluctant one.

Geoffrey Kearney waved back.

The truck, loaded with heavily armed men and a few women, among them Marcie Dane, rolled round a bend in the road and Kearney couldn't see Linda Effingham anymore. . . .

Kearney was grateful for the rain gear, pull-on elastic-waisted trousers, and a pullover hooded top, both pieces dull black waterproofed waxed cotton twill. He had the hood up, rain dribbling off it into his face, as he moved forward along the muddy defile, his black jump boots caked with the reddish goo. His hands clutched the H & K rifle, while beneath the jumper, Kearney wore a shoulder holster that was part of his new equipment. He rarely went for any sort of holster at all unless it were an inside-the-pants model, perceiving most other holsters as just something extra to have to throw away when it was necessary to appear unarmed. But for an operation such as this, with a lot of knocking about over rough terrain, a holster was necessary.

This one was particularly suited to his needs. From the British firm Horseshoe Leather, it was built to accommodate either of the two larger Smith & Wesson semiautomatics in a diagonal carry beneath the left armpit, while balancing out the holster on the right was a specially built extra-length double magazine pouch that accommodated two of the twenty-round extensions that Smith & Wesson had specifically designed for use by American Federal agents.

Slung across Kearney's back, muzzle down against the rain, was the 9mm Uzi semiautomatic carbine. This might turn into a firepower thing, this assault on the FLNA weekly strategy meeting, and should that be the case, the Uzi would be a better weapon in close combat.

Clyde led the column, and about twenty yards ahead at the base of the defile (which was turning into a rivulet by the moment), he raised his right hand, a pistol clasped tight in it, signaling a halt.

With hand and arm signals Clyde conveyed that it

was time to move into the attack formation outlined before boarding the transportation from the staging area where Kearney'd left Linda Effingham behind with the car. Kearney glanced at Marcie Dane—she looked like a drowned cat—and at the indigenous Patriot he and Marcie Dane would be teamed with, one Harry Lane. Harry Lane, a good-natured-seeming, well-spoken black man, had a black scarf tied over his head, almost pirate fashion, and over it the sort of transparent throwaway plastic shower caps often found in American hotels.

Marcie apparently had noticed Kearney's rather odd looks at Harry Lane's headgear and informed him in a whisper, "He works at a textile mill."

Evidently that should have meant something, but Kearney was perplexed as to what.

With Harry Lane and Marcie, who was bareheaded, Kearney moved up the side of the defile. This was done with considerable difficulty because the mud was slick and dislodging even the smallest rock would bring more of the mud cascading downward. Harry and Marcie navigated the climb better than Kearney, both offering him helping hands as he finally made it up.

Out of the defile the going was considerably easier, the long brown winter grass squishy underfoot but not nearly so slippery as the mud. They kept low, crouching as they ran. At last Harry signaled them to drop. There was no cover, except that anyone shooting toward them would be firing at an extreme upward angle. Concealment was taken care of by the high grass, at least for the moment.

As Kearney stared below, he was at once disgusted

and impressed. Spread before him across the small, bowl-shaped valley was a junkyard of enormous proportions, an auto graveyard with partially crushed and demolished cars stacked atop one another four of five cars high, hundreds, perhaps a thousand or more, other cars littered haphazardly over the valley floor. He'd never seen a junkyard so large, but the sight amid the otherwise beautiful countryside was repulsive.

Kearney rolled back the elasticized left cuff of his jumper. About sixty seconds until the attack would begin.

A solitary road, at about three o'clock on the valley's circumference with the opposite end of the valley from Kearney's position at the twelve, led into the junkyard. It looked almost unnavigable, rutted deep with the reddish mud.

But as Geoffrey Kearney watched, two cars, one of them an American General Motors product of some sort, the other a seen-better-days Saab, turned into sight onto the road, heading into the junkyard. As the GM car pulled to a stop, three men got out, one of them carrying what could have been an M-16 or the semiautomatic AR-15, impossible to judge. The Saab pulled up beside it, as if parking in some imaginary slot. Two men and a woman got out, the woman armed with an Uzi submachine gun.

Another car came along the road, this a smallish Japanese import. Then another car, then two more.

Kearney wondered if the meeting was starting tardily this morning because of the rain. He wondered, also, if Clyde would hold off the signal to attack until everyone had arrived. Kearney checked his watch. The minute had come and gone.

One of the modern economy vans turned onto the road, and shortly after its appearance there came a pickup truck, the double-cab style, similar to the one in which Kearney himself had ridden until disembarking at the LD. Before the pickup had penetrated the open central hub of the junkyard, one more vehicle appeared on the road. It was a county sheriff's department car, light bar and all.

"What's holdin' him up?" Marcie groused.

Harry Lane, his voice barely above a whisper, said, "Miss Dane, Clyde knows what he's doing. Loosen up. When it's time to attack, it'll be time to attack. Not before."

This Harry Lane seemed like a cool one, and Kearney had the gut-level feeling Lane would be good in a fight, the sort of man who kept his head and acted, rather than reacted.

They waited, Kearney judging the time in his head as nearly five minutes.

All the while, Kearney kept alternating his glance from the junkyard—no more cars seemed to be coming—to the little knoll at about nine o'clock relative to Kearney's position at six.

And, at last, a red starburst flare was fired from the knoll, fizzling and hissing in the rain.

It was the signal for the other Patriot element, the greater portion of the force, to begin the assault.

There was a long, loud burst of heavy automatic-weapons fire from the opposite end of the valley (Dane had recounted how the Patriots had acquired an M-60 machine gun during a battle with the

FLNA; the gun had been stolen by the previous own-
ers during the robbery of a U.S. arsenal, an increasingly common occurrence in recent weeks). Molotov
cocktails were tossed as Patriots infiltrated near to
the central hub of the junkyard and charged forward,
the glass wine and beer bottles shattering against already wrecked automobiles, doing no real damage,
but heightening the psychological intensity of the attack.

Return fire came from the persons at the central
hub.

Still, Kearney, Marcie, Harry Lane, and the others
of the smaller element under Clyde's personal command waited.

The FLNA personnel at the hub, including the
three men who'd emerged from the sheriff's car, ran
for their vehicles. It was here where the ingenuity of
Clyde's plan shone. It was something Field Marshal
Montgomery wouldn't have been ashamed to use.
And the foul weather actually helped.

As two of the vehicles started onto the road to
escape the junkyard, a new vehicle emerged, on the
road heading for the junkyard. It was a tanker truck,
but driving in reverse, a man hanging on at the rear
of the tanker trailer using a radio to direct the steering of the man at the wheel.

At the midpoint on the road, with three FLNA cars
in motion already, the tanker slowed and stopped.
The man with the radio jumped down, ran to the rear
of the tanker, and operated a crank-type valve. In the
instant that the valve was opened and oil began
spewing onto the roadbed, the truck began to drive
forward along the road, away from the junkyard.

The man with the radio set began running alongside the trailer; he was barely visible from Kearney's vantage point above. As he just disappeared from sight, he flipped a Molotov cocktail into the oil spill. The burning fluid within the bottle ignited the slick coating. The roadbed and flames flared in the truck's wake as it picked up speed.

The roadbed, the only means in or out of the junkyard by vehicle, considering the impossibly slippery mud, had become a napalm-coated inferno.

One of the cars in the lead stopped dead and skidded into the burning oil slick, exploding in seconds. The second and third began reversing along the road, away from the flames.

The truck stopped just before the road bent itself out of sight, both the driver and radio man running as if their lives depended on it. Kearney knew the plan. Their lives did depend on it, because there would now be a grenade inside the cab, set to blow. Once it blew, it would ignite the remainder of the oil in the tanker, the explosion would come, and with any luck a tongue of flame would lick back over the already ignited roadbed and toward the junkyard.

Kearney lowered his head slightly, more out of habit than from a real sense of need.

The explosion came.

The truck cab's roof tore skyward; and before Kearney could draw a breath, the tanker went.

As the black-and-orange fireball belched skyward, Kearney looked to Harry Lane and Marcie Dane.

Harry was making a fast, last-minute equipment check.

Marcie Dane licked her lips, patting her M-16's receiver as if for good luck.

Kearney snugged the butt of the H & K to his right shoulder.

He was to wait for Harry Lane to open fire, somehow doubting that Marcie Dane would wait for anyone.

The sheriff's car was driving across the junkyard. It was the only vehicle still in motion; the rest of the FLNA personnel were assembled in the junkyard, running—they thought—for their lives, toward the slope that Kearney's position and the other four positions overlooked. Kearney's eyes stayed on the sheriff's car, which was weaving in and out of the junk piles, once sideswiping a high-piled stack of partially crushed cars. Some of the Patriot personnel who'd launched the attack were giving chase. One of the FLNA cars—the little van—had been commandeered and was going after the patrol car. Kearney would have chosen the Saab or the little Ford.

The first two of the FLNAers were to the base of the slope. Because of the rain the grass was slick and the going hard and slow. But Kearney looked back to the sheriff's car. If Billy Homan was as venal as he was painted, he'd also have to be clever. He'd be using his police radio to call for FLNA reinforcements.

Would the good deputy, Andy Chitwood, attempt to stop him and risk blowing his meticulously crafted cover? Kearney doubted that.

About nine of the FLNAers were on the slope now, swapping haphazard shots with their Patriot pursuers, but mainly just trying to flee. There was the crack of gunfire from Kearney's left—Marcie! "Damn!" The damage was done, surprise lost now, and Kearney didn't wait for Harry Lane, but opened fire as well, taking down one of the FLNAers with his first shot, missing on the second shot but nailing a man on the third.

Marcie Dane was up, to her feet, running forward, down the slope. "Marcie!" But she didn't stop.

Harry Lane hissed, "Crazy white woman!" And then he was up, joining her. Kearney was already to his feet, throwing in with his companions, no other choice remaining.

But he took one more glance at the valley floor and the sheriff's car.

Chapter
21

*L*em Parrish stopped the car. Despite the rain he'd walk, because, with the rain, making a fast three-point turn on the two-lane driveway leading into the service entrance for the county fairgrounds would be impossible, the mixture of mud and gravel too easily rutted, the likelihood of getting stuck high.

Listening to reason rather than his concern for self-preservation, he'd left his little revolver secreted at home, weaponless as hands in pockets, the baseball cap pulled low over his eyes against the precipitation, he started up the driveway.

Were men and women actually being kept here? Like inmates at a prison camp? It was hard to believe that, because this was America and people were— Were what? Lem Parrish asked himself. Did the concept of innocent until proven guilty even matter when an ex post facto law was being enforced at gunpoint by soldiers without search warrants or arrest warrants, or even probable cause?

He kept walking, the gravel crunching under his feet almost a reassuring sound. It was normal. Sometimes he found himself forgetting what normal had been like, before the days of the Front for the Liberation of North America, the Patriots taking on the job to stop the FLNA because the government could not. The cities and countryside of the United States had become Beirut-like since then, violence and death and repression everywhere. And the government, even before the death of the real President, through the laws rushed into existence by a Congress that was at best misguided, had merely fed the violence and disorder by making the country into a police state in order to counter it.

But the disabling and finally the death of the President had been the nation's ultimate undoing. If Roman Makowski was not in fact in league with the FLNA leadership, then Makowski was the biggest fool of all human history. The cunning politico was many things: some said murderer, because of the violent fate of some of Makowski's political opponents in the early days of Makowski's career and the equally violent ends that befell some of the journalists who had delved into Makowski's life; some said wife beater, because Makowski's wife, who had died some years before, had several times been hospitalized at private institutions after suffering "accidents" that had left her with multiple fractures and bruises; some said communist sympathizer, because Makowski had consistently sponsored bills aimed at socializing everything from medicine to industry, at abrogating the right to keep and bear arms, at drastically

cutting not only defense spending that could be considered wasteful, but vital defense spending needed
only for maintenance of existing systems and salaries
for military personnel; some said corrupt, because
Makowski's personal wealth was always the subject
of rumor; although whistle clean and modest in such
personal financial disclosures as were made public
according to law, Makowski was, according to a few
crusading journalists (some of them dead), vastly rich
from sources as diverse as bribery, illegal campaign
contributions, and even the international drug trade.
But no one ever said Roman Makowski was a fool.

And this vile thing of a man was now occupying
the Oval Office and the good man who had stood for
all that was decent in America was dead in the
ground, even his elaborate state funeral somehow a
final mockery as Makowski, no doubt to some
makeup man's glory, had wept on camera while
reading the real President's eulogy and swearing to
persevere in the real President's work.

But Makowski did not strive to heal wounds. His
very existence, not to mention his usurper's hold on
the reins of power, was in itself a wound, a wound
from which Lem Parrish was starting to have serious
doubts the United States would ever recover.

The drive took a bend, and as Lem Parrish rounded
it, he was suddenly glad, despite the lonely nights
and the lack of anyone with whom to share the inner
workings of his soul, that he'd sent his wife to stay
with friends in Canada.

Men in American combat uniforms and carrying
rifles guarded the fairgrounds entrance. Surrounding

the fairgrounds was a fence that had never been there before, made of chain link and some eight feet tall with concertina barbed wire forming an insurmountable barrier at the top. Behind the fence were crude tents like lean-tos. And men and women were living within the confines of this fence, huddled beneath the lean-tos for the most part, taking what shelter they could from the rain.

Parrish hadn't realized he had stopped in his tracks. But a challenge from one of the armed guards by the gate brought him to reality. "What do you want? You're trespassing on a military reservation!"

He licked his lips, guessing he was in it now. "Ahh, I wish to speak to whoever's in charge here."

"Get lost."

Parrish was at once afraid and angry. "I'm Lem Parrish, the radio-talk-show guy. You want this conversation going on the radio all over Metro or do you want to get me your commander? It's your responsibility, not mine." He'd kept the trembling out of his voice, but not out of his good hand. But his hands, one of them fingerless, were secure within his pockets for the moment and no one would know he was terrified except himself.

"You got ID?"

Parrish approached slowly, now having to remove his good hand from where it was hidden. But the shaking had stopped and he said, "Here," as he showed his driver's license and his press pass. "Now, let me see your boss."

One of the guards looked at the other, then went to a portable field telephone. . . .

. . .

Geoffrey Kearney reached the base of the slope. Three of the Patriots were down wounded or dead, but most of the FLNA personnel were killed.

Time was running out.

He ran along the slick grass until he reached the even slicker mud at the fringes of the auto junkyard, of necessity slowing his pace to avoid falling.

Both magazines for the H & K were empty and replaced with a single spare, but the rifle was slung across his back now, the Uzi carbine replacing it as he moved into the first narrow lane between the junked cars. The sheriff's car had been stopped and the corrupt sheriff and his deputies were on foot. About a half-dozen Patriots were still after them, and it was this battle that Kearney now sought to join. He presumed that all of the Patriots would be careful to avoid killing Deputy Andy Chitwood, the lamb in wolf's clothing.

But for Kearney there was but a single imperative: take Sheriff Billy Homan alive so Homan could be interrogated and Kearney could get closer to the leadership of the FLNA.

There was the time factor to consider, and time could very well be running out. Unless Homan was an imbecile, the corrupt FLNA sheriff would have called for FLNA reinforcements. If he'd successfully reached help via the radio, that help could be arriving on the scene at the junkyard in minutes.

As best he could, Kearney kept to a quick pace while trying to avoid slipping in the mud or exposing himself to enemy fire. From his last vantage point on the slope where he could at least partially overlook the entire junkyard, Homan and his two deputies had been in cover at what would have corresponded to ten o'clock, which meant Kearney had to cross nearly the entire span of the junkyard just to get near them.

He kept moving. . . .

"What do you want here, Parrish?"

The man who stood less than a yard from Lem Parrish, two pistols holstered at his gun belt, one on either side, was the commandant of the camp. And on his shoulder he wore the brassard of the Presidential Strike Force. "I want to see an associate of mine who was arrested for possession of a firearm. It sounds like someone made a mistake."

The man—tall, lean faced, with pockmarked skin and a leering smile—said, "We don't make mistakes when it comes to apprehending gun criminals, Parrish. A gun's a hard thing to miss."

"I understand it was a hunting rifle he'd inherited that he was arrested for having."

"Without knowing the particulars I can't comment. But, I'd say, the gun might have been mounted with a sniper scope."

"A sniper scope?" Parrish repeated incredulously. "You mean a telescopic sight."

The officer—a major—smiled almost good-naturedly. "That presidential order includes any type of firearm that might conceivably be used offensively. Sometimes, Parrish, it's a judgment call. What might be an ordinary hunting rifle in one man's hands might be a sniper rifle in the hands of another man. I may remember this arrest, come to think of it. A nigger?"

"He's a black man," Parrish said, suddenly feeling dirty just standing and talking with this man.

"Same color, just different nomenclature. Gimme his name."

"Greene."

"Hmm. Yes. I remember it now. High-resolution sniper scope mounted on the weapon. You should watch who you make friends with, especially a man in the public eye such as yourself. But your Mr. Greene will receive a fair hearing as soon as his number comes up."

"Has he been arraigned? Bail set?"

"There isn't the time for arraignments these days, Parrish. If you saw the volume of personnel we shift through here, you'd know what I mean. Staggering."

Parrish tried to keep calm. "Can I see him?"

"That's impossible."

"I want to see him, discuss what the charges are filed against him, see to getting him a lawyer. And I understand he was injured during the arrest."

The major shook his head. "Can't see him. I don't make the rules, Parrish, just follow orders like everyone else. If he was injured, and I doubt that he was, we have medics to see to that. And as to a lawyer, you can rest assured his rights will be seen to. Just like with everybody here, the court will appoint a public defender for him at the time of his trial. But you have to remember, it's hard to allege someone's innocence when the physical evidence is right there in front of the eyes of the judge. Each detainee is given a number. And he's told not to lose it or else his trial date will be delayed drastically.

"That's not a punishment," the major went on, "simply necessary. The physical evidence is tagged with that number and so are the detainee's personal effects. If the detainee loses his number, it's a lot of hard work verifying his identity and assigning him a new number and assigning a new number to the evidence and his belongings. And there's always the possibility of a mixup. He could be credited with having been in possession of a different weapon, say a submachine gun." And the major smiled. "So, you wouldn't be doing your friend a favor by trying to see him."

"When will his trial be?"

"If it's the man I'm thinking of and you say he was apprehended this morning, the trial date should be sometime about six to eight weeks from now. We're running behind."

Parrish was trembling, but not from fear; that was long gone. He trembled with rage. "And he has to sit here until then?"

"Hardly sit. Not that many chairs." The major laughed for a split second, then his face sobered. "They get food, toilet privileges."

"The temperatures are dropping. There's a cold wave coming in."

"We have portable heaters arriving in the next few days for just that situation. Nothing to worry about."

"I'll get a court order," Parrish said softly.

"Civilian court orders won't do you much good here."

"You're not trying him by military court," Parrish said.

"It's a combined system. We're acting in conjunction with the newly reorganized Justice Department."

"Find another name," Parrish whispered, trying to control his voice, his anger. "*Justice* is a word that doesn't fit anymore."

Chapter 22

The sheriff and one of his two deputies were behind a cluster of late-model Ford station wagons, the vehicles with various parts—doors, windscreens, fenders—missing, apparently scavenged. As Kearney spotted them, he saw Sheriff Homan raise his revolver to shoot one of the Patriots who had evidently been hapless enough to be captured, the gun inches from the woman's left temple. From body language, although Kearney had the physical description and it matched perfectly—reddish hair, tall, muscular—Kearney could tell that the deputy standing beside Homan was Andy Chitwood. Chitwood was starting to move his own revolver into position to shoot Sheriff Homan before Homan could shoot the female Patriot.

"Freeze—all of you! Shoot that girl and you're dead!"

Homan froze, seemed about to speak. But there was a thrumming suddenly audible on the air. Kearney glanced right and up. Helicopters. Three of them. Military. What the bloody hell was this? Kearney wondered.

He heard Homan's voice. "Those are my boys and your asses are fried."

As Kearney started to respond, the woman Patriot, on her knees at Homan's feet, screamed.

Kearney took a half step forward.

Homan wheeled.

Kearney didn't want to shoot.

Homan brought the gun swiveling around.

"Damn!" Kearney's right first finger started to touch the trigger of the Uzi carbine.

Chitwood stepped between Kearney and Homan.

Kearney sensed it behind him, and, turning, dropped to one knee. Submachine-gun fire tore into one of the Fords as the second deputy opened fire. Kearney stroked the trigger of the Uzi carbine, getting off five semiautomatic shots, then three more, the second deputy's face freezing in a rictus of surprise mingled with death, splotches of red lacing across his chest and up into his thorax as he toppled back, the submachine gun firing skyward.

Kearney was again on his feet. There was Homan to think about and Kearney sidestepped right. As he started to turn around he felt the explosion beginning in his head, felt his muscles start to go out of his control, a light show more brilliant than an American Fourth of July starting in his eyes and a cold, nauseous feeling in his stomach, spreading over his skin, the Roman candles and starbursts turning to black, the thrumming of the helicopter gunships in his ears so loud now that it consumed him. . . .

. . .

His stomach felt it, the lurching and swaying, and he tasted the partially digested doughnut
and coffee he'd wolfed down before the battle, rising
vilely now in his throat. Geoffrey Kearney opened
his eyes.

It was Chitwood staring down at him.

Kearney tried moving. He was lying in a heap
against something hard and unyielding and the motion was still going on and the feeling of being about
to vomit was still there, but no stronger.

His wrists were clapped in handcuffs and there
was something bound around his ankles and his
chest and the pain in his neck and head was so in-
tense as he looked up at Chitwood that Kearney
nearly lost the remains of the doughnut and his consciousness simultaneously.

Chitwood said over the thrumming noise as he
bent his face close to Kearney's, "I saved your life.
Hang tight." And Chitwood, clinging to a webbing
strap leading out of a cleat near his hand, stood up
and walked swayingly away.

Where Chitwood had been, there was emptiness, a
green wash coming over Kearney's eyes and a cold
wind flooding over him through the open fuselage
door of the gunship.

The pain stabbed at Geoffrey Kearney and he
closed his eyes for just a second to get a grip on it.
And he was gone and he knew it.

Chapter
23

Geoffrey Kearney opened his eyes and the pain started again, but the nausea was gone.

He was freezing cold and he instantly realized why. He lay naked on a tile floor of some sort. As he looked up, it was almost as if he were in some sort of pit.

"Hello there, you son of a bitch."

Kearney looked up, and raising his head too quickly was a very big mistake.

But as he looked up, he saw Sheriff Homan.

"You had some pretty neat shit in your pockets, Mr. Kevin Cole from Nevada." Kearney blinked. Kevin Cole? Yes, he was Kevin Cole according to the ID he'd switched to when he'd gotten the shoulder holster and the handgun from the Suburban. Had he changed to Nevada plates? Or was it only one plate? He couldn't remember.

As he tried to sit up and fell for his troubles, he realized that his wrists were still cuffed together behind him. But his ankles were free and the restraints across his chest were gone.

What kind of a place was this?

Fuzzy thinking, Kearney, he told himself.

The sheriff seemed bent on talking, so Kearney didn't try saying anything, using the time instead to gather his wits back from all the wool in his brain.

"I found me this kit with all of these needles in it, hypodermic syringes. You a doctor, a drug addict, or a spy, boy?"

Kearney supposed he was expected to speak. Just who was Kevin Cole supposed to be again? Hmm. Yes, Kearney remembered. Cole was an insurance investigator. The ID would have shown that too. "Insurance."

"Yeah, I believe that, Mr. Cole. Tell me another, but make it better or you'll be hurtin'."

"I'm an insurance investigator. I'm a Patriot and I was here in the East on business and fell in with the local people and—" That wasn't a very creative story, but maybe it would be believable. After all, he'd been armed, caught with the Patriots, and even though declaring he was a Patriot might get him killed, at least it wouldn't betray the mission, and someone else could replace him, use his data to get this far. And there was always Chitwood with his advice to hang tight. Maybe a better story would be needed to do that. He waited for the sheriff's next remark.

It came quickly.

"I got this county sewed up, you miserable asshole, and I wanna know what kinda thing you really are. I coulda let my Presidential Strike Force boys take you after they was finished blowin' away them fuckin' Patriot bastards, but I figured, no, Billy, you oughta ask this boy some questions yourself since he was so eager to take you alive and had this fancy hypodermic kit and all them guns on him. Now, if you disappoint me, Mr. Kevin Cole, I'm gonna kill you the hard way."

Kearney hesitated on purpose, trying to make certain he had the story right and trying to add reluctance to his dramatic presentation. Then he shrugged his shoulders as much as he could. "All right," Kearney declared, dropping the slight twang from his Americanese and adding, instead, a New York accent. "I'm a government agent. National Security Agency. You'll have to check with 'em yourself, man. We don't carry ID. I was assigned to infiltrate the Patriots. So, I was with 'em on the attack. I tried getting information out to my people but couldn't get away. So when I came up on you, I figured if I got the drop on you, I'd keep you from gettin' blown away, all right? So, we all screwed up. What can I tell ya! Check it out, but get me outa this—what the hell is this?" And Kearney looked around him.

It was like a pit, a white-ceramic-tiled pit.

"Well, that's a cute story, Mr. Kevin Cole. That supposed to be your real name?"

"It'll do when you check," Kearney lied.

"Yeah, well, just in case it don't—you wanted to know what this was, this place you're in? Hell, don't they have no swimmin' pools round the National Security Agency? Show the boy what I mean, Chitwood."

"Right, Sheriff." Kearney's eyes—despite the pain

when he moved his head—followed Chitwood as Chitwood walked from beside Sheriff Homan to the far end of the pit. It was a pool, Olympic sized, but with a deep end for diving. Kearney lay in the deep end. Above him as he followed Chitwood to a stop, was a large spigot. "This is what fills the pool, homeboy. It turns on like this." He twisted a circular faucet above it. "Takes twelve hours to fill up, more or less, just a fraction of an inch at a time. And you may have noticed, the shallow end's not very shallow."

As Sheriff Homan spoke, water was already starting to dribble out of the spigot, the volume increasing. "The shallow end's seven feet, Mr. Kevin Cole. Now, with them handcuffs on, you won't swim too good, or tread water either. The only way you'll be able to float's on your face, which ain't too good for breathin'. And there ain't no ladder, so you can't climb out. You'll probably get yourself out of the deep end. Fact, I'd advise it. But, if you ain't no National Security fella, you got two choices, and that's drownin' or tellin' me some story I wanna hear, in which case I'll just have you shot to death afterward. Which is a lot quicker than what you got in store for ya. Chitwood!"

"Yes, Sheriff."

"Turn that damn spigot on all the way, boy, then shut off the lights and lock the door just in case he's some kinda Houdini. Let's have some lunch, then maybe I'll try checking our Mr. Kevin Cole's story out, huh?"

"Yes, Sheriff."

The spigot's volume increased as the squeaky faucet was turned open all the way.

The water splashed against Kearney's naked flesh and felt cold as ice.

He watched Sheriff Billy Homan and Deputy Andy Chitwood until they were so far beyond the lip of the pool that he could no longer see them.

And he heard a click, the lights going out in the same instant. Homan shouted, "Don't slip and fall and crack your skull wide open." And then Homan laughed, but the laugh was cut short as there was the sound of a door slamming, then a click as the lock was set.

Then the only sound was the sound of the water.

Geoffrey Kearney had heard of men with long enough arms or who were sufficiently double jointed or nimble to slide their manacled hands beneath them and under their legs, then pull their feet through and get their hands in front of them.

He was not so gifted.

Instead, cautiously because the tiles were already slick, he got to his knees. He debated getting to his feet or staying on his knees as he worked his way out of the deep end. He stayed on his knees and started crawling.

Kearney slipped, banging his left cheek for his trouble, nearly smashing his jaw against the tiles, struggled upright, crawled on.

Once Homan checked with NSA and found there was no Kevin Cole—Kearney had purposely selected "No Such Agency" because the NSA had the tightest security for their personnel files—but once it was verified there was no Cole, if Homan's contacts went that far, the game would be up.

Kearney laughed. It was already close to up, as close as he cared for it ever to get.

His fate was in Chitwood's uncertain hands now.

At least Linda had to have gotten away or they would have threatened to use her against him. Oddly, he took more comfort in that knowledge than he thought he would have.

"Chitwood," Kearney whispered under his breath. Chitwood had seemed ready to compromise his cover by saving that Patriot woman—although she might have been killed anyway afterward. Would Chitwood risk his cover for a total stranger, or had the "hang tight" remark merely been to keep Kearney silent, so Chitwood himself wouldn't be compromised?

Consciousness and alertness—and pain—were coming back to Kearney rapidly now.

What had the Army helicopters been doing there? Presidential Strike Force, or did the FLNA or Makowski or both have entire Regular Army or Reserve units at beck and call?

It was a puzzle, and he had twelve hours with nothing else to do but solve it or attempt to—and to keep his head above water.

He kept shuffling along on his knees up the slippery deep-end slope.

The water somehow sounded deeper and colder.

Chapter
24

*T*hey could not find a burglar.

There were criminals everywhere. Crime was on the upsurge across the nation, in part because victims were easier pickings—the law had made them defenseless.

But they could not find a burglar.

"If we could only get in touch with Anthony Scapalini," Rosie said almost wistfully. "He did a good job for us that time on Costigan's safe."

Holden looked at Rosie. He remembered Scapalini very well. Because of the timid breaking-and-entry artist's considerable skills, the Patriots' first concrete evidence of a connection between the FLNA and the international drug trade, by which the Front for the Liberation of North America was financed, had been established and Roger Costigan, would-be mayor of Metro, had been defeated. "But your man was a safecracker, anyway. There isn't any safe to get into," Steel pointed out. "What we need is an intelligence commando, not a box man. The tape's inside a little compartment built into the fireplace chimney. Mr. Cerillia must have built the compartment himself. And all somebody has to do to get at it is to reach up inside, slide a brick out, and that's it."

David Holden noticed everyone was looking at him. He lit a cigarette. "The SEALs taught me a lot, about infiltration and exfiltration, all sorts of stuff. And one of the things they taught me was to know my limitations and call in specialized personnel when required. If we can't find anybody with the right qualifications, then I'll try it because we won't have any other options left. And we don't have much time left, either, so it looks like I might have to. But we're probably talking about very sophisticated electronics, silent stuff. The Makowski/Townes crowd wants us to get into Cerillia's house and retrieve the tape because they can't find it themselves. So we won't even know we've tripped any alarms until it's too late. And then our only recourse will be to shoot our way out, and Cerillia's house is located just across the river from Washington itself. Townes could have a whole company of Makowski's Presidential Strike Force people on alert and ready to scramble. We wouldn't be talking a shoot-out; we'd be talking a war. And it won't do us any good to get the tape if we wind up handing it over to Makowski. Hell, I don't know what to do.

"And we can't just feed the information my father-in-law got for us to the media," Holden went on. "Because they're not going to tell the public that Makowski's steady girlfriend is tied in with the Soviet Union's top gangster and through him to corrupt officials in the KGB. And that this same woman is Makowski's information pipeline into and out of the FLNA. It sounds like something out of a spy movie. And the media, for the most part, is on Makowski's side anyway because he's pushing the same liberal agenda that a lot of prominent media figures have been pushing on the American people for the last couple of decades. They might call him heavy-handed, but they're not ready to call him a dictator and a traitor."

"So," Rosie said matter-of-factly, "we're screwed. Unless we can get our hands on Cerillia's tape and get it broadcast so people can see for themselves and don't have to have it interpreted for them."

"Which all brings us back," Runningdeer said cheerlessly, "to finding somebody to get into that house and snatch the tape."

Chapter
25

Geoffrey Kearney had reasoned that allowing himself to fall asleep while the water level was still low was his only choice. Within a few hours the water level would be too high for him to risk sleep and he would need strength and alertness to have any hope of survival, however dim.

The click of the lock stirred him, and the sound of the door opening and closing quickly awoke him. His attention focused on the gray haze from beyond the lip of the pool. It became a beam of light, and in the next instant the light swept across the water and settled on Kearney's face. He squinted his eyes tight shut against its brightness.

"Cole?" It was Chitwood's voice.

"Right where you left me, more or less."

"Look. I can only talk for a second. I'm sorry."

Kearney kept to his New York–accented Americanese. "You're the one who cold-cocked me there at the junkyard, aren't you?"

"If I hadn't, he'd have shot you."

"I might have been better off."

"Look. I don't know if I can get you out of here. I had word from the Patriots. Most of them got away. Your girl friend's all right too. She got away with Marcie Dane. Clyde tells me you're some kind of special agent or something who's been sent to find the head of the FLNA. His name's Borsoi. Dimitri Borsoi. He uses the name Johnson. Metro was where he hung out, but that got too hot for him. He's been in Savannah, Georgia, or at least that was his operations base while he was recovering from some injuries."

"Are you sure he's the number one man, this Borsoi/Johnson?"

"If he isn't, he'd know the number one; and that's for sure. He's connected."

"Can you get me out of here?" Kearney tried to keep panic and hope out of his voice.

"That's the tough part. The whole place is surrounded. If I helped you, then we'd both be trapped."

It was stupid to ask, but Kearney asked anyway. "A key."

"No. I can't. But don't give up. If I can help you, I will. I've gotta go."

"Slow the water down a little."

"I can't." Already the flashlight beam was fading, the voice more distant. "I've gotta go."

"Chitwood!" Kearney hissed.

He heard the door close, the lock click.

He heard the resonant beating of the water as it filled the swimming pool. It lapped against his feet in waves, each wave that infinitesimal part more strong.

Chapter
26

*T*ransportation by air to the Washington, D.C., area was already arranged. The Patriots in Alexandria, Virginia—whom Holden was able to reasonably well trust because he, Rosie, and Steel and his men had worked with them before—were alerted, already mustering as much manpower as possible for the assault on Rudolph Cerillia's home.

And they had to be ready for a full assault because, as much as Holden tried, he could not escape the conclusion that once he was inside the house and had the tape in his hands, every available man from the Presidential Strike Force would arrive in the next instant and there would be what amounted to a small war.

There was an hour to go before leaving for the rendezvous with the small plane by which he, Rosie Shepherd, Luther Steel, Tom LeFleur, Bill Runningdeer, and Randy Blumenthal would travel to Virginia.

Rosie had disappeared a short while ago, attending to last-minute details, and Holden attended to last minute details as well. One at a time he unloaded both Berettas and the magazines for them, field-stripping, and then meticulously cleaning, each pistol, and reloading the magazines after testing the springs for positive function. He did the same with the Desert Eagle, replacing it in the Southwind Sanctions SAS-style thigh holster along with the spare magazine the holster also pouched. He had two of these .44 Magnum semiautomatic pistols now: the one Rosie had brought for him at the conclusion of the affair in Peru that had nearly cost him his life, and the one he had inherited from Rufus Burroughs when the Patriot leader had died in his arms, leaving Holden as his successor.

Rosie understood why he carried the Desert Eagle Rufus Burroughs had left to him and kept the other in reserve. In a strange way, with Rufus's gun, it was as if Rufus were still carrying on the fight he'd died in. It would be nice to think that someday, when peace returned to the United States, Rufus Burroughs would be recognized for the heroic leader that he was and some sort of monument would be erected, not just to honor his memory, but as an inspiration for Americans, of courage, self-sacrifice, and patriotism in the finest sense in which those words—sometimes used so cavalierly—could ever be meant.

But, as it looked—Holden began touching up the edge of the Defender knife—there would never be a monument to Rufus Burroughs's sacrifice—especially not that greatest monument, the restoration of justice. Because the bad guys were winning. If this tape could be retrieved—and the cost would be great to obtain it—and if, after all the effort, it contained the information necessary to damn the regime of Roman Makowski, even then getting airplay for the tape would be a monumental achievement.

David Holden had a way for getting that done, but he had to get hold of the tape.

Rosie entered the tent. She was dressed in faded blue jeans and a black T-shirt under her lined black M-65 field jacket. She shrugged out of the jacket. Beneath it she wore the white Null holster with the little M-60 Smith & Wesson revolver carried upside down beneath her left armpit. She said nothing, only smiled, then started to change. As she began to open the fly of her pants, he noticed that the .45 she habitually carried in her purse was stuffed in the waistband. She set the pistol down and skinned out of the jeans. As she started into the black BDU pants she would wear for the mission, she said almost casually, "I don't see any reason why I can't go in with you."

Holden looked at her across the primary edge of his knife as he continued sharpening. "The same two reasons I gave you the last time you mentioned it: I need you outside the house to coordinate the counterattack once I'm on the way out of the house and the Presidential Strike Force unit hits; and there's no sense both of us getting killed in case this doesn't come off."

"I don't care if I live, if you're dead." She said it as though she were just giving the time of day. And she averted her eyes, turning away as she buttoned the fly on her pants. It wasn't modesty that made her turn her back to him, he knew.

"I love you and I feel the same way; you know that. But if both of us die, the Metro Patriots could fall apart. They'll follow you."

"They follow you, David. That's—"

"They follow me because of you and because of Rufus. They'd still follow you if I were dead. You proved that when Borsoi had me snatched and held prisoner down in Peru. That raid you pulled off on the FLNA facility near Metro on that river island—nobody could have done it any better. Not me, not Rufus, not anybody. If we both die in this, we're saying we're more important than what we've been risking our lives for all this time."

Rosie, her pants only half buttoned, turned around, rushed toward him, and dropped to her knees at his feet, her hands reaching up, touching his face gently. "For once I wish to God we were more important."

He held her in his arms, his lips touching her hair. . . .

Rose Shepherd's sinuses felt clogged and she sniffed as she walked beside David Holden toward the waiting van. Steam rose on her breath and she started zipping her jacket closed. It was only a short ride, along country roads to the airfield; and they traveled openly armed. Both she and David carried M-16s in their hands. But across her back she had the Uzi carbine slung, the semiautomatic Uzi given her by Kelly Martine. The knife Kelly had given her —the handmade "Big Ugly One," as it was called— was sheathed on her pistol belt, which she wore slung over her left shoulder. Both the Detonics .45 and the Glock 9mm were holstered on it.

On David's right thigh was Rufus Burroughs's Desert Eagle .44. Her eyes fixed on it as she only half heard Patsy Alfredi calling from the command tent to them.

"Rosie?"

"What?" She looked up into David's face. God, he was beautiful, she thought. The eyes, the curly hair. It was her luck, the only man she'd ever fallen in love with, the only man she'd ever respected enough to want for a husband, and gorgeous to boot, and all they ever did together was go out and risk getting killed.

"I wasn't listening," she said, forcing a smile.

"Patsy says there's a message just in through the network. From Lem."

"Right."

David waved to Bill Runningdeer, who would be driving the van, and started for the command tent, Rose falling in beside him.

They entered the tent and she was instantly too warm. She started to unzip her coat as Patsy picked up one of the half-dozen clipboards on the table. "All right, David. This just came in from Mitch through the network. From Dane's operation in North Carolina. Actually, from Dane's daughter, Marcie."

"She's his second-in-command, isn't she?" David interrupted, looking at Rose Shepherd.

"Yeah. Pretty good, I guess, but I hear she's a flake. I also hear she's the one who nearly got herself hung the other day." Rose looked at Patsy. "What's she want?"

"She had a personal message for David. I decrytped it. Maybe I shouldn't have." Patsy Alfredi shrugged her shoulders and handed David the clipboard.

David looked at Rose, then began to read aloud: *"David, I hope you remember me. We met at your wedding and then at that lawn party when you got your Ph.D. Elizabeth and I were best friends all through school, two rich girls who thought they were the prettiest things on two legs and probably were. Elizabeth gave up the parties and the money and married for love. If I'd been smart, I would have found a man and done the same thing. I found a lot of guys, but never what you two had. Until recently. Elizabeth and I kept up over the years, but I never knew about Elizabeth's death until it was too late for me to come to the funeral. And I guess I thought that calling you or coming to visit would be just a reminder of something you'd want to forget. I've learned since then that when you love somebody you don't want to forget them.*

"I've been following your career since Elizabeth's death. I was never political. Maybe I thought you'd gone off the deep end a little. I was wrong. I need your help. I met a man named Geoffrey Kearney. He uses a lot of different names. He's a British Intelligence agent—just like in the books, honest. He came here to fight the FLNA, just like you do. And I love him. He was captured by the FLNA and the Presidential Strike Force and I know where he's being held. But no one here is willing to risk getting him out. I'd go, even though I don't know much about guns and things. But Mr. Dane won't let me. I hate to put it this way, but for Elizabeth's sake, so I can have what she had with you, even for just a little while, please help me. And hurry. They will kill

him soon. I know that. Please, David. I'm begging you to help me.''

David looked up from the clipboard. He smiled a little. "Long message, huh?"

"What's her name?" Rose Shepherd asked.

"Linda Effingham."

"Are you gonna help her?" Rose asked.

"Ahh—I remember her. Really pretty girl. One of these people who laughed at things just to keep the party going. Elizabeth used to talk about her every year when we'd get her Christmas card. But Elizabeth never talked about how lucky Linda Effingham was, the expensive cars, the expensive clothes, not having to scrape for a living and juggle the bills between paychecks. But I knew Elizabeth thought about it," David went on, reaching into Rose's pocket for a cigarette and her lighter. "I guess, in a way, Elizabeth was telling me she loved me when she didn't talk about Linda's life-style. But sometimes, when we were really having it hard, I'd see her dig through the boxes where we kept the Christmas ornaments and the old cards and everything. And she'd be reading the letter Linda'd always write on the inside of the card when you folded it open. She read about the places Linda had gone, the people Linda had met.

"I never let Elizabeth know I saw her read the card again and again," David almost whispered by now as he lit the cigarette and exhaled. "Yeah. I'm gonna help her. And there's a practical side to it too. If this guy really is some kind of hotshot intelligence agent, he just might be our burglar—if we can get him back to Linda alive."

Rose Shepherd lit a cigarette for herself and shrugged out of her coat.

David was a wonderful man.

Chapter
27

"**M**y father wouldn't come. He said it was crazy to even think about it. The people who should be working on getting this English guy out are Clyde's people down in Harrington."

David Holden let the name click through his mind. Then, "That's Clyde Burns, right?"

"You know him?" Marcie Dane asked.

"Of him. He's a good Patriot leader, the way I understand it. Pretty much like your father. Why do you want to help this Kearney guy and your father doesn't?"

"That's not it. My dad would help him, but we don't have the people. Neither does Clyde. Clyde's people got the shit shot out of 'em when those Army helicopters came in. But I don't have a choice. This English guy—hell, he told me he was Canadian, at first, then after a while he was from Nevada—but he's the guy that bailed out my ass when those assholes were gonna lynch me to a tree."

David Holden asked her, "How good is he? I mean, you and your dad—you've seen a lot."

"I know what you mean. Real good. If they got him alive, I don't see how."

Holden nodded, but didn't like the sound of that. "Where's Linda?"

"Back in the car. I figured she'd be safer there."

David Holden nodded and started across the field toward the gray shadowy hulk he recognized as a Chevrolet Suburban. Chester Little, who'd piloted them down into this farmer's field, was changing the tire on the cargo plane. It had punctured and gone flat as a result of something they'd run over during landing. But Chester Little was a good pilot, and aside from a bumpy moment or so, the landing had been a safe one. Runningdeer, LeFleur, and Blumenthal—probably more help than the stonily silent Chester Little wanted—were helping him fix it.

Steel and Rosie flanked Holden and Marcie Dane as they approached the car.

A dome light came on as the driver's side door opened and Linda Effingham stepped out.

Even in the dusky light of the sunset she wasn't as he remembered her. No Chanel suit or designer original peasant dress. Jeans, a shirt half out of them, hair combed but not styled. The years hadn't been as kind to her as they'd been to Elizabeth. But, seeing her, David Holden almost cried, and he took her in his arms and kissed her cheek and held her. "I came as soon as I got the message."

"Oh, David. You—I wanted to call when I found out about Elizabeth, but I thought I'd start crying and then—"

Holden held her close. "Tell me everything you can about your friend," he began, letting go of her, half turning away. "If we can do anything, we'll have to do it quickly." And he looked at Marcie Dane. "Is there a place where this plane can land near Harrington? I mean, I guess that's where he's being held."

"Yes. Both times," Marcie Dane told him.

Holden nodded. He realized he was biting his lower lip. Words were hard. He simply looked at Linda and said, "Talk to me."

"He's a wonderful man and I love him, David." He wanted to tell her to just tell him what he needed to know, but he feared he'd sound like Jack Webb or something with "just the facts" and the thought made him want to laugh, but if he laughed he'd lose it. He let her talk. "And this Sheriff Homan—he works with the FLNA? And, well, he must have captured Geoff."

"Then you don't know for sure he's alive," Rosie said.

"Oh, but I'm sure he is."

Rosie pressed. "I'm not trying to ruin your life, but you don't know he's alive. I hope is he is too. But if he isn't, a rescue operation will just get a lot of other people hurt or killed."

And David Holden saw Linda Effingham staring at him. He wasn't listening to Rosie or even, for the moment, thinking about this Geoff guy. It was in her eyes, in the shadows growing around them. It was about Rosie. As if to tell her, Holden grabbed Rosie's hand and held it. And he wanted to for another reason, because Linda Effingham and his wife had always looked close enough alike to have been sisters, and if he didn't hold Rosie's hand he didn't know what he'd do. . . .

It had a new-car smell edged with cigarettes. They sat inside the Suburban in the darkness and Linda Effingham talked. "I know he's alive. He's got to be, David. You wanted to know just who he is. Well, at first I thought he was a businessman, but there was something more to him and he wasn't like any of the guys I knew, not at all. He's so good-looking it hurts to look at him, but he isn't even conscious of it, David. He's like you always were. Just a man—as if that weren't enough.

"And then, suddenly, I learn about all this secret agent shit because he saved my life and was slick at it; it was like he did it every day. And a lot of stuff happened to us and eventually he told me who he really was, what he really was, and that he shouldn't be telling me but would anyway. And I realized that he really, honest to God, loved me like I loved him. He's from England. As a little boy he just wanted to grow up and fight the bad guys and make the world better and suddenly he was a man and he was a spy or something. And he got this assignment, to come here and find this man named Borsoi."

Holden wondered if blood could freeze. His felt that way.

Linda Effingham kept talking. "He was supposed to kill this man named Dimitri Borsoi or whoever the head of the FLNA was. He figured it was Borsoi and we tried getting this Sheriff Homan—the mother-fucker—tried getting this Billy Homan to lead us to Borsoi. That's why Geoff was there! That's why he got captured, because he didn't want to kill this Homan fella because he—Geoff, I mean—Geoff had these hypodermics with a kind of truth serum in them? He was going to get Homan to talk and then track down Borsoi. So I know he's not dead."

She stopped talking so abruptly, it was almost as if she'd run out of words.

Marcie Dane, a lot more clinical sounding, said, "He'd be one of two places. Either the Army guys who took him off took him somewhere and we can't get him, or he's in the county jail. I'll know in a little while, maybe."

David Holden didn't say anything. . . .

The radio message, when it finally came—on the CB off a sideband—was clear enough, even though the words didn't make any sense. "It's Clyde's people." The message was a series of numbers. Already, as Holden merely listened, looked at his watch, and realized that his own time was running out, he could get the rhythm of the pattern in the code.

By one of the snap-on dome lights Marcie was writing down the numbers in groups. "I'll have it in a minute," she said after acknowledging the message over the CB and racking the microphone.

"Lincoln says man to die in two hours or less. In pool. Can do nothing without blowing cover. Side door YMCA can be jimmied. Can give no more help."

"Lincoln?" Rosie repeated.

"Andy Chitwood, a deputy sheriff, a Patriot."

"Why Lincoln?" David Holden echoed Rosie Shepherd.

"They're both Republicans," Marcie said as though she were stating the obvious.

"In the pool?" Steel asked.

David Holden shook his head. "Do you know where this YMCA is?"

"No," Marcie answered.

Rosie snarled, "Oh, that's just wonderful. Then how the hell are we supposed to find this Brit?"

"Clyde—Clyde Burns?—he said he'd loan us some reconnaissance."

"Maybe Mr. Burns has a pool pass," Luther Steel suggested in a rare attempt at humor.

"Maybe," Rosie agreed.

Marcie Dane wore a knit cap pulled down so low over her ears, it was almost over her eyes, and the collar of the high-school jacket was snapped up high. With a cigarette hanging out of her mouth and her hair tucked up under the cap, she almost did look like a guy.

Rose Shepherd, in borrowed clothing—a plaid scarf over her hair and tied under her chin, an old winter coat, and elastic waist pants that were too big for her—sat in the passenger seat of the pickup truck, weaponless and smoking a cigarette.

Marcie Dane was at the wheel. "We hear a lot about you, that you're a real badass on those FLNA scum bags, Shepherd."

"Yeah, that's me," Rose told her. "My ass is so bad, Marcie, sometimes I gotta change ass disguises six times a day to keep from bein' recognized. You sure you got the street right on this place?"

"Clyde says we drive three blocks west and two blocks north and we're there."

"This is assistance with reconnaissance?" Rose Shepherd asked rhetorically. "Sometime, maybe I can assist him," she said pleasantly.

They crossed the intersection, some of the yellow lights still functioning to illuminate the street, and Rose Shepherd saw the sign that read YMCA, but stuck up over the sign was another sign, just hand lettered, reading, PRIVATE—DON'T TRESPASS! BY SHERIFF'S DEPT. ORDER. "What's he using this place for, this Homan guy, the sheriff?"

"Clyde thinks he uses it to torture prisoners, maybe kill 'em. Can't do it at the jail that well."

"God, times are tough when a scuzzball sheriff has to move outa the jail just to have some fun. I'm lookin' forward to meeting this turkey," Rose Shepherd hissed. Then, "Don't slow down, Marcie, keep driving. Take us around the block, but circle by going two blocks up." There were three sheriff's patrol cars in front of the flat-roofed red brick building. Evidently, if this Englishman was really there and alive, sadism was a lot more fun than fighting crime.

Chapter
29

*I*n male drag Marcie Dane climbed in behind the wheel of the pickup truck. In the same moth-eaten old-lady coat she'd worn a half hour before, Rose Shepherd slipped into the passenger seat.

David and Luther and Bill and Tom and Randy were getting under the tarp in the pickup's bed.

And Rose Shepherd considered how lucky she was. Marcie Dane was coming along because she would drive the truck, which with any luck would be their wheels for the getaway. But Linda Effingham, who didn't know much more about guns than which end the bullet came out of, was at the old druggie airfield just inside the county line where Chester Little had landed the plane. Rose Shepherd felt lucky because—at least usually—she didn't get stuck with staying at home pretending with the tea set and the dress-up clothes while the guys were out playing hardball in the dirt.

The old-lady coat she wore was way too big for

her, which made it just the perfect size. Her M-16 wouldn't conceal under it, but the Uzi carbine and everything else would. "Drive, sweetie," Rose Shepherd told Marcie Dane, laughing. "And don't go showin' me your Russian hands and Roman fingers 'cause my boyfriend's in back and he's so cool. And get that oldies station back on the radio, stud."

Marcie Dane laughed and threw the pickup into gear. . . .

Rosie had spotted three police cars parked in front of the building when she and Marcie Dane had driven past it the first time. There were still three police cars there. David Holden let the tarp drop all the way down again, Luther Steel, lying beside him, saying, "If this Deputy Chitwood isn't what he appears, and this is a trap . . ."

"That's why LeFleur and Blumenthal are backing us up," Holden told him, wishing he believed that was an answer rather than a put-off. "If this Kearney guy is what Linda Effingham says he is, he just might have the skills we need to get the tape out of Cerillia's house."

"Maybe." Steel grunted. "Whatever, David, I admire a man who sticks by his friends."

Holden just looked at Steel's gray shadow in the darkness. . . .

"Now," Rose Shepherd ordered.

Marcie Dane started pumping the truck's clutch in and out, the truck lurching violently. Her right hand played the key in the ignition switch, turning it into the start position. The grating sounds that resulted were as loud as pistol shots.

With another lurch Marcie brought the truck to a halt.

Rose Shepherd just sat in the passenger seat, her left hand through the opening at the front of her borrowed coat, on the butt of the hammer-down, chamber-loaded Detonics .45.

Marcie tried starting the truck again, intentionally wrong, then turned off the key and climbed out. She raised the hood. In the passenger-side West Coast mirror Rose Shepherd's eyes stayed on the red brick YMCA building. From where the truck had stopped, by the curb near the parking lot, she could see clearly both the main entrance and the side entrance that had been suggested as their means of entry, as well as a portion of the roof. They were attracting no attention.

There was the impulse to think that this might be easy, but she rejected that. Things were rarely easy. She pulled the old plaid scarf back a little from the right side of her face, clearing her peripheral vision.

Marcie was pretending to do something under the hood of the pickup truck.

Rose ticked off the seconds. The longer they waited here, the greater their chance of discovery by a passing city police car or someone else, but the longer they went without being noticed by the sheriff and his personnel inside the building, the better the chances that this Billy Homan was more concerned with the Englishman than preparing for a rescue attempt.

Although Rose Shepherd shied away from thinking overconfidently, she hoped the Harrington County sheriff was.

Finally, Marcie Dane approached her side of the truck, gesturing to Rose about going to the red brick building to find a telephone, in reality saying, "So far so good. They haven't spotted us."

"Or they haven't let us know they'd spotted us. Don't forget about that. Be cool."

Marcie nodded, pulled her knit cap down a little lower—but none of her hair was showing—and started for the building, trying to walk like a man, hands stuffed in the pockets of her loose-fitting jeans, her stride wide, her shoulders hunched up and a cigarette in her mouth. There was a good touch, too, what looked like a wallet in her left hip pocket— just like something a man would carry—but it was a DeSantis wallet holster for a .25 automatic.

Rose never took her eyes off Marcie, who was almost up to the side door now. No one was coming out of the building to stop her.

Rose Shepherd opened the door of the truck and stepped down. From a distance her combat boots wouldn't look like boots and the too-loose elastic-waist pants dropped well over their tops. The coat and the pants and the scarf were thrift-store items, another of the many services—along with the pickup truck—provided by Clyde Burns's Patriot cell.

She started walking toward the building, rapping on the side of the truck bed twice to let them know what she was doing—a prearranged signal. Her stride was purposely short, to add the appearance of age, her shoulders slightly bent. She clutched the double-handled purse tight against her abdomen, because beneath it, free from the voluminous folds of the tentlike old-lady coat, the .45 was still in her other hand, but the hammer cocked and the safety on.

She filled her mouth with saliva—she was chewing gum—and made her voice as fragile sounding as she could, as she called out to Marcie Dane. "Is there a telephone, honey?"

Marcie shook her head, not trying to fake a voice.

"It's gettin' cold out here," Rose continued, closing the distance to Marcie Dane, who was standing now at the side door.

And suddenly the door opened, a man in a sheriff's deputy uniform—khaki shirt and pants, brown waist-length jacket, gun belt but no hat—emerging from the doorway. "What the hell you want, kid?"

Rose Shepherd preempted Marcie speaking. "My grandson and me. Our truck up and died, mister. Can we use your phone and call his father to come get us?"

"There ain't no public phone here, lady. Try down the street and maybe you'll find a gas station."

"Not at this time of night. Please?"

He had his back almost turned to Marcie Dane as he stepped farther out of the doorway, the door still open. "Get outa here and move that damn truck. This is county property. Now move it, or I'll ask for your curfew permits. You got curfew permits?"

Rose Shepherd quickened her pace a little. "I'm a citizen of these United States. What do I need some permit thing for?"

"Old lady, you're in trouble." He started to turn toward Marcie Dane, and as he did, Marcie Dane had the wallet holster out and rammed the muzzle of the gun up against his forehead. As the deputy started to react, Rose Shepherd dropped the old-lady gait and got behind him, the .45's muzzle burrowing in behind his right ear. "What the—"

"Touch that gun, dogbreath, and your brains are all over the parking lot."

Marcie Dane was already getting his revolver as Rose Shepherd, the purse hooked over her left elbow, reached her fingers to her lips and whistled once.

"You people are in deep shit."

"No—I'm not standing on your face," Rose snarled. "At least not yet, pal."

Her right foot was wedged against the open door. . . .

David Holden, Luther Steel, and Bill Runningdeer broke into a dead run across the sidewalk and through the parking lot, in Holden's fists Rosie's M-16, his own slung across his back. Steel had Marcie Dane's assault rifle.

As they neared the doorway, Holden could see the deputy, down on both knees, hands getting cuffed behind him, Marcie Dane holding a shiny nickel-plated revolver about three inches from the man's head.

And the door was open.

Runningdeer joked, "I'm going to feel damn silly luggin' this crowbar around."

"Maybe there'll be a door inside you can jimmy," Holden suggested.

They reached the doorway, Rosie already ordering

the deputy up to his feet, pushing him through, Marcie Dane right behind her.

Holden, Steel, and Runningdeer passed through after them. "Bill." Steel nodded.

"Right, boss." And Runningdeer snatched the radio from the pouch at his belt, hissing into it, "Liberator One to Liberator Two. Come in. Over."

Blumenthal's voice came back with a lot of static. "Squelch button," Holden advised. Rosie was shrugging out of the coat, throwing it into a corner of the empty gray hallway where they now stood. She started out of the gray pants she wore over her BDUs. "This is Liberator Two. We're in position. I repeat. In position. Over."

"We're inside and moving. Liberator One Out."

Holden stepped up beside Marcie Dane. "Deputy. You know who I am."

"You—you're—"

"I'm David Holden. What does the media say I do to people?"

"K-k-kill them."

Holden handed Rosie her assault rifle as she tore the scarf from her hair. Then he drew the Desert Eagle .44 and thumbed back the hammer, resting the muzzle of the weapon against the tip of the deputy's nose. "Guess what I'm going to do to you if you don't tell me where I can find your prisoner." He was careful not to use the name, or refer to what Americans like himself would consider a British accent. "Tall guy, about my coloring, wearing a black rain suit and carrying an H & K 91 and an Uzi carbine and a pistol. You got him at the junkyard. Where is he?"

"In the swimming pool."

"The swimming pool?" Holden repeated.

"Look—it was Homan's idea, to make the guy talk. To—"

"Show me," Holden whispered, shoving Homan's deputy ahead of him down the hallway. "And if we die, guess who dies too."

Chapter
30

*T*he water was up to his chin when he leaned as tightly as he could into the far corner of the shallow end of the pool. And it was up to his chin only because he stood on his toes.

His feet and legs were cramping and Kearney inhaled deeply, let himself down beneath the water, careful lest his own buoyancy tug him away from the corner, because he would be powerless to control his body.

His lungs ached.

He almost had the cramp out of his left foot.

He felt something reaching, grabbing hold of his hair, and as he looked up, the surface of the water was bathed in light. He was pulled up, his head pushed roughly against the edge of the pool as he gasped and sputtered for breath, his eyes squinted tight against the light.

Billy Homan let go of his hair and Kearney nearly slipped beneath the surface, but held himself there in the corner, the icy water nearly to the level of his lower lip. "I found out. NSA don't know any Kevin Cole, boy. I make it you got yourself about five minutes before the water's up to your nose. How long you gonna be able to stand on your toes, anyway?"

"Fuck you," Kearney snarled. There was no reason to deny himself a little bravado. They were going to shoot him or let him drown anyway, and either way he'd be dead. And if he got Homan angry enough, Homan just might pull him out of the water and he might have a slim chance.

"You talk tough. And I know why. Figure I'll take you out of the water here and slap ya around. Well, I won't. You tell me who you are and I'll keep my word and shoot you. But if I don't believe the story, same as if you don't talk at all. I just walk out, shut off the lights, and come back in about an hour and get my handcuffs back."

"I hope they rust," Kearney snapped, swallowing water, spitting it out.

"God, you're hysterical, boy. Who are you? Why the injection kit? Who sent you?"

"Bite it."

Homan grabbed Kearney by the hair and shoved his face underwater, Kearney just having the time to gulp air, but not enough, his balance nearly going.

There was a drumming in his head. It was getting louder.

Then suddenly the pressure of Homan's hand was released and Kearney started to the surface, but his footing was gone and his legs swept up from under him and he was floating, on his chest, his face in the water. He twisted his head right, gulped air and water, nearly choking.

He could hear Homan, though, laughing. . . .

"It's here. But the light's on, see. So the sheriff's gotta be in there."

David Holden pushed the deputy back from the sign that read, POOL.

Rosie Shepherd was beside him. Luther Steel and Bill Runningdeer, with his Uzi submachine gun, were on the other side of the door.

"Keep a gun on the deputy," Holden told Marcie Dane.

"I'll shoot his damn brains out if our boy's dead."

Holden made no comment, nodded to Steel, Steel reaching for the door handle, giving it a twist, the door moving inward, Holden stepping away from the jamb, kicking the door inward hard, going through left to right, knowing Rosie was on one side of the door, her rifle ready, knowing Steel was crossing from right to left, that Runningdeer would be on the other side of the door, the Uzi ready.

Holden's M-16 was in a hard assault position as he dropped to his knees beside a stack of flotation boards.

A burly man in a sheriff's uniform, his right sleeve rolled up past the elbow, was standing beside the far end of the pool, caught in midlaugh, two men in deputy sheriff's uniforms flanking him.

There was something flesh-colored floating in the pool. A man, Holden realized in the next split second, face down.

"I got him!" Steel shouted, then, "Bill!"

"Right, boss!"

Steel ran toward the pool, his M-16 already gone, his pistol belt falling to the floor, his arms shrugging out of the shoulder holster. Boots and all, he dived into the swimming pool, making long, powerful scissors kicks and breaking the surface midway across the width of the pool.

Steel closed with the man who was floating face down there, rolled him over, and lifted the man's face out of the water.

Holden shouted, "Rosie. Runningdeer. Help Steel. I got these guys." As Rosie Shepherd and Bill Runningdeer ran to aid Luther Steel with the drowning man, David Holden looked at the sheriff and his two deputies. One of them had to be this Chitwood, the Patriot plant in the department. "Give me the excuse. Please."

Neither of the three men moved.

Steel lay back on his elbows, just breathing. Runningdeer was administering mouth to mouth. Rosie, kneeling beside Kearney—it had to be Kearney—shouted, "I think Bill's got him breathing!"

But would Kearney be able to do the job? Holden wondered. And, without knowing why, he suddenly thought of Elizabeth, that if somehow it were possible that she knew Kearney would live to go back to Linda Effingham, Elizabeth would be happy for knowing it. . . .

David Holden sat in the front seat of the sheriff's department car so he could keep an eye on Chitwood, whom he didn't fully trust regardless of what was said about the double-agent deputy. Geoffrey Kearney, still coughing a little, wrapped in emergency blankets taken from the sheriff's cars, sat in the backseat. Runningdeer had the other deputy from the pool area and Rosie and Luther Steel were in charge of Sheriff Homan himself and the deputy who had led them to the pool after Rosie and Marcie Dane had gotten the drop on him. Marcie Dane, who'd wanted to shoot Homan dead on the spot, drove the pickup truck alone.

Kearney, his British accent showing between coughing spasms, was questioning Chitwood. "How do you know for certain that—" Kearney coughed again. "How do you know that this Borsoi fellow is the number-one man?"

"All the decisions about FLNA operations in this area come through him. He's the man the people who come in at Siamese Shoals are to report to, at least the more important ones."

"That still doesn't spell out that he's the overall leader. He could just be the top field commander, which is what it's pointed to all along. He's the one in charge of the blood-and-brains department and someone else is pulling the strings and running the operation. Borsoi's records, as far as I'm familiar with his background"—Kearney coughed again—"his records show that he's a field agent. A damned effective one, but a field agent, not a controller. It's hard to swallow that he's so changed character."

Chitwood said, "That's all I know, anyway."

"How do you contact him?"

"Me? I don't contact him. The sheriff does that. Through some kind of system in Savannah. I don't know how it works, except the sheriff makes a phone call—always from a public phone so it can't be traced without a lot of hassles—and he gets a call back. I guess sometimes it isn't Borsoi, but some younger guy the sheriff can't stand, calls him a punk. That's the extent of what I know."

"Would you have let Homan kill me?" Kearney asked.

Chitwood cleared his throat. "If I blow my cover, we'll never get Borsoi. Just 'cause you want to get Borsoi, it doesn't mean you will. But eventually, I'll get to meet Borsoi and then I get into his confidence and unravel the whole thing from the top down."

Kearney didn't speak for a moment, then said, "You're an ambitious man as far as this is concerned, Chitwood. And maybe you have the abilities, but maybe you don't. Anyway, you have your job and I have mine. Next time, don't set me up. Or I'll kill you, ally or not."

Chitwood didn't speak, just kept driving.

"What if the sheriff disappeared?" David Holden suggested.

"To get me further along?" Chitwood asked. "No. Because they'd figure Homan spilled his guts and everything was compromised."

Then Kearney spoke. "Stop the car and signal for the other cars to stop." Holden twisted around in his seat, trying to read Kearney's face in the darkness. In the next second he realized he didn't have to read it. "You said you found my clothing and my weapons, Dr. Holden. Where do you have them?"

"Trunk of this car. Why?"

"We're going to solve this Homan problem right now, unless you have some objections."

David Holden closed his eyes for an instant. "Stop the car, Chitwood. Signal the other ones to pull over."

Chitwood glared at Holden for an instant, then began slowing down, blinking his lights for the car ahead to pull over. . . .

They were two thirds of the way out along the roadway to the airfield where Linda Effingham waited with Chester Little, the pilot who would ferry them to the D.C. area. The operation would have to be postponed, assuming Kearney was to do it. David Holden wrestled with this and with what was, he knew, about to happen.

He wondered, were the good guys and the bad guys becoming so alike that, whoever was victorious in the end, it wouldn't matter anymore?

Barefoot, visibly shivering, two blankets wrapped around him, Geoffrey Kearney stood a few feet from the hood of the sheriff's car. Homan was on the other side.

At the center of the hood were two handguns, one of them Homan's revolver, the other a Smith & Wesson 9mm semiautomatic, Kearney's gun.

Kearney said, "Homan, you're a vile, evil son of a bitch. You enjoyed watching me die. Don't tell me you didn't."

Homan said nothing.

Kearney kept talking. David Holden felt Rosie come to stand beside him, her hand holding his arm. Kearney said, "I don't care what happens to your deputies. They can rot. But I'm giving you the same two choices you gave me. Talk or die. If you talk, you can walk off and no one will stop you. If you don't want to tell us all about the FLNA and who your contacts are, then go for your revolver. You saw it put there. It's loaded and ready to go. If you kill me, I have the word of Professor Holden and the others that you and your deputies will be left here alive and unharmed.

"Use your mouth or use your hand. I can't stand up that much longer, Homan," Kearney concluded.

Homan started to laugh. "You Limey asshole. You play guns with me you're playin' for the last time."

"I take it you won't talk."

There had been a syringe kit in Kearney's things, Holden knew. Maybe the drugs took too long to work or Kearney didn't think Homan really had anything to say that was worth listening to or maybe Kearney was just disgusted with it all and just flat out wanted Homan dead because Homan had been about to kill him there at the pool.

"I'm gonna enjoy finishin' what I started, boy."

"Then stop talking about it and do it," Geoffrey Kearney said quietly.

Homan reached for the revolver.

Kearney moved so rapidly, the blankets fell away from him. There were two shots, almost simultaneous, but Kearney dodged left.

Homan didn't move for several seconds, just stood there holding his gun.

And then Homan fell over dead. . . .

The deputies, Chitwood among them, were tied up with their own handcuffs and left by the side of the road. And so was Homan's body. The car carrying Blumenthal and LeFleur had reached the airfield first. Chester Little already had the cargo plane's engines idling.

They needed fog and a little man in a French policeman's uniform and a kepi.

Rose Shepherd watched as Geoffrey Kearney, wrapped up in the blankets again, opened the blankets, folded Linda Effingham within them, and kissed her.

She knew why David had gone to help Kearney. It was all crystal clear.

She looked at David Holden standing beside her. "I love you," she said. "I always will."

David held her hand.

Chapter
31

Marion Charles Hofsteader stood beside the apartment's living-room window, midafternoon sun streaming through the sheers, backlighting him as he lit a cigarette, the smoke curling upward as the forced-air heat vent below the sill caught it, dissipated it. He ran the hand without the cigarette through his crew cut, not turning around as he said, "I have twenty-seven men and women left who haven't quit the Patriots. I've talked to most of them. They'll back whatever you want to do, Holden."

David was pacing between the couch and the window. He stopped pacing for a moment and lit the cigarette he'd been holding on to for the last ten minutes, then tossed Rose back her lighter.

Rose Shepherd watched the four men with her in the living room. Blumenthal, LeFleur, and Runningdeer, up all night, were sleeping in the next room. Like David, she'd caught naps a few times and then slept a few hours straight after arrival in Alexandria. She was barefoot and her feet were tucked up under her, the legs of her black BDU pants pulled down to where they covered her feet almost. She hugged her bare arms around the sofa pillow, a little cold with just the black T-shirt she wore, but determined not to get up and miss anything.

Luther Steel sat on the floor beside the coffee table, cleaning his SIG-Sauer P-226. He looked up and said, "Then I guess it's up to Mr. Kearney, how we do it, isn't it?"

David didn't say anything.

Geoff Kearney—he was almost as good-looking as David, but only almost—sat in the reclining chair, stockinged feet up, a cigarette burning between his fingers. "I said I'd come and I said I'd try it. That still holds. I owe you people my life. You've even shared data with me concerning Borsoi and Makowski and this drug dealer Guzman and the Russian, Kirovitch. So, it's the least I can do. And if that tape is as important as you think it will be, it's worth the risk."

"Then we'll go tonight," David said, exhaling smoke from his borrowed cigarette. She was glad David was back to bumming cigarettes from her. "The longer we stay in this area, the greater chance we have of being found out, or Chester Little and the plane getting discovered out at the field. Are you up to it for tonight?"

Geoff Kearney nodded, stubbing out his cigarette. "I'm a little sore in a few places, and I'm definitely not in the mood for a dip in the pool." He smiled. "But yes, I'm physically able. Tonight it is. You're right, Holden. The longer we're here, the greater chance of blowing the mission. Tonight."

Hofsteader turned away from the window. "I'll make the arrangements with my people."

Luther said, "I drew up a rough layout of the house and grounds. I was invited to Mr. Cerillia's house twice and the diagram should be pretty close to accurate."

"If one man can make it in, any problems with two?" David asked Kearney.

Rose sat bolt upright. "Happy for the company, Doctor."

"How about two men and a woman? And none of this sexist crap, okay?"

David looked at her, then at Geoff Kearney.

David said, "If you want to."

She leaned back into the couch, feeling colder than ever.

Chapter
32

*T*hey'd watched the news at eleven before leaving to board the converted soft-drink truck that would take them away from the apartment over the restaurant where M. C. Hofsteader had housed them.

There were two items of interest in the news, both of them expected for some time, but neither of them welcome. After hearing them—Rose had watched David's face, how his eyes hardened—David Holden picked up his weapons and, without saying a word, left for the truck.

Charlie Lang, the FLNA conspirator (arrested after the assault on the Cedar Ridge Islands base, which Siamese Shoals had apparently replaced as the entry point for FLNA terrorist personnel into the United States), was dead. Called "a key Federal witness in the ongoing campaign to stem the tide of violence perpetrated by the so-called Patriots," he had been found hanged. A Patriot conspiracy was suspected.

More likely, Roman Makowski's version of American government was to blame.

The second item dealt with the Patriots more directly. "In the wake of last night's ambush murder of Harrington County, North Carolina, Sheriff Billy Homan at the hands of Patriot gunmen, the Justice Department announced today that a special FBI Ten Most Wanted List has been inaugurated just to deal with Patriot violence. Heading the list, with a bounty of one million dollars on his head, is former college history professor Dr. David Holden. Holden, it may be recalled, first appeared as the leader of the Patriot cell near Metro after dropping from sight to escape an investigation concerning his possible conspiracy in the deaths of his wife and three young children. Described as a 'radical right-wing activist with bizarre racial theories,' Holden and mistress, former Metro Detective Rose Shepherd, number two on the Most Wanted list, are described as heavily armed and dangerous. It is theorized that if, indeed, Holden was involved in planning the death of his family, the Shepherd woman, discharged from the Metro force for her brutal handling of juvenile offenders and for charges of sexual misconduct, may have been Holden's accomplice in the murders.

"Shepherd was reportedly the lover of former Metro police officer Rufus Burroughs, whose wife was killed at the same time as Holden's wife and children, in what Justice Department authorities are describing as 'a suspicious coincidence, to say the least.'

"Burroughs, a black, dropped from sight early in the period of Patriot violence and may well have been murdered, authorities say, by Holden and Shepherd because of Holden's racial beliefs and so that Holden could advance himself in the Patriot organization; or, as one official put it, 'It might have just been in a fight over the Shepherd woman's affections.' "

Chapter
33

All of them in the back of the soda-pop truck were dressed in black, all of them armed with every weapon they could practically carry—because twenty-seven Alexandria Patriots, plus Hofsteader and themselves, just weren't enough to fight off the Army Makowski and Hobart Townes would send in to keep them from getting away with the tape.

"When we have the tape," David began, as if the word "if" had suddenly been striken from the English language, "we can get it broadcast. There's a man," he said, looking at Kearney, "who works with us and has broadcast connections. The government arrested one of his co-workers recently on a trumped-up gun charge. It was a warning to him, this man Lem Parrish, that he should keep quiet. He's been an outspoken critic of the Makowski administration and the lies about the Patriots being involved in the real President's death."

"I'm surprised they haven't killed him already,"

Geoff said thoughtfully. "He's a radio broadcaster, isn't he? How can he get it on television?"

"I didn't quite know how to manage it myself. But then I realized the opportunity was staring me right in the face. I had to push to get the job done last night or tonight. There's a football game tomorrow night, being broadcast live out of Metro. That's why we had so little time. We can feed our tape into the instant replay equipment. I spoke with Parrish just before we left to get you, and I spoke with him again this morning. He has enough people in Metro and in New York, where the live feed's going through, that he can guarantee us five minutes before the government pulls the plug on the satellite—unless they blow it up or something. There should be about sixty-five million people watching that game, the minimum. The ratings for pro ball have hit the ceiling since everybody's gotten afraid to actually go to the games anymore because it means leaving the house and might get them home after curfew.

"It's the best chance we'll ever have," David said.

"I've always liked American football," Geoff said.

Rose's hands were sweating inside her gloves.

Chapter
34

*F*BI Director Rudolph Cerillia's home was in a modest Washington suburb, but happened to occupy a considerable amount of land, more so than any of the neighboring houses. It sat square in the middle of a little over an acre, and because of his position in Federal law enforcement, when he purchased the house it was thought necessary to build a fence around it. This, against Cerillia's objections, but necessary in an era of terrorist death threats against American officials, was paid for by the taxpayers out of a presidential contingency fund. Not even the harshest critics of Cerillia's appointment to the post objected publicly.

The fence, in a compromise with Cerillia, was made to look decorative rather than forbidding, consisting of wrought-iron bars within a framework, the bars spiked at the top in the common decorative fashion and placed eight inches apart, the framework one-by-two wrought iron, the height of the fence ten feet rather than the twelve originally advised by security personnel, and minus the barbed wire at the top.

With the elaborate fence, the house Cerillia lived in—by himself in the time immediately preceding his murder—was all the more modest by contrast. A two-story brick affair with gabled roof and ivy climbers, looking more like the residence of a philosophy professor than the man who was America's top lawman, the house would eventually be torn down. That was inevitable. Property values in the area, as Steel recounted, had tripled in the last seven years and three houses could be built on the acre lot (which was wider than it was deep) that would each fetch more than Cerillia had originally paid for one house and lot together.

"The grounds are wooded, but the trees were planted, landscaped in. So none of the tree cover is very dense," Steel emphasized. "The Geophones are virtually everywhere, now, according to Hofsteader's intelligence." It was the dozenth time they'd gone over the plan since its formulation that afternoon, agreeing to the plan only after verifying that the equipment needed to carry it out could be had from materials the Patriots had recaptured during various battles with the FLNA. The FLNA had been particularly well stocked in the D.C. area after several remarkably successful armory raids, one of them on the armory at Little Creek, Virginia, near Norfolk, a facility housing equipment used by SEAL Team Two. "The helicopter comes right up the street. I fire the Korean War relics."

Steel looked at Holden and Holden nodded. "The

helicopter engages the troops surrounding the perimeter. Twelve men, so the pilot's going to have to get in and get out fast if he doesn't want to get killed."

Kearney said, "And while it's attracting everybody's attention, we do our thing. We hope."

"And Hofsteader's men make their assault on both flanks of the perimeter."

Blumenthal joked, "Why do I have to pretend to be Rosie? That's what I wanna know!"

Rosie touched him on the arm, smiling. "Because you're the closest to my height—and besides, you have the nicest figure. And that extra black scarf of mine looks terrific on you. Other than that, you're dressed like the rest of the boys."

"Then we're ready," Holden said.

As if punctuating his words the truck stopped. . . .

"There can't be anything much more than the chip camera video surveillance that we already know about outside the fence perimeter or it would drive them crazy," Geoff Kearney said under his breath. David nodded in agreement. Rose Shepherd's fingers moved quickly, retying the black bandana at the nape of her neck. She felt awkward in the body armor she wore over her BDUs, but she'd feel worse getting shot, she told herself.

Kearney moved out from the concealment of the hedgerow and along the roadway in a low-crouching run, David behind him, Rose Shepherd, the Uzi carbine strapped tight against her chest, the M-16 across her back, the Big Ugly One knife in her right fist, at David's heels.

It was like attacking one of those perfect middle America suburbs seen in the movies—houses, garages, decks, Weber kettles, tricycles, station wagons, barking dogs—but intelligence Hofsteader's Patriot cell had gotten suggested that everyone on the block fronting the late Rudolph Cerillia's house had been moved out, at gunpoint when necessary. But even if that were true, and the dogs barking in backyards were tape recordings and the tricycles were gathering cobwebs, and coals glowed in the kettles, Geoffrey Kearney and David were probably right, there was nothing much beyond standard video surveillance. Because there would have to be stray dogs and cats and occasional deliverymen and even if the Presidential Strike Force picked up the newspapers and the mail, someone had to bring it.

And the security was designed to keep them from getting out, not getting in. She kept repeating that to herself without ever verbalizing it.

They paused, all three of them, beside a Buick station wagon. There was a Volvo sedan parked farther up the driveway. She could hear, just faintly, a television set playing from inside the house. Was it all a fake? Were the televisions turned on by remote control from a central command post, or did someone have that as duty, walk into homes people had been ripped from and turn on some lights and the television set and maybe the clothes washer or the dishwasher for good measure, just washing the same already clean clothes and dishes over and over again? What was real anymore?

Rose Shepherd realized she had lost the ability to tell.

The Defender knife was in David's right hand. Geoff Kearney held a Cold Steel Bowie.

David and Geoff started to move again, and Rose Shepherd followed.

The basic plan was a combination of David's tactical input and Geoff's knowledge of electronic surveillance equipment and his commando background. One of the local television stations' helicopter pilots was a Patriot and was willing to go under—if he did not, he would be a marked man—and use the helicopter to aid the Patriot cause. Luther Steel would ride the chopper.

Blumenthal, supposed to be her—and the thought of that still made her smile—and LeFleur and Runningdeer would move up through the same penetration channel she and David and Geoff Kearney were using now, only a few minutes after them. Meanwhile she and David and Geoff would already have entered the grounds.

If the plan worked, it was brilliant; if it didn't, they were dead and the tape would be lost.

But they were prepared for that contingency too. Geoff Kearney carried with him a vial of acid to pour over the tape lest it should fall into enemy hands. And all three of them had agreed that, if the only alternative were capture by Makowski's Presidential Strike Force, they would take their own lives first. Because what would happen were they captured was unthinkable.

They paused in their race toward the fence beside a Cadillac Brougham positively reeking of wax, parked in the driveway two doors from the boundary with Cerillia's house.

"This is a setup," David hissed through his teeth. "Nobody leaves a brand-new car with a fresh wax job in the driveway overnight when frost is expected unless he doesn't have any choice. Look into the garage." The door was open, and in the glow of the gaslight-era-look front-yard lamps dotted down the block on both sides of the street, it was clear that there was an empty parking slot inside the garage.

In the distance, as she peered over the Cadillac's trunk lid through the Baird night-vision goggles, Rose Shepherd could see two men armed with M-16s patrolling the front gate. The goggles afforded a forty-foot field of view and amplified ambient light twenty-five hundred times. With the goggles it was almost bright enough to read, and the lights from the houses had pulsating coronas around them. Just visible from her vantage point were a third and fourth man in the shadows some distance farther along the fence, almost as if whoever had set up the security were making it obvious how far one would have to travel before finding the next sentry.

And in a way, Rose felt sorry for these men, even though they wore the hated insignia of the Presidential Strike Force. Because each man on sentry duty had to be expendable. That was clear.

"Across the front yard and alongside that garage sound good to you both?" Kearney asked.

David nodded. "Let's go."

Rose didn't feel any response from her was required. She'd go where David went.

Both men started to move out, Rose grabbing up her gear bag and following. . . .

. . .

David Holden got out the clam gun, bracing
it against the beautifully sodded lawn running alongside the garage. It fired all but silently, the cylinder
filling with dirt. He pulled the clam gun up, using the
sawed-off broomstick handle Rosie had made to
punch out the dirt. Holden inserted into the lawn the
first of the L20A1 EOD simulators while Kearney fed
out the wire. . . .

The last of the EOD simulators was planted
now, all of them wired in series to the radio receiver,
Kearney checking the connections as Holden discarded the clam gun into a hedgerow. . . .

Geoffrey Kearney had always seen the advantage of electronic security—to the person trying
to penetrate it—that those running it became dependent upon it and less dependent upon men. But each
of the Presidential Strike Force sentries stationed
around the perimeter was carrying a radio. And what
was imperative was not that no one should realize
the grounds had been penetrated, but that they
shouldn't know from which direction. For that reason the guards had to be eliminated.

Kearney had tried the suppressor-fitted 10/22 in
the apartment, playing the radio loudly and firing
into a pillow. Like others of its type he had used, it
worked so wonderfully well that all that was heard
was the clicking mechanical noise of the .22 rifle's
bolt opening and closing. Of all suppressor/gun
combinations, it was the most silent.

But there was only one of these and there were

four men to be taken out, which meant knife work too. Holden and this wonderfully bewitching girl, Rosie, had that.

Lying flat beside a large willow tree, Kearney sighted on the first of his two targets, still mentally ticking off seconds for the coordinated strike.

Four seconds left. . . .

Rose Shepherd was counting. Three . . . two . . . one. She ran forward as quickly as she could, and as silently, too, the Big Ugly One in her right fist. The sentry started to turn around as she'd known he would and she threw herself at him, her left shoulder impacting him at the chest as her right hand and arm arced over her and in front of her face.

The goggles protected her eyes and the bandana over the lower portion of her face protected her mouth and nose from the blood spray as the hatchet-thick blade of the Big Ugly One cleaved the right side of his neck, severing the carotid artery. He fell to the ground with an audible thud. She could see David dragging off the body of the man who'd been his target. . . .

David Holden wiped the blade of the Defender knife clean against the woodland camouflage BDU blouse of the dead man beside whom he was kneeling. He sheathed the knife under his right armpit behind the double magazine pouch carrying spares for his Beretta pistols.

With the night-vision goggles he could easily see the face of his Rolex.

He made it about two minutes remaining before

the air and ground assaults began, with their built-in redundancies. He'd tried planning for everything, and with Kearney's input—Kearney was clever and, best of all, audaciously imaginative—he told himself that all the bases were covered.

But were they?

His SEAL Team training had been so many years ago that Holden sometimes felt he was trying to defeat space-age technology with stone-age measures, but Kearney's knowledge was as up to the minute as a morning briefing.

The part about how to defeat the pulsed infrared and microwave transmission on the fence, not to mention the taut wire, was extraordinary.

David Holden rested back on his heels and waited.

Chapter
35

*T*he M-20 rocket launcher was a Korean War antiarmor weapon that could penetrate eighteen inches of armor plate (of Korean War vintage), but, when impacting ground rather than a tank, would make a crater roughly three feet in diameter and a foot or so deep. But most importantly, David Holden hoped, it would activate every single Geophone buried in the estate grounds beneath the winter-brown sod and pine needles and in the dormant flower beds. Geophones, originally designed to detect earthquakes, had been modified to serve as security control devices so they could detect a solitary human footfall several feet away.

He hoped they were that sensitive.

Rosie and Geoffrey Kearney flanking him, Holden watched the sweep second hand of the Rolex.

The instant before it passed the twelve, he heard the discharge of the starburst flare. And, as the sound died, he heard the drumming of the rotor blades on the air. The blue-and-white Bell Long Ranger traffic helicopter was skimming over the street, toward the gate and the driveway and the sentries there.

An assault rifle opened up from the helicopter. It would be Hofsteader, the Alexandria Patriot cell leader. Fire returned toward the helicopter from the sentries at the driveway gate.

Holden rose to his full height and slowly walked toward the fence, Rosie beside him, Kearney moving toward the fence more quickly.

"About another thirty seconds is my guess, Holden."

David Holden nodded.

The improvised gunship swept over the fence line in a low, fast arc, the downdraft from the rotor blades making a storm of dust and leaves and pine needles, alarms beginning to sound as the debris activated the pulsed infrared and microwave systems, the downdraft itself tripping the taut wire. With any luck a good fifty to seventy-five percent of the security board was lit up by now.

Holden flipped the safety cover, then tripped the toggle on the radio signal transmitter. And then the rumbling began, like distant booms of thunder. The EOD simulators, wired in series, buried into the ground with the clam digger, were detonating, one right after the other.

More alarms, of a different pitch and intensity, began sounding across the grounds.

"Over the fence!" Holden ordered, Rosie flipping the rope ladder up, reaching through the fence, pulling it down over the barbed wire added at the top, Kearney securing the hook at the swing end to the base of the fence, stabilizing the rope ladder as David Holden jumped onto it, making the climb in under four seconds, rolling over the barbed wire on the cushion of vinyl secured beneath the rope rungs, dropping to the far side of the fence in a crouch.

Gunfire from the right and the left. Small explosions. Hofsteader's twenty-seven remaining Patriots were attacking the perimeter from both its farthest ends.

Rosie Shepherd was over the fence, Kearney flipping over just behind her, Rosie already freeing the hook from the base horizontal brace, Holden pulling the ladder over, rolling it as they ran on. "Don't forget cameras."

As if in answer he heard a burst of automatic-weapons fire from Rosie's M-16.

They ran across the wood chips right beside the fence and into the sparsely planted Virginia pines and cedars, mortar rounds impacting the far sides of the fenced-in perimeter, the M-20 rocket launcher being fired from the helicopter, the .87-kilogram explosive charges detonating in a ragged line along both sides of the driveway leading to the house, at once activating the rest of the Geophones and restricting any vehicular movement within the compound.

Holden, Rosie, and Kearney moved through the trees, Holden's M-16 tight in his left fist, an egg-shaped M-61 high-explosive fragmentation grenade in his right fist, the pin already pulled as he tore it from his armored body vest. He spotted the glint of a video camera lens in the flash of a distant M-20 round's detonation. "Watch out!" Holden gauged the distance, let the spoon pop in his hand as he counted. When the count hit two, he lobbed the grenade underhand in a high arc. At the count of five, still in midair, the grenade exploded. The camera would be destroyed.

Rosie was running ahead, nearing the side of the house. Holden dashed after her, Kearney ranging far to their left, engaging two PSF troopers coming from the direction of the house.

As Holden looked toward Rosie, he saw her stumble, go down, and come in a roll. There was so much noise—the explosions of the M-20 rounds, the gunfire from both sides of the property, the alarm sirens blaring—that the only way Holden could tell Rosie was encountering resistance was from the muzzle flashes. She was firing back. Holden tore free another grenade, drawing his right arm back and hurtling it overhand toward the left side of the house where the enemy fire seemed to be coming from. As the spoon popped, it caught Holden on the right cheek. But he was already running, throwing himself toward Rosie, bulldogging her down as the grenade impacted and blew. A shower of dirt and debris rained down on them.

Holden was already up to his knees, shouting at Rosie, "Are you hurt?"

"Just hit my vest and winded me." They broke into a run for the house, Kearney already at the blown-out dining-room windows. Kearney jumped and flipped a sound-and-light grenade through the opening.

As the grenade flashed and whistled, the Bell Long Ranger made a pass over the driveway, the M-18 smoke bombs detonating. Smoke—white, red, and green—billowed in the helicopter's downdraft. But the night-vision goggles protected Holden's eyes and he'd be inside Cerillia's house in seconds, so there was no need for a mask.

Holden took the middle, Kearney and Rosie flanking the window. Holden fired a long zigzagging burst upward, into the living-room ceiling through the open window, then ran for the window, jumping to the sill, thankful for the heavy-palmed fingerless gloves he wore. There were icepick-sized shards of plate glass everywhere.

He cleared the windowsill and hit the carpet in a roll, glass crunching as he moved, keeping his body low as Rosie and Kearney started the crossfire.

To his right was the hallway leading to the front door, the door open. To his left, the stairway leading up. Farther left and back on the far wall was the fireplace mantel.

Holden started for the fireplace after a glance at his Rolex. The agreed-upon thirty seconds of crossfire ceased. He dropped into cover beside a torn-apart wooden stereo cabinet, ready to cover the staircase and the doorway, but there was movement on the staircase above. Holden stripped away his night-vision goggles lest someone of the enemy personnel should use a flash-bang and the intensification from the goggles blind him.

The house seemed dark and Holden squinted his eyes against the abrupt loss of light, to give his vision the chance to adjust.

More movement. His normal night vision was returning, but not fast enough. Holden fired a burst from the M-16, then another and another, dumping the thirty-round magazine, ramming another one in place.

Holden reached into one of the musette bags he carried slung across his shoulders, extracting the Bilsom Com-Impact earmuffs. The muffs were made for shooters, designed to allow normal conversational-tone noise but filter out loud, sudden noises. They worked well against the high-frequency noise of sound-and-light grenades.

With the poor light, protective goggles would have made him blind, so he had no choice but to rely on alertness alone to protect his eyes.

As he looked back, Rosie and Geoff Kearney were coming through the window frame, one at a time, both of them already having shed their night-vision goggles and donned their hearing protectors. Rosie held her M-16 in her right fist, the Glock-17 pistol in the left. Kearney covered the window as Rosie ran toward Holden, dropping and skidding on her knees to hunker down beside him near the stereo cabinet at the base of the stairs.

Holden fired a burst up the stairs, Rosie ducking past the base of the staircase and taking up a flanking position on the other side beside a heavily over-stuffed couch, much of the stuffing gutted out of it.

"Go for it!" Holden shouted.

Kearney crossed the room in a low crouching run, a borrowed M-16 in his right fist. He reached the brick mantel for the fireplace.

Holden saw it, heard the subtle bumping sound as it rolled down the steps. "Flash-bang!" Holden covered his eyes, the shrieking whistle of the grenade a dull, high-pitched roar. Holden counted out the time of the flash, then reached to his web gear for one of the M-61s. "Watch out!" Holden tore the grenade free of his gear, the pin pulling simultaneously, then lobbed the grenade up the stairwell.

Holden and Rosie, opposite him, tucked back. There was a roar and smoke belched down the staircase, plaster dust thicker on the air than the smoke, chunks of ceiling material collapsing onto them, the sound of glass shattering, pictures falling.

Holden glanced toward the mantel. Kearney's left hand was inside it, up the chimney. "Almost got it!" Kearney shouted, as if reading Holden's anxious thoughts.

"Kitchen! Look out!"

The door swung open as Rosie shouted the warning and Holden stabbed the M-16 toward the dark-stained wooden door and fired, chunks ripping from the wood, but a long burst of automatic-weapons fire stitching across the littered living-room carpet, more glass shattering, chunks of the staircase railing ripping out.

"Masks!" Holden ordered, reaching to the gas-mask bag strapped across his chest, pulling out the mask with one hand as he pulled off the earmuffs with the other. But he wondered if it would be too late. They were encountering greater resistance within the house itself than he had anticipated. There was a bump-and-roll sound as Holden pulled the mask over his head.

"Fragmentation!" Rosie shouted, diving for what cover there was.

Holden dived back, his rifle out of his hands and

still beside the base of the staircase, the concussion of the grenade making the floor vibrate, whole segments of wallboard collapsing.

Holden rolled onto his back, getting the mask into place as the next grenade was lobbed through the kitchen doorway. He was gambling this one was gas.

But in case it wasn't—Holden pulled the muffs back on. The grenade detonated. He heard Rosie scream. He looked up. He couldn't see Rosie or Kearney, the plaster dust too thick and off-white vapor rising from the center of the floor. Tear gas, he surmised. "Rosie!" The larger of Holden's two Berettas was in his left fist. "Rosie!"

"I'm all right!"

Where was Kearney?

There was no time to wonder.

Holden threw himself across the gap between his position and the base of the stairs, reaching for the plaster-dust-covered M-16 with his right hand, rolling. Men were rushing through the kitchen doorway, and he knew they'd be coming down the stairs too. "Rosie! The kitchen!"

"Got it!"

Holden, the Beretta 92F in his left hand, the M-16 in his right, opened fire as the first men came down the stairs. . . .

Geoffrey Kearney shook his head to clear it. He'd gotten the mask on, but something . . . His forehead felt sore by the left temple. But he could see straight.

He was lying on the floor beside a large over-stuffed chair, most of the stuffing either cut out or shot out.

His rifle.

It would be beside the brick mantel. He'd had the compartment open, been about to reach for the tape. He saw a man running past him through the kitchen door, then another. Kearney grabbed for the Smith & Wesson 9mm, stabbing it toward the running, booted feet, firing into legs as they passed him, hearing curses. Something fell on him and Kearney beat at it. A man, fists hammering at Kearney's gas-masked face. Kearney fired the 5906, four times, the body thudding upward, rolling onto Kearney's right arm.

A pair of combat-booted feet over him, a rifle butt crashing down. Kearney dodged his head right, the rifle butt impacting the floor. Kearney's left hand tore the Cold Steel Bowie from the fabric sheath at his left side, ramming the nine inches of quarter-inch-thick carbon steel straight up between the man's legs and into the scrotum.

There was an inhuman shriek.

Kearney tore his right hand free of the dead man, losing the pistol. The suppressor-fitted 10/22 was still slung to Kearney's back—he'd felt every contour of it as he lay on it—but there was no time to reach for it as another of the PSF personnel came after him, fired an M-16, Kearney throwing himself left, but too far still from the fireplace to reach for his M-16. Instead he reached for a large shard of pottery on the floor beside him, flipping it into the face of the Strike Force man as the man fired again, chunks of wallboard beside Kearney's head breaking away under the multiple projectile impacts.

Kearney was to his feet, his right hand opening the B & D Fazendeiro, then arcing upward as the man wheeled toward him, the tip of Kearney's inverted blade catching the Strike Force man at the base of the chin, ripping, the man's head snapping back as Kearney's left fist hammered forward through the blood spray, into the Adam's apple, crushing the larynx. As the man fell back, just to be sure, Kearney made a backhand rake with the Fazendeiro across the man's throat.

Kearney wheeled as Rosie Shepherd shouted, "Geoff—down!"

Kearney threw himself toward the fireplace mantel, flat, gunfire tearing across the room from both sides just over him.

He saw his chance, the kitchen door wide open. With his left hand he snatched one of the American M-61 grenades from his webbing, the pin pulling as he tore the grenade free. Kearney backhanded the grenade through the open doorway, then rolled right, his left hand closing on the M-16 as the concussion came, more pieces of the ceiling collapsing as Kearney rolled right again. He was up, to his knees beside the opposite end of the couch behind which Rosie Shepherd crouched. The M-16 at hip level, Kearney started to spray. . . .

David Holden started up the staircase, a fresh magazine in both the M-16 and the Beretta. He shot a man five or six times in the face with the Beretta as the man leveled an M-16 toward him.

At the midpoint of the staircase where it took a bend, Holden pulled back, stabbing the Beretta around the corner and turreting it right and left, firing it out, reasoning that they might think he was out of ammunition for his M-16.

Holden stabbed the Beretta into his pistol belt, shifted the M-16 back, and pulled a grenade off his web gear, lobbing the M-61 up the remainder of the staircase.

The grenade detonated, the stairs shuddering under him, starting to give way. As the belch of smoke and dust blew past him, Holden shifted the M-16 to his left hand, thrusting it beyond the corner, firing it out, waving the muzzle left and right and left, emptying the thirty-round magazine.

The entire bottom portion of the staircase was starting to shift and Holden grabbed the rail and flipped it, the rail giving way under his weight. Jumping, Holden crashed down to the living-room floor in a tuck roll.

He looked up as he drew the second Beretta, the only loaded gun on him.

Kearney and Rosie were closing toward the kitchen door, Kearney flipping a flash-bang through the doorway, the door itself so shot to pieces that it hung in shards off one hinge.

Holden rammed a fresh magazine up the well of his M-16, taking up a position at the base of what little remained of the staircase, ready for anyone else who might still be alive above. . . .

Rose Shepherd crouched behind the overturned reclining chair, a coffee table pulled up walling her in, but affording her little protection from rifle bullets, she realized.

Kearney had his pistol in his left hand and was pulling his Bowie knife out of one of the Strike Force troopers. "Hurry it up!"

He was at the mantel again, half disappearing into the chimney, emerging a second later. "Got it!"

"David!"

"We're ready?"

"Ready in thirty seconds," Rose called back. With the little B & D Grande penknife she'd scrounged out of her purse, she cut the fabric name tags off the BDUs of two of the dead men. She turned around and watched for an instant as David activated the radio signal. . . .

The Plexiglas in the chin bubble of the Bell Long Ranger was spiderwebbed from multiple impacts.

He was out of M-20 rockets.

Hofsteader's forces on both sides of the compound had to be doubly decimated.

In the distance, about two blocks away at the outside, he could see a long line of fast-moving vehicles with flashing light bars, closing. And there was a light, like a second moon in the sky, growing, coming toward them.

"Mr. Steel! I just got the signal. They got the tape!" Sadek Muhammed, the pilot, shouted.

"Move in and down—we need this fast, just like when you used to be in Vietnam getting the Air Cav guys out."

"I'm goin' in—hang on!"

The helicopter slipped left and started down, Steel

wondering if his stomach would take much more of this without losing the small dinner he'd put into it.

The only functioning weapon Steel had left—everything else out of ammo—was the SIG-Sauer P-226 in the DeSantis holster under his armpit. Luther Steel tore the 9mm free of the leather, his eyes searching the street below them for what he hoped would look like two men and a woman in black BDUs. "Come on, guys!" Steel hissed under his breath.

That second moon, growing in intensity, was a spotlight off a helicopter. "Come on!" Steel shouted into the slipstream. . . .

Beside the window, Kearney already through, Rosie climbing out after him, David Holden shifted his M-16 to his left hand and reached to his vest. He snatched at one of the M-61 grenades, hurtled it toward the staircase, then another toward the kitchen door and another into the center of the living room.

Holden bolted over the window frame, throwing himself to the ground just outside as the grenades detonated in rapid succession, the ground trembling under him, debris raining down on him, his gloved hands over the back of his neck and head.

Bolting to his feet, Holden glanced at the Rolex on his left wrist. He pushed the second switch on the radio-signal device.

Blumenthal, LeFleur, and Runningdeer would wait sixty seconds and emerge from beside the fence, running for the helicopter, carrying openly a videocassette.

Holden heard a whistle, saw Kearney faintly, ran toward him. Rosie should already be changing. . . .

Rose Shepherd was out of the flack vest. She dropped it to the ground, with other hand already starting to unbutton her pants. There was a light in the sky, growing.

She was running out of time.

She let her pants drop to her ankles, rolling down the slip and the A-line Army uniform skirt, hoping any wrinkle would fall out.

She bent over, with the Big Ugly One knife slashing the laces of her combat boots, kicking out of them. The boot socks she wore over her panty hose —she pulled them off, standing on the balls of her feet now as she got the BDU blouse open and shrugged out of it. She straightened the uniform tie, then dropped into a crouch, opening the small, Kevlar-lined fanny pack she'd worn. She pulled out the spit-polished black heels and started cramming her feet into them—they were a half size too small. She had big feet for a woman but guessed big flat feet were just part and parcel of being a cop as she had been.

Next she shook out the carefully rolled uniform jacket. Shrugging into it, she shifted the Null holster beside her left breast to make certain that it wouldn't profile. Without buttoning the jacket she bent down for the hat. "Yuck," she hissed under her breath, pulling the black bandana from her carefully pinned-up blond wig, then the hair net she'd worn beneath it to preserve the hairdo. She put on the hat.

There was a black uniform purse inside the pack;

and, inside it, she had the Detonics .45 and her little Cold Steel Mini-Tanto. She exchanged the Glock for the .45, then shoved the Big Ugly One and the sheath for it into the purse, closed the flap, slung the purse to her shoulder, and started to button her jacket.

Already changing as they ran, David and Geoff joined her within the stand of pines.

"How's my face?"

"Beautiful."

"No, dammit! Dirty?"

David looked at her intently. "No."

She spit on her fingertips and wiped a smudge off David's left cheek.

Geoff was already skinning out of his pants, pulling them over his boots, the camouflage BDUs of the Presidential Strike Force beneath them.

David pulled off his BDU blouse and threw it into the trees. He pulled on the baseball cap after removing a paste-on mustache attached to its bill. She caught sight of the Presidential Strike Force brassard on his shoulder.

There was a thrashing sound almost directly overhead, growing louder, the glare of a spotlight over them, not on them.

She had her uniform jacket buttoned, slung her Uzi carbine and the magazine pouch. There would be David's shoulder holster to carry, as well as Geoff's, and the two bags with the rest of their collective gear, David finishing the packing.

"If anybody notices you, we're in deep shit," David observed.

"Yeah, well, we're in deep shit already," Rose

noted, stuffing the .45 into the waistband of her skirt beneath the uniform jacket.

"I'm ready," Kearney announced.

She looked at him. Like David's, his hair was a little long for the military, but it was dark unlike David's salt and pepper wig and mustache. God, he'll still be gorgeous when he's old, Rose thought. He slung his M-16. "Halpern was a corporal. Here, turn around." The tube of instant glue from her purse in one hand, she settled the rank insignia onto the sleeve beneath where the luminous guideline was drawn in to get the right distance down from the shoulder seam. She did the same for his left arm. He turned toward her and she stuck one of the name tags she'd removed from a body in the house over his left breast pocket flap. "David. You're a buck sergeant. Jones, R."

"Jones, R.—got it." As David spoke, she began applying the rank insignia on his right arm, then his left. She could hear the chopper landing. She applied the name tag, then tossed the instant glue into the trees.

"Litterbug." David smiled. "If something goes wrong, I love you. Remember."

She nodded, kissed David on the lips—really hard—and told them, trying to make her voice sound confident, "You guys look good. Let's go."

The helicopter had swept in above them and landed in the clearing between the pines and the all-but-demolished house. Rose Shepherd put on her lipstick, dusted a little powder onto her nose, then ran toward the chopper as David and Geoff disap-

peared in the other direction. She straightened the
damn hat. . . .

      Presidential Strike Force personnel moved
about the grounds in small teams, David Holden and
Geoffrey Kearney splitting up, using their flashlights
as the others did to search the grounds, joining them.
As of yet no one had found the clothing and other
gear.

A knot of PSF officers and senior noncoms were
clustered around the helicopter gunship. Military Police vehicles and troop transport vehicles were everywhere.

But the knot broke as Holden watched over his
shoulder from near the front steps of the house.

A bullhorn echoed, "I need Halpern and Jones, R.,
up here by the helicopter front and center right
now!"

David Holden shrugged his shoulders toward the
men he was with and took off at double time, toward
the helicopter.

Out of the right corner of his peripheral vision he
could see Kearney coming too.

There was a major standing beside Rosie, who, in
her captain's uniform, was holding a clipboard.

Holden fell in before the major. Kearney fell in to
his left.

The major turned toward them, snarling, "Disarm
these two!"

Some of the men with the major and Rosie approached, and took Holden's Beretta from the holster
at his hip, and his M-16.

"Neither one of you two looks familiar. You in the second platoon?"

Holden didn't know what to say, but was starting a lie as Rosie interrupted. "Sir, I have orders to get these men to headquarters as quickly as possible."

"This officer," the major began again, "has warrants for both your arrests. Theft of government property and various violations of the articles of war."

Holden wondered which ones the major had violated by killing innocent civilians, as the PSF was wont to do.

"That pistol may be one of the M-9s from the missing shipment," Rosie said in her captain's voice. "I'll need it as evidence."

"Unload that weapon and put it aboard the chopper, Deames," the major snapped at a young lieutenant with a long scar down his left cheek.

"Yes, sir. Corporal!"

Rosie and the major conferred between them for a few seconds.

She stepped back, rendered a neat salute, the major returning it with a sloppy one like something out of a low-budget World War II movie.

Rosie dropped the salute.

Cuffs were going onto Holden's wrists.

He was shoved toward the helicopter, Kearney beside him.

Through the Plexiglas, at the controls, he could see Lou Bandini, the GI who was a Patriot and had stolen the gunship for them.

Kearney climbed aboard the chopper.

Holden climbed in. He could see Rosie's gear just

inside the forward portion of the fuselage. She had the tape.

He started to breathe, but wasn't ready to just yet.

He could hear the major saying to Rosie, "You tell Mr. Townes, Captain, that I don't like having men snatched out of my command."

"I can tell him that, sir—do you really want me to?"

And the major actually laughed. "Maybe you'd better not. You busy later?"

"No, sir."

"Will you be at HQ for a while?"

"Yes, sir—and I haven't had dinner yet."

The major smiled. "It's a date, then."

He took Rosie's elbow, starting her toward the chopper, the speed of the rotor blades seeming to just slightly increase. Rosie held her hand to her hat.

Holden started to look away and laugh, but then he saw a man—an officer—running from the direction of the house, and just barely, over the now noticeably increasing whirr of the rotor blades, was able to hear him.

"Major—it's a trick! Jones and Halpern are dead in the house!"

One of the PSF men beside Holden started to raise his M-16.

David Holden, wrists still cuffed behind him, threw his body weight against the man, his hands clawing for the testicles, grabbing and ripping, his head snapping back. He felt and heard something crack and it wasn't his skull.

Rosie was drawing away from the major. He was reaching for her.

Kearney kicked a second PSF man in the crotch, then knee-smashed him in the face, the body tumbling out of the chopper.

Holden started for the open fuselage doorway.

The major was drawing his weapon.

Rosie already had hers coming out from under her uniform jacket, stabbing the .45 toward the PSF major's face and firing twice, the rear of his head rupturing outward and upward.

Holden shouted, "Airborne now!"

The helicopter's rotor blades suddenly increased to full takeoff power as Rosie dived toward the gunship opening.

Her upper body was in the doorway, Kearney dropping to his knees, then back, extending his right leg to Rosie. She grabbed his ankle, pulling herself in.

Lieutenant Deames reached for her from the ground. Holden was in the doorway, and even though he knew he'd lose his balance and fall, he struck out with his left foot, into the lieutenant's face, driving the PSF officer back.

Holden fell, his left elbow hitting the deck hard as the chopper slipped to port, rotated about 180 degrees on its axis, then arced slightly downward, then up, over the trees.

Gunfire from the ground below—Holden threw his body over Rosie's. He looked up. Kearney was unlocking the cuffs at his wrists. Both Kearney and Holden had standard handcuff keys taped to their left wrists beneath their watchbands.

Rosie Shepherd started laughing as the helicopter gained altitude.

"Are we slick or what, guys?"

Kearney used his key to release Holden from the cuffs. David Holden rubbed his right elbow.

"Huh, are we slick?" Rosie rolled onto her back, her skirt almost up to her crotch, holding her stomach, laughing, her right hand still holding the .45.

"You're nuts—slick, but nuts," David Holden told Rosie Shepherd, on his knees beside her, the rush of slipstream from the open fuselage door cold. He took the silly hat from her head, tossed it through the opening.

She looked up at him and laughed.

Holden took Rosie in his arms and kissed her so hard that, if Rosie Shepherd had been an ordinary woman, he would have been afraid she'd break.

Epilogue

*T*he night was overcast and reception was exceedingly clear because of it.

"And Dzikowicz fades back for the pass. Schmidt has it—he fumbles! That's a twelve-yard loss for the Dragons! I can't believe that, Jase. Dragons wide receiver Yanos Schmidt fumbles the ball on the forty-five yard line for a twelve-yard loss? That's incredible!"

"Ted Dzikowicz didn't look too happy about it, did he, Walt? And suddenly, with fifty-five seconds left on the clock, the whole ball game changes."

"It looks like a spread formation for the Tigers, now as the clock runs out. And all eyes are on Tyrone Bladesdale, the Tigers' promising rookie and one of the most charismatic players in the league."

"That's right, Walt. Tyrone Bladesdale, six foot five, 243 pounds, a high school and college track star and a former member of the United States Olympic wrestling team, a man of infinite contradictions—"

"And some say infinite abilities, Jase. The quarterback fakes a hand-off to Bladesdale. It's the old cherrypicker play—desperate times require desperate measures—and the left halfback fakes to the right and explodes on number thirty-six, safety Aaron Heinz. There's a huge gap in the defense there and—wait! Bladesdale takes the hand-off from Stan 'Boomer' Evans and follows the left halfback. That looks like thirty yards, Jase! And Bladesdale's brought down on the twenty-five yard line by the Dragons' smallest man, Larry Fenstermacher."

"They're checking that with the tape. Yes. It's the twenty-five yard line. The Tigers still have the ball, but they're running out of time. Fenstermacher almost didn't make the flight out here to Tiger Stadium, Walt. He was en route to the airport and was stopped by Presidential Strike Force personnel for suspected curfew violation. His curfew pass was mistakenly packed in one of his suitcases, sent on ahead earlier in the day. I understand it took a personal call from Dragons manager Herb Wilton to Presidential Security Chief Hobart Townes to get Fenstermacher aboard that airplane."

"And I also understand, Jase, that both Security Chief Townes and President Makowski are Dragons fans, so that probably helped the young defensive safety as well. Forty seconds to play and the Tigers are still alive. And the fans are going wild down there—despite the fact that curfew is approaching the stands are still filled."

"Mary Beales, one of our statisticians, tells us that it's estimated that sixty-five million people are watching the game from home tonight on television, Walt, including President Makowski."

"The Dragons are ahead twenty-one to fourteen. The Tigers won't get any second chances. They need a touchdown and the two-point conversion to win. 'Boomer' Evans is giving the count. The ball is snapped! Todd Rouster, the Tigers' split end, is in motion, breaking free. And Evans has the ball! He passes! Rouster's got it! He's got it! On the goal line, ladies and gentlemen! On the goal line. Rouster makes a phenomenal catch—just as he steps out of bounds! Touchdown!"

"Todd Rouster, twenty-seven-year-old split end from the University of Georgia, the man who almost never played football because of a bicycling accident when he was seven years old, makes the catch of the decade!"

"Or has he, Jase? It looks like—yes! The officials appear to be disagreeing about whether or not the ball was caught in bounds!"

"Instant replay will decide, Walt. Slow motion. The fans are going crazy down there!"

"We have that instant replay now!"

The television flickered.

Rudolph Cerillia's face filled the screen. "I am Rudolph Cerillia. If you are watching this tape, I have been murdered on the orders of Roman Makowski, the man who has assumed the Presidency of the United States. The real President's life, as I make this tape, hangs in the balance because the forces of Roman Makowski are on the move to take the real President's life. Roman Makowski, using Nancy O'Donnell, lobbyist from the People for a Better America, as his contact to international drug dealer and terrorist Arturo Guzman, works in direct cooperation with former KGB confidant, smuggler, and crime boss Alexei Kirovitch.

"Makowski, Nancy O'Donnell, Arturo Guzman, and Alexei Kirovitch are inextricably tied to the Front for the Liberation of North America, as is Hobart Townes, Makowski's security chief, who now runs both the Justice Department and the Army. Whether or not Makowski joined forces with the FLNA after assuming the Presidency or was a co-conspirator earlier in the FLNA's assault on American liberty is unclear.

"The FLNA is sponsored by dissident factions within the Soviet KGB and is not, as best as can be determined, an official instrument of current Soviet policy. On the contrary, as intelligence from the Soviet Union suggests, Soviet society may have in store for it an assault similar in nature to that already under way against American society. The FLNA is financed by profits from the international drug trade, supplemented by monies derived from child pornography, white slavery, and donations from certain individuals and corporations, both foreign and domestic. Among notable American FLNA supporters one can include the following: retired senator Herbert Welch, automotive executive Lionel Winstead, newspaper publishing magnate Charles Randall, broadcast executive Elmo P. Docsteader, actress Lydia Blaine, and scientist Chester Babinski. These persons and others have actively advanced the FLNA's assault on America through propaganda, disinformation, and heavy financial contributions either as direct monies or in the provision of so-called 'safe houses,' transportation, false identities, et cetera. These and other facts, including dossiers on each individual named, including Makowski and Townes and numerous other Federal officials (both elected and appointed), have been duplicated and will be disseminated to newspapers, television and radio networks, and magazines both nationally and internationally. The truth will be known, the evidence is hard, concrete and admissible in court.

"These persons will never get to trial because they have already subverted the American system beyond reconciliation.

"There is one ray of hope. The Patriots, most notable among their ranks Professor David Holden. Holden and other Patriot leaders like him have systematically fought at great personal risk to champion the rights of the American citizen and to defeat the FLNA, which is why the focus of attention by Federal and local law enforcement has been the apprehension or assassination of the Patriots rather than the FLNA. They wish to silence the Patriots and to neutralize the last remaining obstacle to FLNA control and power.

"Support your fellow Americans who believe in freedom. Remember who the enemies of freedom really are. Demand that your local newspapers, television and radio stations disseminate the truth—"

A phone rang in the background of the tape.

Suddenly it seemed as if Rudolph Cerillia had jumped but no movement was seen. He was sitting differently and his face looked like a face that saw death.

"I have just spoken with eyewitnesses to the death of the President of the United States. These eyewitnesses are named in documents that will be forthcoming at a time when naming them will not be signing their death warrants. These documents were written when these persons agreed to embark upon a daring rescue mission to save the President. They were unsuccessful, but their efforts are not diminished because of the outcome, however sad.

"But the names of the men and women, the organizations, all the information I have recorded here tonight on this tape, now has the strength of deathbed testimony. I realize, as I had before only suspected, that I am the next target for—"

The tape was cut off. A sign reading NETWORK VIDEO DIFFICULTIES appeared.

David Holden reached into Rosie's purse for her cigarettes and her lighter.

Beside the purse was a stack of preaddressed envelopes, packets of information preprepared by Rudolph Cerillia. Their location had been indicated on the videotape before the beginning of the taped message and had been recovered before Holden and the others made their return to their camp near Metro. There they gave the tape to Parrish to pass on for broadcast during the game.

Rosie now stood by the tent flap, her hands in the pockets of her uniform skirt, her hair down.

Luther Steel, sitting beside the television set, covered his face with his hands.

Geoffrey Kearney folded Linda Effingham into his arms, just holding her.

David Holden lit the cigarette, then returned the lighter and the pack to Rosie's purse.

Patsy Alfredi, Mitch Diamond, Lem Parrish, and some of the others crowded into the tent began to talk quietly among themselves. Patriot activity would now intensify. There was a raid on an FLNA supply depot scheduled within hours.

David Holden walked to the tent flap. The sports announcers were apologizing for the interruption in programing. The Tigers were going for the two-point conversion.

David Holden curled his arm around Rosie Shepherd's shoulders and she leaned her face against his chest. He offered her a drag on the cigarette and she took it, inhaling deeply.

"There'll be a revolution now, to overthrow Roman Makowski," Holden whispered.

Rosie nodded. "I know. God help us."

There was loud cheering and Holden looked toward the television screen.

The Tigers had made the conversion.

Holden touched his lips to Rosie's hair and they held each other.

"God help us," she whispered again.

David Holden was suddenly very glad Roman Makowski was watching television that night.